I DON
MONDAYS!

COLETTE KEBELL

SKITTISH
ENDEAVOURS ™

I Don't Do Mondays!
A SKITTISH ENDEAVOURS BOOK:

Originally published in Great Britain by Skittish Endeavours 2020

Skittish Endeavours Books are supplied and printed by Amazon

Printed and bound by Amazon www.amazon.com

Thanks to:-
Design © www.Lizziegardiner.co.uk; illustrations © Shutterstock.com.
Proof-reader and Copy Editor: Emmy Ellis of Studio ENP

For more information on Colette Kebell see her website at
www.colettekebell.com
or
follow her on Twitter @ColetteKebell
and/or
https://www.facebook.com/ColetteKebellAuthor

Acknowledgements

I would like to say thank you to my amazing beta readers, these were Denise Sutherland, Sarah Owen, Caroline Meurice and Annie McDonnell and I thank you so much for taking the time and trouble to steer me in the right direction with my editing and book as a whole. I also have to mention Sarah Owen, Julie Newman and particularly Angelina Kalahari for their selfless assistance with my back cover blurb.

CHAPTER 1

'I don't do Mondays.'

The woman was Amanda Parker, a beautiful twenty-three-year-old blonde who was lying naked on the bed in the master suite at the Waldorf Astoria. Her family had old money, and they made it clear she wouldn't see a single penny of it. Her primary occupation was to party, doing the occasional modelling, and hoping to have another spot in a celebrity magazine. Which one, was not important.

'How come? It's not that you have to get up and go to work.' Carlton Allerton, owner of Allerton Groceries, and worth several billion in assets, although mostly made by his grandfather, was the man sharing her bed.

'I don't know. People always disappear, rushing to go to work. Monday morning is dead. Too quiet for my liking.'

People have to work for a living, albeit most of us, but he didn't say it out loud. The last thing he wanted was to start a quarrel. Amanda could be temperamental.

Instead, he said, 'What about having a shower together? We've been lying here doing nothing since six.'

'Nothing since sex, you mean. Are you checking the time?' Amanda asked.

'Not at all, but I'm getting hungry, and I still need to fully wake up.'

'You didn't seem asleep when we were making love,' she teased him.

'Give me a break, Amanda. You know very well this is borrowed time. We can't keep going like this.'

The woman suddenly looked him straight in the eye, her voice now firm and sharp. 'Then do something about it.' It wasn't the first time they'd touched that topic, and most likely not the last one.

'It's not so easy, and you know it.'

Carlton sat on the bed and turned the television onto *Bloomberg* to see the latest news on the Asian market. A man in a suit and a yellow bow tie was explaining why the Nikkei had slipped, reversing early gains from the past few weeks. The Federal Reserve meeting was due in a few days, and the investors were cautious.

'I know you care more about your money than me.' Amanda's expression stiffened. 'And don't give me that crap that you have to work this morning. You're dodging the issue. This is you; always avoiding confrontation whenever you can.'

Carlton got up from a bed that was far too large for only two people and walked towards the bathroom. The soft carpet under his feet was warm, contrasting with the air-conditioning blasting at full speed. In the background, the man in the bow tie explained that a rupture in one of the most essential pipelines would likely result in a surge of gas prices.

He hesitated for a second and then opened the sink tap.

'Are you preparing breakfast?' Amanda asked, reaching him and turning the tap off. The boundaries between conversation and argument were always foggy with her.

'What in hell are you talking about? We are in a hotel; they bring us breakfast.'

'I see. It will take a while to have you fully domesticated, but I'm sure I'll do a good job on you.'

You bet. Carlton didn't retort. Although Amanda was by far the best experience a man could have in bed, she was also too much of an embarrassment. Her flirtatious nature brought attention to her, and as a result she was on the cover of too many magazines. Amanda allegedly had a relationship with that famous Hollywood actor who never won an Oscar, followed by a notorious rapper and countless other partners.

Carlton was irresistibly attracted to her, but their relationship needed to be confined to a hotel bedroom. Or to his own bedroom occasionally, or even the back seat of his Rolls-Royce, come to that. But that was it. No public appearances with Amanda and the newly instated CEO of Allerton Groceries.

He didn't want that sort of attention anymore. Not now and perhaps not ever.

Carlton knew it, and Amanda knew it. Neither of them were ready to relinquish their current arrangement, hoping the other changed their mind or at least adapted. Not yet.

He entered the shower; Amanda followed. She wrapped her arms around his neck and kissed him slowly. Carlton grasped her bottom and lifted her against him.

You won't change my mind.

They skipped breakfast, and Carlton, once he had his suit on, called for his driver. When he reached the lobby, the Rolls-Royce was already waiting for him.

'Where should I take you, sir?' Ben asked.

'To headquarters, please.' Carlton checked the time on his Blancpain and flicked through the initial pages of *The Wall Street Journal*.

'How are Tony and Simon?' he asked without lifting his eyes from the paper.

'Very well, sir, thank you for asking. It's Tony's first day at school today. My wife took care of that. The boy said he didn't want to go and had a bit of a tantrum this morning.'

'Ah, school. Time flies. Nothing to worry about, they'll love it.' Carlton didn't care about the driver's kids. He didn't really want to know who they were or what they were doing. But it was in his nature to always have an edge on people, remembering those little details. As his grandfather said, business was made by people, and finding a way of showing those people he cared led to further business. He was refining an act.

'Don't have any kids, if I may say, they are only trouble,' Ben stated.

7

'Thanks for the advice.' Carlton's tone didn't leave room for misinterpretation—the employee had crossed a line; exchanging a few words with the boss was allowed, but the rule was "never talk about personal matters". Employees were fired for less.

Concern clouded the driver's eyes, reflected in the rear-view mirror.

'The rest of the newspapers are in the folder, as usual.'

Carlton put down *The Wall Street Journal*, picked up *USA Today*, and flicked through the headlines, letting go of the driver's intrusion into his private life.

'What is all that commotion?' Carlton asked once they reached the headquarters.

A crowd of tourists and bystanders were assembling at one side of the building.

'I am not sure, sir, but they don't look like protesters of any sort. I'll make some enquires.'

Carlton entered the building and didn't respond to any of the 'Good morning, Mr Allerton' nonsense from the employees. They were numbers, plebs, not too different from the people outside on the left corner. The only difference was that the employees were an unavoidable evil he had to deal with.

Carlton went directly into his office and put the newspaper on his desk. Soon afterwards, a secretary knocked at the glass door.

'Your grandfather is waiting for you in the boardroom,' she announced.

Carlton didn't acknowledge her, still intent on reading the news, but quickly glanced at the secretary's bottom when she exited. Banging the personnel was a big no-no; they'd soon dream of a career and have expectations. And if things went pear-shaped, they'd sued you. His secretary was going to keep her mouth shut, she was good at that, but why take the risk? Carlton flicked through his emails, and ten minutes later, he went to the boardroom.

'We have to keep a lower profile,' Jason Allerton barked. The man was in his late seventies. He started working young. He was five foot five tall, slim as a pick, a full head of ghostly white hair; his double-breasted pin-striped suit had seen better times. Despite not having an official title in Allerton Groceries, he still held a significant number of shares.

'When you say *we,* I assume you mean *I* have to.' Carlton knew what was coming, another tirade from the old man.

'You're damn right I mean *you*! Look!' Old Allerton threw a handful of gossip magazines over the long boardroom table towards his grandson. 'We sell cheap stuff, our employees don't give a damn about the customers, and rightly so, we pay them just enough to get by; we don't have a customer care service and we have been nominated many times in the papers as the worst supermarket in the US. That is okay, we still make plenty of money, and customers cannot do without us. When customers enter our shops, we constantly remind them they are poor. The shoppers know damn well that if they had some money, they'd shop somewhere else. They have no choice. But this?' He picked up one of the magazines where Carlton was pictured half-drunk, entering his Rolls-Royce after dinner in a two-Michelin-star restaurant. 'This is unacceptable! We have to be the grey men; people don't have to give us a second look. They obviously know we have plenty of money, but we don't flash it in their damn miserable faces like this.'

'Grandpa...'

'I'M NOT FINISHED. For over fifty years, nobody cared about us, and when I say us, I mean the ownership of Allerton's. Now we're making the news, and not only in the gossip magazines.' Jason Allerton's face was becoming redder and redder. He walked towards the opposite side of the room, facing Carlton, and grabbed *The Wall Street Journal*.

'Here, now we're getting articles about us. People are complaining about our business; last night they even dared to put graffiti on the side of our building. When people are too upset, that is when businesses go bankrupt. Cut the crap, Carlton. No more front-page spreads in the gossip magazines, get rid of your beloved cars, and get something soberer. I've had enough!'

'What is the point of making money if we're not allowed to spend it?' Carlton's tone was harsh and direct.

'Oh, but this is where you're wrong, young boy. I don't care if you buy a thousand villas around the world or if you have a car collection bigger than Jay Leno's, if you throw money down the drain or burn your inheritance on whores and cocaine. Just don't get caught showing it off when you're the CEO of this company. And you know very well why you hold that title. No more news. If you get in the papers one more time, it has to be for some charitable work. Do we understand each other?'

'Perfectly.'

Old Allerton didn't wait any further. He gave an order, and that was enough for him; nobody ever failed to comply.

When Jason Allerton left the room, Carlton threw the magazines on the floor. What a bastard. He dialled Amanda's number.

'Still in the hotel, babe?'

'Yeah, what's up?'

'Don't move, I'm coming back. Get undressed.'

CHAPTER 2

Ginger hated Mondays.

Especially those Mondays when she had to work, and the premise was, for that day at least, that she already had a full agenda. No question, it was to be a hectic day.

'This is Ginger,' she said, answering the phone. No *how can I be of assistance,* none of that pleasantry rubbish; she was supposed to be a boss, busy with international meetings and company mergers. At least during that call.

'Good morning, this is Andrew from the Global Investment Bank. We are calling for a referral, a Mr Matthew Torkington.'

Ginger shook a bunch of paper and typed on a computer to give her some background noise. 'Yes, sure. He told me to expect your call. What do you want to know?'

'We are in the process of hiring him, so we'd like to ask for a reference. Was he a good employee? I see from his CV he worked for you for about four years.'

He hadn't. Ginger barely knew the guy, but that was one of her 'temporary' lines of work: doing referrals for strangers in need. They could add on their CV a few years of employment in Ginger's fictitious company and avoid telling the new employer why they had been fired in their previous job. In exchange for a fee, of course. Ginger did the whole shebang, doctoring LinkedIn, adding a few fake endorsements, creating new departments in her imaginary company to fit the candidate's role.

'Excellent employee, we are sorry he decided to leave us.'

'What made him look for another job?' the man on the other end of the line asked. He had a warm, calm, but inquisitive voice.

'He's a talented guy and eager to climb the ladder, it's just that at this time we don't have the right position for him. I'm sure you've read the news about the merger. We should have been selfish and kept him in his current position for another year, but that wouldn't have been appropriate behaviour. We talked about it at length...'

'So, you knew he was looking for other opportunities?' Andrew asked. The surprise in his voice was evident.

'Sure, actually, I encouraged him. I don't like to see talent go to waste. We might try to poach him back into our ranks in a couple of years, just so you know.'

'Well, we shall see about that. Any weaknesses I should be aware of?'

That was a tricky one. The candidate was not the sharpest knife in the drawer, had a bit of a drinking habit and a temper. 'He's a visionary, and I really mean it. He's a couple of steps ahead of all of us, but when he talks about his ideas, he explains them as if they were common sense. It took us a while to recognise his wisdom; don't let that happen in your company.'

'We will not.' Andrew's tone was assertive and enthusiastic. 'I really thank you for your time.'

'Any questions, call me back. I'm swamped but, in this case, I can make an exception.'

They never called back, not for further information nor to complain she'd fed them a pile of bull.

That was not Ginger's sole occupation. She barely passed college in Tennessee six years previously; she was one of those people who were talented but froze when it was a matter of doing an exam. She still remembered her days at school as the worst kind of nightmare and a dark period in her life. When she eventually cracked up during the last year at college, she gave up the dream of becoming a teacher. Whenever she could, she worked, but most of her earnings came from the "alternative" line of businesses she had created. Not all of them exactly legitimate.

Faking referrals was one of them.

'Are you working on some other scheme of yours?' Mia asked, entering the office at that very moment.

Ginger turned from her computer to look at her boss. 'By all means, no. It was a personal call, sorry about that.' It was an innocent white lie to avoid her boss getting suspicious, more to justify it to herself than to Mia.

'You know, that's why you came here in the first place, because all that funny business of yours put you in serious trouble.'

'True. Mia, I really appreciate you keeping me here as your secretary, but you know the reality: things are looking grim, out there and in here. You know my rent almost doubled? Just like that! The bastard knocked at my door, and that was it. If I didn't like it, he said, I could move. Which I would, if it wasn't that it's the same all over Brooklyn.'

That was the ugly truth. Real estate was skyrocketing. There was little that could be bought for less than six hundred thousand dollars, nothing really decent below a million, and the landlords were squeezing their tenants. Sometimes to make them move, other times just for sheer greed.

Mia shrugged.

Ginger knew the reality wasn't too different for her boss. After Mia lost her job as a corporate lawyer, nobody hired her. Damn, nobody was hiring anybody in that period, and the only options she had was to give up on her New York dream and go back to Maine with her tail between her legs or reinvent her career.

The little cash her boss had left went into a three-year lease for that tiny office on Myrtle Avenue, placed between a kebab shop and a ninety-nine-cent shop. The place was a former barbershop, and people still entered asking for a haircut. Legal aid didn't pay six-figure salaries.

'I know, it's tough. Not what I imagined doing when I was at university,' Mia said. 'But these side businesses…'

Ginger was another desperate who had walked in in search of legal advice. From there, things had evolved. Mia needed a paralegal and a secretary, and Ginger was looking for a place to lay low for a while.

The phone rang, and Ginger picked it up. 'Carlton on line two.'

'I'll take it in my office, but we'll continue this discussion later.' Mia ran back to her desk, leaving the door open.

'Hello, darling, are you still in Washington?' Mia asked.

Ginger could not avoid listening to the conversation. Her boss' voice always shook a bit when she was talking to him.

'And when did you land? Excellent. So, you can join me and my friends this evening. You always procrastinate when it's a matter of meeting them… Say again, please?'

Mia's voice firmed up. She sipped some water from a plastic bottle. 'They're not losers, and they're my friends. I appreciate you're tired, but meeting new people didn't ever kill anybody'. She paused.

Ginger was well aware that statement was far less than accurate. She had a folder on her desk on precisely that subject matter.

'Okay, see you later.' Mia hung up and opened her laptop.

Ginger stared out of the window. She looked at the people walking in and out of the bar on the opposite side of the road. She recognised some of the faces and thought how peculiar it was sharing their customers with that bar. Unfortunately, far too often, people chose the bottle instead of getting legal advice.

They'd switch from the bar to the clinic, eventually, although only when they were in much deeper trouble.

'Why can't Carlton simply accept my friends?' Mia asked from her office. 'They aren't losers!'

Maybe because he's a patented asshole. 'I couldn't say, Mia,' she replied.

Mia shrugged and went back to work. *'I do hate Mondays'.*

Ginger got busy on the phone, embroiled in another of her schemes.

CHAPTER 3

Mia's plan for the evening was to simply chill out at Corrigan's, her favourite wine bar in Brooklyn. She hoped her boyfriend, Carlton, could stick around for a while and get to know her friends. That was, until some sort of grocery crisis struck in the middle of the evening and he'd have to leave.

She loved Carlton.

They'd met when Mia still worked as an associate at Carnegie, Stephens, and Honeycomb. Corporate law was a demanding job, and Mia was clocking eighty hours a week. She had barely time to eat and had a bastard of a boss. Her life was simple: bill as many hours as she could, go home, and crash on her tiny sofa in her small Manhattan apartment and start all over again, really early, the morning after.

She was convinced it was the right price to pay to get somewhere in life. Sacrifice a decade doing a tedious job, then either become a partner or earn enough money to start her own firm, and her own American dream would come true.

Carlton's company was one of her clients, a large supermarket chain that paid far too many taxes, who eventually decided to switch to her firm. They were the best in the financial sector, hundreds of associates working around the clock to find loopholes in the system, so their clients only paid what was due and not a penny more.

It was unusual that a client took a direct interest in what their lawyers were doing. Most of the time, they were happy to pay the bill and forget about the lawyer's existence. On the contrary, Carlton took a particular interest in how the firm calculated their taxes and, more often than not, he stopped for a chat with Mia, either at the coffee machine or by her office.

The fact that she was an extremely attractive dark-haired woman, with a slender figure and a beautiful smile, played some part in it.

Carton was in his mid-thirties, just four years older than her, and he was a handsome man. Tall, with curly hair and a square jaw. Most of the time he kept a two-day stubble that made him appear even sexier in Mia's eyes. He always wore tailor-made suits from Bond Street, London.

The first time she met Carlton was at the office. They had dumped a ton of documents on her desk, where she usually drank her first coffee of the morning. That day, she went with her cup to the business lounge, a large area with ergonomic armchairs, sofas, and other amenities. You could get some evil looks if you just sat there: an associate was not supposed to waste perfectly good billable minutes by drinking coffee.

Carlton was sitting nearby, and they started chatting. They spent half an hour talking, and something clicked between them. To Mia, Carlton didn't seem to be the bastard womaniser depicted in the newspapers. Several years back, Carlton's grandfather took a very different direction in how supermarkets worked. No more "the customer is always right" nonsense. The strategy was simple: if you had rock-bottom prices on goods, everything else could be overlooked. It didn't matter if the supermarket's employees were the rudest on the planet. It didn't matter if they organised weekly sales, often causing a stampede at the door at opening times. What was important was making money and the certainty that customers would stand every sort of abuse as long as the price was low enough. That was when Carlton took over.

Carlton was often both in the financial and gossip section of the papers and, after that chat, Mia kept reading avidly about him. Whenever he went to the law firm, he never failed to stop by and say a few words until one day he invited her out for a drink. From that moment onwards, she had her own prince charming, like in any good fairy tale.

'Hey, we're supposed to drink this evening, not spend our time daydreaming.'

Mia jumped at the voice behind her.

'Xander!' she said, hopping out of her chair and kissing him on the cheeks, 'I haven't seen you all week, what have you been up to?'

'The same old stuff. Writing, painting, delivering parcels. Didn't make a breakthrough this week, if that is what you're asking. What's your poison?'

'Just a beer for the moment,' she said. 'Jennifer is late, as usual. Mind joining me?'

He sat in front of her and signalled Joe. He pointed at Mia's beer, stuck up two fingers, made a circle with them, to confirm that it was a second round, followed by the OK gesture. He could have simply asked, but that was Xander.

'What about you? Any luck in getting back into being a corporate lawyer?' Xander asked.

'Not really. I keep sending CVs all over Manhattan. I've begged, cried, asked for favours, but nothing so far. I guess I'll have to stick with the clinic for a while.'

'Did you try outside Manhattan; I mean, a smaller firm?' Xander was the one with practical sense. He had a dream, like everybody else, but he also had a pragmatic attitude.

'Outside Manhattan is a void, career-wise, babe. It's here or nothing, and I'll eventually get back on my feet.'

'Yeah, I'm sure you will. Still just you and your crazy secretary?'

'Ginger? I haven't figured her out yet. She promised to be on the straight and narrow, but today I caught her up to her neck in another of her schemes. I should have fired her, although last month she actually helped pay the rent.'

'We have to do what we have to do,' Xander said.

Mia looked at him pondering his own words as if he'd told the ultimate truth.

'Is your boyfriend going to join us or is this place not upper class enough for him?'

Mia passed a hand through her hair. She'd tried numerous times to merge her two worlds. Carlton on one side and her friends on the other. Without success. She turned the empty beer bottle between her fingers, thinking about what to say next. She didn't want to apologise for what she didn't consider her fault. 'He said he'll be with us; he actually sent me a message. One day you'll explain to me what you have against him.'

'Maybe, one day. Here are our beers. Thank you, Joe.'

Xander was a true New Yorker. Never once been to the Statue of Liberty, never been out of NY because *everything you need is just around the corner*, and he'd never admit to not knowing something. One favourite game was to bring up random subjects, possibly the most unusual facts, only to see Xander quibbling on the matter. The theme was not relevant, talking about minor Swiss watchmakers, he knew the details; dinosaurs, he was an expert. Ask him the direction to an obscure ethnic grocery shop, he would tell you exactly where it was. Even if the shop in question didn't exist and was invented on the spot just for fun.

Mia knew he also struggled through his life. From listening to him, someone would be led to believe he was a successful writer and a painter, but most of the money he made came from being a delivery guy. Mia had read some of his stuff, and he was indeed a talented writer, but, like many, he was looking for a quick buck rather than working for something in the long term.

He wrote thriller novels. From what Mia recalled, after countless rejections from the top publishers, he decided to publish independently. He could have been considered an attractive man if only he didn't put so much effort into dressing like a homeless person.

'Hey, did you finish that dystopic of yours? It's been a work in progress for what, two years? I want to read how it ends.' Mia kept pushing that button; she was an avid reader of his work.

'Yeah, I know, it's parked somewhere on my laptop. I'm not in the mood in this period.' Behind those thick-rimmed glasses, Xander kept ranting about the public: his best work didn't get noticed, and when he wrote dime literature, as he called it, he could actually earn some good money.

'Here comes Jenny', Mia said, pointing to the door.

'What was the emergency this time? A shootout or a car accident?' Xander asked with a smirk.

'Don't be nasty, nothing unusual in her arriving at the last minute.'

'Hello, fellas,' Jennifer said, 'sorry I'm late. Today was manic...'

'Tracheotomy, broken bones, or vintage shopping in Williamsburg?' Xander asked.

'You caught me. What gave it away?' Jennifer placed a couple of bags on an empty chair and raised her hands in surrender. 'But it was nonetheless busy at the hospital, too. Hey, we're in a wine bar, what are you doing with beers?'

Xander raised his bottle. 'Just waiting for you, babe, to start the party.'

'Wine is good for your arteries, trust your doctor. We were supposed to meet that elusive boyfriend of yours, right?' Jennifer said.

Carlton had promised he wouldn't miss the appointment this time.

'Maybe he's embarrassed to meet us here,' Xander commented.

'Don't be daft. Carlton is actually a good guy, nothing like how he's depicted in the press.' Mia felt the urge, one more time, to defend her boyfriend.

'Okay, what shall we have today?' Jennifer turned towards the blackboard. 'I've had a nightmare weekend, I deserve a Sassicaia.'

'Good for you, I'll go for a Rosso di Montalcino.'

'Never abandon the classics,' Mia said. 'Well done, Xander, we know you like traditions. I'll start with a Bellavista for now, and then I might switch to something else. Unless our doctor here has any objections about mixing up wines?'

'Nah, we have billions of brain cells, killing a few won't really matter.'

Mia received a text message. It was from Carlton; apparently, there was a crisis in the Midwest. The text said he was going to be late. She knew Jennifer spotted the disappointment on her face. Xander checked something on his phone.

'Damn!' he exclaimed.

'What's up?' Mia asked, wondering if his bad news was worse than hers.

'I sold twenty erotica today, and nobody bought my horror masterpiece.'

'They are readers, what do they know?' Jennifer interjected.

That was a classic argument with Xander; like Mia and probably the vast majority of their generation, they were there for the instant killing. Trying to get it right the first time, as fast as they could. In a society where everything happened instantly, where people could get the latest news on the phone immediately, nobody really wanted to invest years in building a real masterpiece. Time was precious in New York, and the fear of not being able to reach the top was far more significant than the desire of doing an excellent job.

They had finished their first glass when Carlton arrived. Some people in the bar stopped talking and looked at him. It wasn't usual to get celebrities in their little bar, and Carlton was always in the news. Finance, gossip, or both. Coming out of his Rolls-Royce in front of the bar also did the attention-grabbing trick. Carlton walked in as if he owned the place in his pinstriped suit. Mia signalled to attract his attention, and her two companions turned in his direction to spot the newcomer. Jennifer let a soft 'Wow!' escape her lips.

Carlton kissed Mia on the cheeks, and then she introduced her friends.

'What's up? You seem upset,' Mia asked.

'I think after a day like this, I deserve a large glass of wine. What's the best here?'

Xander had a mask of panic on his face as the three friends usually shared the bill at the end of the evening.

'White or red? They should have a Masseto, Tenuta dell' Ornellaia, or a ninety-seven Yquem,' Jennifer said, racking her brain, 'but those are only rumours, we never dared to ask for a bottle, not at a couple of grand a pop.'

'I'll take the Masseto whatever-it's-called,' Carlton said, and then addressing Mia, 'It's just three months since we opened the new headquarters, down on Third Avenue, and someone has already put graffiti on it. I hate those guys; they should be shot!'

'On Third Avenue, you said?' Xander intervened, 'I saw it in the news. That's not graffiti, you've been blessed by one of Kowalski's works. Thousands of people will make pilgrimages to your front door only to see it.'

'Kowalski?' Mia asked nobody in particular. 'I love his work, he's so sarcastic!' She knew her boyfriend had a strong, different opinion to hers, but that artist was a genius. He'd left his mark all over the States, although the best work was usually in Los Angeles and on the West Coast. New York had never had one of his works previously, until now.

Xander was already on the phone searching for the image.

'Here it is.' He showed the picture on his phone as if it were the catch of the day. It depicted a homeless Statue of Liberty, sitting on the road and begging, while a fat, rich man was stealing her coins.

Mia understood why Carlton was upset.

'It's on a side road, fortunately, although I can't understand how they manage to do it and get away with it. I mean, this is Manhattan, not an isolated corner in the Bronx,' Carlton said.

'Well, you have a piece of art on your doorstep,' Mia added.

'That's not art, that's vandalism. Art is a nice Rembrandt on a wall!' The tone in his voice didn't leave room for misinterpretation. He was pontificating.

'I disagree on that,' Xander said, trying to keep his cool. 'With that concept we should only listen to classical music. No room for jazz, pop, or even punk. Mind you, I was barely born when the punks were around, but it's a form of expression.'

'Punks. You used the correct word. What gives those punks the right to ruin my private property?' He loosened his silk tie and unfastened the top button of his shirt. Carlton could be very assertive at times.

Mia knew where this was going. Neither of the two men were ready to give up their own point of view for the sake of a pleasant evening together. It was pure antler clashing, and despite her attempts at changing the subject, the two went on arguing. Mia was on the fence, and Jenny was sipping, silently.

Kowalski was one of Mia's personal heroes, reminding people with his artwork what was wrong with society. On the other side, she was torn, because she was in love with Carlton. They fit together nicely, apart from the occasional argument about… art. That was possibly the only subject they argued about. At the end of the evening, and a couple of bottles later, Jennifer and Mia were spared the exhaustion of listening to the two men bickering. Carlton received an urgent call and had to leave.

'Did he pay the bill?' a worried Xander asked.

'Indeed,' Mia said, 'although I doubt he's going back to the office. I mean, he drank the whole bottle. Most likely he's going to fall asleep in his Rolls. The driver will take care of him.'

They all laughed.

'A Masseto on our table and not being able to even have a sip.' Xander frowned, his face the mask of tragedy. 'We're reaching the decay of morals, our society is on the verge of collapsing…'

'Wow!' it was Jennifer's turn to comment, 'that's the alpha male I'm talking about. Well done, Mia, and well-deserved. I'd be at his feet every day of the week, that is, if he wasn't already taken.'

'He's an asshole.' Xander wasn't ready to give up. Not yet.

'Who's up for a last round of wine?' Mia asked, hoping not to trigger another diatribe on Carlton.

'Why not? Tomorrow is my day off, I can have a lie-in,' Jennifer said.

Mia didn't remember the last time she'd had a lie-in.

COLETTE KEBELL

CHAPTER 4

Mia received a message from Carton at 7.30 PM on the spot. He was waiting outside.

She closed the door behind her and looked around. It was only when Carlton lowered the tinted window on the passenger's side and waved, that she wondered what was he up to now? The brand-new black Mercedes S-Class, illegally parked in front of her, was going to be her ride for the night.

'What happened to the Rolls? Did you lose your job?' she asked as soon as she sat inside. She hurriedly put the seatbelt on. A very persistent *ping* coming from the dashboard was a reminder that safety came first.

Carlton gave her a quick kiss and replied, 'I thought it'd be nice to have a night out in the name of sobriety. The ride helps to keep a lower profile.'

The disapproval was clear on his face whilst he examined the neighbourhood.

'Since when did you become wise and concerned about your public image?'

Carlton's eyes lingered on her exposed knees.

'Since this morning. You know, with great power comes great responsibilities, although this whole thing sucks a bit,' Carlton said. 'As the new CEO of a budget supermarket chain, I have to keep a low and soberer profile. It's good for the business not to be seen splashing money on expensive cars.

Come on, let's make a move, we have a reservation.'
The engine was already running, and he left the
parking spot without indicating, causing havoc
among the traffic behind.

'Where are we going this time?' She planted her
feet firmly on the floor and grasped the handle on
the passenger-side door.

'Gustave Chignon at Bryant Park. They've
recently got their third Michelin star, and I thought
of checking them out.'

'So, bang goes Captain Sensible.' She laughed.

'What do you mean?'

'You just said you need to keep a sober profile,
and we're going to a restaurant that charges five
hundred dollars a head, wine excluded. What would
your customers think about that?' she poked fun at
him.

'I haven't signed up to be a monk. This time it's
Gustave Chignon, next time I'll take you to a Burger
King.' By the tone of his voice, he didn't seem
pleased by the remark. He kept his focus on the road
ahead, zigzagging among the traffic as if he had to
catch the midnight train to Georgia.

'I could murder a burger right now.' Teasing
Carlton was far too easy. At times he was simply
very predictable in his reactions.

'So maybe we should,' he said, but it was
apparent by how he was trying to strangle the
steering wheel that he wasn't amused.

'Up to you, babe. I had significantly lowered my expectations when it's a matter of restaurants, recently.'

The next twenty minutes passed in silence, except for the occasional glimpse of road rage in Carlton. Mia was lost in her thoughts, gazing at the Manhattan skyline, wondering how and when she'd have an occasion to return to a real job that paid real money.

They left the car at a twenty-four-hour parking garage at W 43rd street and walked towards Bryant Park. The restaurant was next to the HSBC tower.

'Good evening,' a young, attractive brunette at the entrance said. 'Do you have a reservation?'

'Sure, the name is Allerton.'

'Of course, you are." The brunette stared at Carlton and smiled expectantly for several seconds, completely ignoring Mia.

She knew that look, daydreams of yachts, private jets, and making love with the most desired bachelor in the city. She wondered if she did the same when she first met him.

The waitress picked up a pair of menus from the counter and led the way into the restaurant. The spacious rooms were modern in style; the couple followed her through walnut tables and dark-brown leather chairs. The walls were adorned with ornate mirrors and contemporary artwork, making the atmosphere warm and cosy.

'I'd like to try the five-course tasting menu,' Carlton said to another attentive waitress who arrived a few seconds after they sat, 'and a bottle of Crochet Sancerre.' Then, addressing Mia, 'And you?'

'I've barely had a chance to read the menu.'

'Would you like five more minutes?' the waitress asked politely. At least this one kept her distance and didn't drool over Mia's boyfriend.

'Yes, please.' *The menus are becoming more and more complicated as the years pass.* What had happened to the old-fashioned way of giving a name to a plate? The *Peach Melba*, the *suprêmes de volaille Jeannette*, *fraises à la Sarah Bernhardt* like Escoffier used to call his dishes. Nowadays, plates of food didn't have a name anymore, they were becoming a long list of ingredients on the menu. In the worst cases, like the one Mia had in her hand, they even explained the way they cooked the food. Be it sous vide, poached, or fumigated in hay.

'Let's hope they don't put edible flowers on it,' she mumbled.

'What was that?'

'Nothing, darling. I think I'll go for the tasting menu as well.' She didn't mention they could have picked up a bottle of Crochet Sancerre at Corrigan's for a mere thirty-five dollars instead of the whopping two hundred and sixty-five.

'Good choice, Mia. I always think the tasting menu is the best in these kinds of places. It lets you better understand the chef's style and where he's going with his ideas.'

Mia stared at the open kitchen, five meters away from their table. There was a large glass window separating the chefs from the public; they worked at a frantic pace. They seemed miserable. She picked up her phone and did a quick search on Gustave Chignon. A second look at the kitchen confirmed the chef was nowhere to be seen. He was probably too busy attending a culinary show on television.

The first course arrived, and the waitress launched into a sophisticated explanation of the ingredients, where they were sourced and foraged and how they were cooked. What Mia could see on the plate were three minuscule Jersey potatoes, two slices of radish, one green bean, and a sort of brownish puree, allegedly made with liquorice and celeriac. A tiny drizzle of sauce, or better a few drops, was possibly what the menu listed as a rabbit and Madeira bisque.

'Exceptional,' Carlton said, full of anticipation.

'At least no foam or dry-ice fog is coming from beneath the plate. I was hoping they had some edible soil and reconstructed carrots which tasted like quail.'

Carlton placed the cutlery on the table. He wasn't amused. 'Are you being sarcastic?'

'Who, me? Not a chance, but then what do I know, I'm a simple girl from Maine. I wouldn't expect steak and chips but, hey, look at this plate.' She pushed together some of the ingredients. 'There isn't even an entire radish in here. A quarter of it, I reckon.'

'Mia, it's the mix of flavours that counts, the texture of the food and the combination of ingredients.'

She took a bite, ignoring the patronising tone in Carlton's voice. 'Which is definitely interesting. I'd say whacky, but who am I to judge?'

'Here, have some wine with it. You're talking yourself down. You're a brilliant woman and you've been a successful lawyer.'

Mia couldn't believe what she was hearing. She was fuming and could have strangled him right there. 'I have been? Meaning that now I am a loser for what I'm doing?'

'You know I didn't mean it like that. You're the first to say you're not enjoying what you're doing, and you want to go back to corporate law.'

'I don't dislike what I'm doing, it's that I'm earning peanuts, and after years of study I'd like to have a more rewarding career.' Mia was unsure of her own words, though. 'Yeah, I hate my job. I can't believe I'm spending my time going to court for DUIs, people who forgot to pay their rent and get evicted, bitter divorces, and couples who argue over pennies.'

In the meanwhile, the second course arrived, depressing Mia even further. The plate was made of three tortellini (why always three?) with a pinch of parmesan and a truffle. The chef probably had to use one of those Sherlock Holmes magnifying glasses to place the cheese correctly. On a side plate, a poached samphire stick and a mushroom and Madeira sauce.

This time she had a whole girolle mushroom, although the chef, for unknown reasons, decided to cut it into four pieces. A couple of cubes of jelly orange and a parsnip puree completed the dish. Carlton muttered something about the balance of acidity. Mia gulped another glass of Sancerre.

'Divine. The combination of the texture of the samphire and the thin pasta that melts in your mouth...'

What in hell was he talking about? Even old-fashioned manners of not speaking with a full mouth was out of the question, due to the fact there wasn't enough food on the plate for a mouthful.

'There is also that employee of yours, Ginger, who you hate,' Carlton remarked.

'I don't hate her; she is indeed a challenge on occasion. I haven't found a way to rein her in yet, especially when she launches one of her schemes.'

'Is she still doing that? Just fire her,' Carlton said as if there wasn't any other logical, reasonable choice in the world.

'I'll consider it.' The fact was, Ginger had saved her little firm a couple of times by putting her own money into the business. Questionable cash from some of her unorthodox lines of business, admittedly, often on the boundaries of legality. When she'd done that, she'd never asked for anything in return. Not a share in the company, although the earnings were so scarce, they could barely pay themselves a salary, nor any kind of recognition. Getting rid of her wouldn't have improved her position one bit and possibly would have made matters worse.

'How long is it going to take you to get back into corporate law, in a *proper* firm?' Carlton pushed.

Her job and her status bothered him; it was his pet topic since he'd become CEO. Maybe his grandpa was nagging him, as usual; it wouldn't be the first time from what she knew. Old Allerton had little choice, given that Carlton was the only child in the family with some business sense. His brother had a job in the company as Chief of Architecture and Strategy, a right-sounding name for a position with no power whatsoever. And his sister, well, she was too busy going shopping on Fifth Avenue to care about the business. As long as her credit card was topped up, she wasn't a contender for any leading position in the company. His own father disappeared somewhere in the Midwest with an exotic dancer and was stripped of any corporate earnings. His personal savings disappeared soon afterwards, with the exotic dancer. Carlton hadn't heard from him in ages.

'I don't know, how should I? It doesn't depend on me, the market is rubbish, and nobody is hiring,' Mia tried to justify her lack of success. She hated living in Brooklyn but most of all she hated being ordinary. Her biggest fear was becoming like her parents.

Mia's dad worked as a journalist for a small local newspaper and was now retired; he was a handyman in their little town to raise some extra money. Her mother had a bakery and had worked there for as long as Mia could remember. No, she rejected the idea of having an ordinary life.

That was why she'd studied hard to get a scholarship to Harvard. Why she had moved to New York in the first place and worked like a Trojan. She'd landed one of those jobs at a hundred and fifty thousand dollars a year, bonus excluded, dealing with corporate taxes. Or how to avoid them. It was a sweatshop, but that was the life she chose, trying to be the best at what she did. Then everything went wrong; one of their major clients, a bank, went bust, then another couple of clients followed suit, and the firm, Carnegie, Stephens, and Honeycomb, closed entire departments to survive the turmoil. They made her and a few hundred other associates redundant before she could become a partner, and the firm continued their business without her. Their loss, although Carnegie, Stephens, and Honeycomb didn't want to hear any of that. As an outcome, she had to change her lifestyle, giving away her minuscule apartment in Manhattan, and had to settle for another minute apartment in Brooklyn. And she had to reconsider her expectations of a brilliant and fast career track.

It wasn't just the firm she was working for that was in trouble. Other firms "optimised their assets", "slimmed down", and preferred being "dynamic and flexible", and the result was that tons of lawyers were now battling for the few positions available. Being a woman didn't help. For half a second, especially when she saw at what rate her bank account was falling, she considered moving out of New York altogether; she could have still practised law, but somehow corporate tax wasn't such a hot subject. Mia was not ready to give up her dream, not yet.

Nobody or nothing was stopping her. Now it was only a matter of how and when, but she could work on finding a better place. She always did.

'Maybe you aren't trying hard enough,' Carlton said. 'I cannot believe there isn't a law firm out there who wouldn't hire you. Did you try Lowe and Barrington?'

'Of course.'

'Tomlins, Daniels, and Co.?'

'That one as well, and all the other top firms. I also asked the university if they could share contacts. I begged for free work just to have my foot in the door. Nothing.'

The third course was an uneventful lamb and beetroot plus other *stuff* Mia couldn't remember. The fourth course was eaten in silence, and the fifth was a deconstructed *floating island.*

'What is the purpose of a floating island if they serve you the custard separately and the island doesn't float?'

'That's the point, my dear, they deconstruct the dish, but when you eat it, it tastes the same,' Carlton lectured.

'I still don't get it. The only purpose, I believe, is to make the chef have an intellectual orgasm. Look how clever I am, I can deconstruct a dish, forgetting that for whoever eats it, there is no difference whatsoever.' Mia was annoyed by the whole direction the evening had taken. She had been anticipating a night out in a fancy restaurant, but in the end, she got overpriced food and had to sustain an interrogation on her job applications. If Carlton pushed her any further, she'd explode.

'I see you don't appreciate haute cuisine. Maybe it was my mistake,' Carlton said without sounding too convincing.

'Indeed, my fault. You should have taken me to have that burger. Given how the evening is going, I'm actually craving one.'

Carlton asked for the bill, which arrived seconds later. Those waiters were good and understood when a bill was to be brought to the table in a hurry.

A flood of flashes invaded them as soon as they came out of the restaurant. There were at least twenty photographers taking pictures of Carlton and Mia.

'Who's the pretty lady?' a journalist asked, sticking a microphone under Carlton's nose.

'She's my fiancée,' he answered without any doubt in his voice.

Mia stared at him as if her partner were an alien. She hadn't expected that and, most of all, she couldn't believe he was telling a reporter before even discussing it with her. Carlton put his arm under hers and almost dragged her away from the crowd in the general direction of the parking lot.

The photographers kept running ahead to get a better shot.

'Is a date for the wedding already decided?' the same journalist asked.

Carlton kept walking at a fast pace, but again, he answered, 'Not yet, but stay tuned. I will hold a conference as soon as we've decided.'

Mia was looking around, lost. She was surrounded by photographers. There was no escape from that crowd.

'What's your name, lady?' someone shouted.

Mia lowered her head and kept walking. Finally, they entered the parking lot and got some peace.

'What the bloody hell was that?' Mia screamed once they were safely inside the car.

'Paparazzi. They seem to be everywhere these days.' Carlton shrugged, as if nothing had happened. He turned the ignition key and reversed the car, almost hitting another vehicle in the process.

'I saw who they were, thank you very much. I mean, what's that story about being your fiancée? My face will be plastered all over the tabloids tomorrow. People will start showing up at my office and asking questions.' Mia was on a roll. 'And I think I deserved to be asked, rather than being informed at the same time as others, if not at least consulted, about something like that, before hosting a press conference.'

Carlton was in the wrong. She couldn't believe how egotistical he was at times. As a result, their drive to his apartment was of a somewhat tense, but quiet nature. After parking in the underground garage, they arrived at Carlton's *bachelor pad*, as Mia often referred to it. There were little or no personal items on display, just boy's toys and a fully equipped, though hardly used, kitchen. Strike that, there were indeed plenty of personal items on display, but nothing made it feel like a home. She perused, for the umpteenth time, the signed baseballs enclosed in Perspex, the artwork, most of which were eighteen century or earlier and caused no feeling whatsoever to emit from her, and then there were the boxing gloves and the like. She still couldn't comprehend how such an intelligent man, one who, as she had just discovered, was obviously intent on marrying her, could keep his place so masculine. For sure she could put her own spin on the furniture once they got married.

Carlton rushed off to the fridge to open a bottle of Dom Perignon and returned swiftly with two glasses. He deftly handed a glass to Mia, loosened his tie, and undid the first button of his sartorial white shirt, then he descended to one knee and, raising the glass, said, 'I'm sorry, Mia, I'm a complete idiot. I promise, tomorrow, without fail, the first thing I shall do is go out and buy you the biggest, most gorgeous rock I can find. And I will propose properly.'

Mia looked down at him, unable to comment. But that was Carlton, she said to herself. One moment he could be the most utter jerk, and the moment after the most romantic guy in the world.

Carlton continued, 'Then tomorrow evening we shall eat at Kobayashi, that new Japanese place which is receiving rave reviews from *The New York Times*, to celebrate our engagement and announce it to the world'.

'You bloody hell already did it.' She laughed, then kneeled on the floor herself and kissed him on the lips. 'Come on, let's kill that bottle of champagne before it gets too warm.'

Carlton stood and so did Mia. They kissed again before toasting to their own engagement.

Though Mia had relented and accepted the situation she now found herself in, she still couldn't help thinking why he'd even announced anything without consulting her. The moment took hold of her, though, and when Carlton, after a couple of glasses of champagne, suggested an early night, she readily took his hand and followed his direction. Carlton was romantic, and Mia wasn't about to throw that feeling away, not that night.

After a rather attentive session in the bedroom, Mia felt she needed a shower and so extracted herself to the bathroom. She spent minutes looking at her reflection in the mirror. Married to Carlton Allerton, Chief Executive Officer of Allerton Groceries, and the best bachelor in town. She didn't fully realise to what extent that would have changed her life, but she was ready to accept whatever fate had decided to throw at her. *Maybe they will take notice in my next interview.* She giggled thinking about her job situation. *No, I would hate finding a job like that.* She wanted a career, but not at the expense of her own dignity. She still had plenty of work to do with her clinic and concluded the job search had to wait until after the wedding and the honeymoon. That triggered an entirely new train of thought. *Where to go? The Maldives? A trip to Italy?* She wanted something memorable, not like her parents, who spent their honeymoon… *Damn! My parents.* That was an issue she had to sort out sooner rather than later.

When she exited the bathroom, Carlton seemed nonplussed entirely about her, and so she took a cab to her own apartment, where at least she'd have time to consider her situation, on her own, without his or any other interruption. Mia had a fitful night's sleep from that point on but felt more in control, having returned to her home.

She didn't it know yet, but her life was going to change radically.

CHAPTER 5

Mia had a peek at the latest Kowalski's work. There were a few other bystanders around, someone was taking pictures, and the painting was amazing. It was really a work of art, and she couldn't understand how he'd managed to paint it; nighttime for sure, but this was Manhattan, and the spot he had chosen wasn't a dark alley in the Bronx but right near a main street. She took a picture to post later on Instagram. Carlton wasn't a fan of social media so there would be no argument there.

She entered the Allerton Groceries building.

The secretary approached Mia, apologising. 'Mr Allerton has an important meeting, it's likely to be at least half an hour wait.'

She was directed to a lobby with a black leather, too-hard-to-be-comfortable sofa. Mia checked her emails. The secretary returned in front of her computer; she was undoubtedly trained not to strike up any conversation with customers and, at that point, Mia didn't think the secretary knew she was Carlton's girlfriend. Fiancée, according to the media.

She peeked out of the window overlooking Manhattan. It was a crisp and clear night, and the view was stunning. Not even the senior partners in her old firm could afford such a view. On the left side, the conference room was barely visible. A long walnut oval table. People sitting and nodding at what Carlton had to say, and her boyfriend standing next to a projector. Mia was too far away to make sense of slides, graphs, and a map of Europe.

The meeting ended abruptly a few minutes afterwards, and the people left the room in a hurry, surely with lots of strategies to devise. Carlton was as beautiful as ever; he emanated power from every pore.

'Bloody lab rats!' he said, coming towards Mia. He kissed her before even giving her the chance to say a word.

'What's up, trouble in paradise?'

'Nah, we have an acquisition in progress, and I had to set them straight. Now they know what to do, let's hope they don't mess up,' he said, still holding her in his arms.

'I thought it was about supermarkets, not performing in the Midwest.'

'That one, too, but it can be easily rectified. We're reducing the workforce and making the balance straight for our investors. The meeting was mostly about the acquisition of a company.'

Her mind cast back to her previous job. It was so easy to get rid of employees; a quarter not delivering the right results, and innocent people would get the axe. In that moment, she related more to the unfortunate unknown individuals who were going to lose their jobs than to her boyfriend. She glimpsed again at the picture of Kowalski's work on her phone. It seemed to her that during the years the artist had spoken to her directly, as if there was some mysterious connection. When she left Maine for Harvard to pursue her dream of becoming a famous lawyer, Kowalski was depicting elegant lawyers with a shark's head feeding on their client's flesh. And a painting found in an alley in San Francisco about that girl's dream of working pottery. She almost cried when she saw it because art was the choice she had abandoned. She shrugged the thoughts away and returned to pay her attention to what Carlton was saying.

'It's about the acquisition of a frozen food chain in California, right?'

'Right.' Carlton seemed to carefully consider his answer. 'We acquire it, we split it into pieces and sell them, we keep some lucrative shops, and it should be a done deal in six months' time. Are you ready to go?'

'I am indeed,' Mia said

On that occasion, they took the company limousine and spent the rest of the time cuddling until they reached their destination. Actually, it was Mia hugging him, Carlton was busy texting some instructions on that deal of his.

'How is your job hunting going?' he asked suddenly, his gaze lost on the crowd in the street.

'The same as the last time we touched the topic. Nothing on the horizon, and I'm surviving. What I'm doing now pays the bills. I'll be back in a law firm eventually.'

'Why don't you come to work for me? In our legal department? Bill is retiring, and we need some fresh blood. You could take his place.'

Bill was the senior legal consultant at Allerton Groceries. He was in his early sixties and as sturdy as a rock, an old-school guy. He set up his own firm in NY when he was in his thirties and had a bit of a past in litigation. Mia had actually studied a couple of his cases at university. Bill Ross wasn't yet a legend, but indeed he had been one of the major players in his youth. He sold his firm for umpteen million dollars a few years back and went to work for Allerton for an undisclosed amount of money. Rumour had it that was several million a year.

'I… I am shocked. Do you really want me to work for your firm? This isn't a joke, right?'

'Never kidding on work-related matters. Never kidding ever, now that I think about it, but yes. We have nice a position waiting for you there, a sound title and taking Bill's place full time. He's retiring; you'll have our legal department all for yourself. You're talented, and I don't like you wasting your time as you're doing now. You could even hire your old firm and then sack them the day after just for fun.'

That was an unexpected offer. 'I was mostly in corporate taxes, though…'

'I remember that, but you can learn the new stuff nonetheless. You're a clever girl.'

'I don't know what to say…' Flabbergasted was the only word that came to her mind; in a matter of days, she could be back on track with her career. A couple of years of hard work, and she'd have the vice president of the legal department on her business card. All that without too much effort, she knew how those things worked. Corporate lawyers did only part of the job themselves; if things became tough, they hired a third party anyway.

'It's something you should consider, especially if you're going to be my wife,' he said.

Can a lawyer ever be speechless?

There might have been a few moments in life where Mia found herself without anything to say, but last time it happened to her was at school, in fourth grade, when she hadn't studied for a lesson. The look on Mrs Clark's face, her teacher, spoke volumes. Since then, she'd promised herself never to be caught off-guard, always having something to say, an opinion, or even empty words to fill a silent gap.

'I'm speechless...' Mia repeated and then, 'it's going to be a big jump.'

'Don't think too long; eventually, I'll have to fill that position, and we're in the middle of an acquisition.'

She hugged him and kissed him on the spot. 'Thank you for the opportunity, I promise I'll think about it.' *Maybe my life is changing for the good.* In that moment, she knew everything she had dreamed of could well become a reality. *Funny how dreams are always the same—a career, a lavish wedding, a family.*

Perhaps on that front, I lack imagination, but she felt happy nonetheless.

The building was in midtown Manhattan.

'I'm glad I got changed. People are so elegant tonight,' Mia said.

'You look beautiful, too, and that dress is perfect for the occasion.'

The last of my high-end purchases. She couldn't afford a black Valentino with her current salary.

'What's the charity?' Mia asked.

'Compassionate American Purse. I've been a member for a few years now. We take turns in organising events and fundraising.'

'What's the cause?' she asked.

'There are several, actually.' He passed a hand through his hair. 'The aim is to improve peoples' lives. Creating jobs, which is the difficult part, but also to provide immediate relief to the ones in need.'

'You mean food banks? Or the other sort?'

'Yes, that is one of the initiatives,' Carlton continued, 'since the beginning. To be honest, I'm not a hundred percent knowledgeable on where all the money goes, that's a task for whomever manages the charity, but we get decent tax relief out of that. Philanthropy is the next big thing, and we need to be seen doing our part.'

'You should do it because it's the right thing to do, not because it makes you look cool.'

'I apologise if I didn't express myself correctly.'

There was more to the event than Mia had imagined. First of all, it was on the top floor of a skyscraper. Few of the present, on the large terrace admired the Manhattan skyline and the Empire State Building. Secondly, it didn't resemble at all a charity event. Elegant people milled around, smiling, chatting, and drinking wine.

A bored couple sat on a pair of stools near the bar.

'Come on, relax and let's mingle.' Carlton took her by her hand.

'Is there going to be an event of any sort? I don't know, an auction or a way of getting funds?" She had never been at a charity event that resembled a party. There was music in the background, and a few people were tentatively dancing in the large open space.

'Of course, they should start shortly, and I'll also make a donation in your name, my dear future wife."

Married!

Me!

Who would have dreamt of that? I mean, obviously I was dreaming about that, most of the time, but in my mind I imagined it would happen much later, maybe around my forties. And here I am, with the best catch in New York asking ME to marry him. If only he had done it correctly, on one knee, I would have been thrilled to bits.

Carlton was having casual chats with guests, and he appeared extremely relaxed. Mia wondered if he was restraining himself. *Come on, Carlton, let go.*

You just asked me to marry you, you should be as happy as a clam.

Whilst her companion was still busy talking about market shares, she went to the bar and asked what wines they were serving.

'Wine?' the waiter replied, as if she'd asked for Ambrosia. The young guy regained his composure. 'Of course, of course. We have different vintages of Dom Perignon Reserve, also in rosé and white brut, we've got Krug Clos d'Ambonnay, Louis Roederer Cristal "Gold Medallion", and Cristal Vinotheque Rosé…'

'I mean, do you have anything that is not a champagne?'

'Not a popular choice here, milady. Champagne is what *they* drink, full stop. The other popular choices are whiskey.'

No other wines? Mia felt on the wrong planet. 'Okay, let's crack open a bottle of Gold Medallion. I saw it in a picture once, I'm curious about its taste.'

'Wise choice, milady.'

Carlton reached her by the bar. 'So, what do you think?'

'I… I don't know,' she whispered.

'If you don't like it here, we can go somewhere else,' he said. 'Why are you whispering?'

'Do you know any of these people?' she asked.

'As a matter of fact, I do, most of them are actually friends of mine. Let me introduce you. Some contacts might be useful in the future.'

A few names were dropped and, oh boy, it was la crème de la crème of the young New York.

'Ladies and gentlemen...'

A young, elegant man in his thirties was on the podium trying to grab the attention of those presents by pounding on a glass with a golden pen.

'Ladies and gentlemen, the auction is going to start, so please make ready your cheque books. Tonight, we are going to auction your girlfriends and boyfriends to help the less fortunate singles in this room with a starting bid of twenty thousand dollars. No, there is no option to give up your husband and wife for free...'

Someone laughed, others looked disappointed.

'Just kidding, of course, but I bet you thought about it, tell the truth. The first item on the list is...' The young man removed a remote from his pocket and turned on the mega screen behind him. 'The famous Gustave Chignon will cook for you, at your home, for an entire week. Starting bids at ten thousand.'

'Fifteen!' a woman shouted.

'Twenty thousand,' replied another.

'My new favourite chef,' Carlton said.

'Don't you even think about that,' Mia whispered in his ear.

'Well done to the gentleman on the right, you and your family can enjoy this fabulous prize for a mere twenty-five thousand dollars. Sold!'

A few people clapped.

The auction went on with a luxury vacation in Dubai, another one on a mega-yacht in Monte Carlo that one of the participants to the auction had made available for the occasion, but what, at that point, stole the show was the possibility of doing a cameo as a stormtrooper in the next *Star Wars* movie. That was until the following item they put up for auction.

'And now, ladies and gentlemen, we are entering into the top prizes for the evening. Prepare to raise those hands of yours and do, at the same time, some exercise. The next item in this auction is a painting from the famous street artist, Kowalski. The piece has been cut from a door in Baltimore and represents Steve McQueen jumping with his motorbike over the wall built by Donald Trump on the Mexican border. Any opening bids?'

Mia remembered that piece very well. The Steve McQueen image was the one depicted in *The Great Escape*. The original painting had been done on a backstreet door of a struggling restaurant. The overall idea was to encourage people to go and visit less fortunate areas in Baltimore. In reality, the owner dismantled the door a few days after and sold the painting for an unspecified amount of money. It was a small painting, though. Nobody said anything. Not a word, not even pleading the fifth amendment.

'One thousand dollars!' Mia said.

A few people turned in her direction; she herself was surprised she had even opened a bid for an amount of money she didn't have.

'Ten thousand dollars,' someone shouted from the back.

'Fifteen thousand!'

Mia whispered to Carlton, 'It is a very nice painting.'

'It is rubbish. And I disagree on the message from that vandal.'

'It could be nonetheless a good investment. Kowalski's value has constantly risen during the years. If you don't like it you can keep it in a safety deposit box. Or lend it to me. I could gladly keep it in my apartment for safekeeping.'

'I'd rather burn my money than buy that... *thing*.'

And that ended the discussion, despite the clear hint from Mia. The painting sold for twenty-two thousand dollars, which wasn't much given the auctioneers should have considered it was a charity auction. Twenty-two was a realistic valuation for a Kowalski of that size on the open market.

'We now have a group of items from the famous Yankee's player, Mickey Mantle. Two signed balls, one of those is from the sixty-one World Series Champs Team, a signed game bat, and a Yankee's jersey also signed by him. Obviously, the lot comes with a certificate of authenticity. Do I hear a first offer of twenty thousand?'

A man in the front row raised his hand, and Carlton outbid him a few seconds later with an offer of twenty-five.

Mia's jaw dropped when they reached fifty thousand, and she was unable to close it until the final bid, a hundred and ten thousand, assigned the prize to Carlton.

A number of people around patted him on the shoulder.

That would have been six months' worth of salary and bonuses in her previous job. Probably ten years in her current employment. Or five Kowalskis. She managed to say a 'well done' but, for the second time in a week, she was speechless.

She was not impressed when Carlton bid five thousand dollars for a case of fine Californian wines on her behalf.

CHAPTER 6

A secretary knocked at Carlton's office door.

'Come in, Rebecca.'

He was behind a large desk made out of an aeroplane wing piece; the top was covered with tempered glass. His laptop was open directly in front of him, displaying the latest stock report, while the two monitors at each side showed, respectively, the company intranet home page and the quarterly business review presentation he needed to deliver to the shareholders. He didn't bother with sending the Earnings Statement to the press; that was a job for the Chief Financial Officer. Things were going well for Allerton Groceries, up two percent from the previous day. After the statement had been released, Carlton was sure they'd increase even further.

'You have a visitor, an Amanda Parker. She is waiting in the lobby.'

'Okay, thanks, let her through in five minutes, please.' He pondered the reason for the unexpected visit. He was again in the news after he'd announced his engagement to Mia and he was sure his lover had turned up at his office to mark her territory. He had made it clear to Amanda many times that, in his opinion, she wasn't wedding material, and Amanda knew it. Why had she suddenly decided to drop by the office?

With the Earnings Statement going out in a few days, the last thing he needed was for another scandal to be in the news. He closed his laptop and sighed.

Amanda entered the room. 'Nice place you have here. You never invited me to your office.'

'What do you want?' Carlton asked.

He tried to remain calm, but when she removed her overcoat, revealing she was wearing only black lingerie and stockings, he froze. Amanda threw the coat on the sofa near the door and moved towards Carlton as if she were on a catwalk. She stopped right in front of him, on the opposite side of the desk, and positioned her hands on her sides, as if to challenge him.

Carlton took an in-depth look at the woman in front of him. So far, he liked what he was seeing. He picked up the phone, without taking his focus off Amanda's body, and speed-dialled his secretary.

'Yes, Mr Carlton.'

'I'm not to be disturbed for any reason whatsoever.'

'Understood, Mr Carlton.'

He slowly put down the phone and kept watching her.

'Is it not customary to offer a drink to your guests?' Amanda teased him.

He got up from his black leather chair and went to a modern walnut cabinet. He took two square glasses and a bottle of twenty-five-year-old Macallan. Something you could never find on any shelf of any Allerton's supermarket. He added a couple of ice cubes and poured the whisky. Amanda sat on his chair and placed her feet on the cold desk.

'Whisky? I'd have preferred a bottle of champagne,' she said, taking the glass from Carlton's hand. With a slick movement of her feet, she removed the Jimmy Choo red sandals.

He leaned on the table. 'I bet you would. We don't have a full working cellar in this office, I apologise.'

'You are a cold-hearted bastard, you know? You could have used that to chill the bubbly.' Amanda tasted the old whisky, posed the drink on the floor, and with her legs, she enveloped Carlton, who was a few inches away right in front of her.

They made love there and then. Carlton was only hoping that Amanda's loud orgasm wouldn't attract too much attention.

The phone rang, but he ignored it at first. It kept ringing, so Carlton got up and sorted himself out, then he tossed the overcoat towards Amanda. 'Get dressed.'

'Ah, is it going to be that way?' she said bitterly.

'Not at all, we are going out. I need some advice,' Carlton said, adjusting his shirt and tie. He used one of the windows as a mirror to check that everything was in place. He then passed a hand through his hair to comb it as best as he could.

Jason Allerton stormed in at that precise instant; he glanced at the semi-naked woman still sitting on the sofa, with her overcoat in her hand, and shouted, 'Get out of here.'

The woman glimpsed for a second at Carlton, who nodded briefly. She put her overcoat on and exited.

Jason Allerton had a few magazines in his hands and appeared to be taken aback by the presence of Amanda in his grandson's office. 'What the hell is going on here?'

'Good morning, Grandpa.'

'I told you to sort yourself out, and this is what you are doing?' His skeletal finger pointed at one of the magazines he was holding. 'Who is this Mia Crawford?'

'She's a lawyer, and she's pretty. You said to sort the matter out,' Carlton replied calmly.

'Don't tell me who she is, I read it all from the news. A Brooklyn lawyer, and she is doing legal aid work, for Christ's sake.'

'A very honourable profession, I might say.' Carlton turned his back to his grandfather and looked at the skyline outside the window. The weather was chilly, and he could clearly see for miles.

'So, you haven't learnt anything in all these years? If you have to screw around.' Jason Allerton pointed back at the sofa. 'At least marry someone with money. Are you in love with this woman?'

Carlton still had Amanda's perfume filling his nostrils and thought about the young lady who had just left his office. Then he realised old Allerton was talking about Mia. He never thought about love, not recently. Relations were something that happened; he got involved, and then they eventually ended. Was he in love with Mia? He couldn't answer that question, and he wondered if it was at all relevant. His father had affairs; all his friends were doing the same. Even the old bastard used to screw around when he was younger. He also got caught and had to pay the consequences. He never considered that marriage was something more than a mutually beneficial arrangement. Mia would be a good mother, she was gorgeous and intelligent, and they had great sex. So, yes, maybe he was in love, as much as he could be. He cringed at the idea of being married but he was well into his mid-thirties, and perhaps the old man was right: it was time to think about having an heir. Mia was a fantastic candidate. A prenuptial agreement to keep the family fortune in his hands, in case he got caught cheating, was mandatory. Mia was in love, no argument there. With a newborn baby around, the old bastard would relax his grip on the company and let him do his job correctly. He was already taking the company on new paths.

'Yes, I do love her,' he eventually said.

'Ah, love.' The contempt in Jason Allerton's voice was clearly audible. 'The most stupid things have been done in the name of love. What happened to that Caroline from the Hamptons? You loved that one as well, didn't you? Are you still in touch with her?'

Caroline was Carlton's last official girlfriend, from a few years back. He knew why his grandfather, actually, both him and Carlton's mother, liked her. She had old money, mostly invested in real estate and mining companies scattered all over the world. They had occasional sex whenever he went to his mother's property in the Hamptons, but those visits had become rare as time passed.

'I'm not going back with Caroline if that is what you're trying to suggest.'

'It's a damn shame, my boy. You'll understand that love is not real. There isn't such a thing. It's a game of compromise to reach your goals, be that affection, sex, money, or power. The only relationships worth having are about the latter. You can have sex anyway, within or without being in a marriage, so why not make the most of it?'

'Sounds a bit cynical,' Carlton retorted, although he knew what his grandfather meant.

'Not at all. Life is cynical, we're only trying to survive here and put our own stamp on things. Life is too damn short to be wasted with romance and sentimentalism. Get a grip, Carlton, you'll soon realise that being married means compromise, every single day. From what toothpaste you have to use, to what film to watch in the evening, and even how you should dress. On the other side, you have full control on how you shape a business; nobody can make you compromise there if you don't really want to. Enjoy your time with this attractive lady, but for Christ's sake, don't marry her.'

Jason Allerton stood from the armchair and walked out. There was an unusual silence after he'd left, and Carlton decided to have a glass of gin, while his grandfather's words were still echoing in his head.

Carlton could not recall when he started behaving like him. The guy had three divorces under his belt in his early days and, from what he remembered, he hadn't had a partner for the past ten years. Surely, he was getting his pleasure occasionally, but he kept that extremely quiet.

Carlton looked at the white ceiling. He was becoming more and more like his grandfather, but there was a time when he was different. There was a time when he cared about people and those around him. And it wasn't true, he admitted to himself finally, that he had never been in love. He'd met his first and possibly only love when he was still at university. Cynthia was one year older than him, and she was studying medicine. They had dreams of changing the world; they'd often discussed how he and Cynthia could be an example to the rest of the country. Carlton would eventually take the reins of Allerton Groceries, providing good quality food at reasonable prices, part of the profits to be used for charity work. Cynthia really wanted to make a difference in the world, talking all the time about organisations such as Médecins sans Frontières and others. It was a dream Carlton shared and believed in. In that period, clashing with old Allerton was a daily task. His grandfather didn't think about anything else but profit. Then Carlton's mind went to the accident.

The roads were covered in snow, and he had drunk more than he should have. He didn't recollect much of what happened that night, only flashbacks when they hit a tree, the blood in his eyes. A few images of paramedics loading him into an ambulance and then the void.

Cynthia, three months pregnant, spent two days in a coma, but too much damage had been done. The baby was lost.

It was after his recovery that he started with the booze, the fast cars, and the women, resulting in the end of his relationship with Cynthia. Mia reminded him of her, although for different reasons. His fiancée was not oriented into charity work or saving the planet, but she did indeed have that potential. She could have been Cynthia's best friend.

He shook those thoughts from his mind and picked up the phone.

'Amanda, are you free this afternoon?'

She was.

CHAPTER 7

The following morning, Carlton had devised himself a plan. His first port of call was going to be Amanda. He'd realised that without her assistance, he didn't have a chance in hell of impressing Mia after such a failure of an engagement announcement. He showered, shaved, and was busy on his cell before even having arrived at the office. Okay, he had fed Mia a little white lie, the ring thing wasn't going to be the first topic on his agenda, but he was going to deal with it when he met with Amanda.

'What the hell do you think you are doing on my doorstep after pulling that stunt? It's been all over the press, and I no longer want anything to do with you,' Amanda spat out upon opening her door to Carlton. 'What an idiot. I came to your office, made love with you, and this is what I'm getting?"

Carlton realised Amanda hadn't read the news until then. When she'd visited him at the office, he mistakenly thought she was fine with him getting engaged, that their arrangement would continue as usual. Caught by surprise, he couldn't utter a word.

'What's this story about you getting married, Carlton?'

He caressed the woman's face. 'I think it's time for me to settle down. It's good for business.'

'So, where does this leave the two of us?'

'I'm getting married, I'm not planning to be faithful,' Carlton snarled. Then he bent towards her and tried to kiss her.

Amanda sharply turned her head away, and Carlton's lips landed on her cheek.

'You are going to pay for this, big time,' she whispered in his ear.

The threat didn't pass unnoticed.

'Oh, come off it, babe. You and I both know where we stand. We enjoy each other's company and have good, exciting times together. You've never let me know anything other than you're a free spirit.' In the back of his mind, he was justifying his behaviour by drawing on the knowledge he had about his father's relationships, either marital or otherwise. He reckoned Amanda, on the other hand, had yet to decide whether she wanted more from him or not.

She closed her dressing gown and said, 'Come in.' She led the way through the lounge and went into her bedroom.

Carlton followed and explained what he had in mind, talking to her through the door.

Buying jewellery for someone else.

Amanda giggled at the idea. She was indeed a free spirit. She chose a Roberto Cavalli dress, a generous gift from one of the magazines she modelled for, a pair of high-heeled shoes, and a cashmere overcoat. She didn't do anything with her hair, leaving it scruffy. Still, she looked beautiful, although wild.

'Where are we going?' Amanda asked.

'Van Cleef & Arpels. Is there any other place where you could buy jewellery?' Carlton replied from the door. He was admiring a black-and-white nude picture of Amanda on the wall. 'I'm the luckiest bastard in the world,' he muttered.

'I could name a few who rightly have a claim to that spot,' she replied. 'I've never been to Van Cleef. Jeez, that sounds expensive.'

'I asked one of my secretaries to make an appointment. We'll be pampered.'

As soon as Amanda came out of the bedroom, he had the desire to make love to her but resisted the temptation.

When they entered Van Cleef & Arpels on 5th Street, Carlton announced himself, and a sales clerk ran to the back of the store to inform a Mr Gentry. The man was the store manager.

'I've understood from your secretary you're looking to find an engagement ring. How nice that you brought your fiancée with you,' he said, looking at Amanda.

The woman chuckled, and Carlton, flushing, hurried up to explain. 'Oh no, she is just…'

'Come on, dear, don't get embarrassed.' Amanda moved closer to him; her hips touched his. 'I know you want to keep it secret at the moment, but eventually we'll have to tell the world.' And said so, she giggled like a little schoolgirl.

Carlton stared at the floor, and Mr Gentry wore his best poker face.

'Very well, sir. If you'd like to follow me, I'm sure you'll find something suitable in our Boutique.' The man led the way to an elegant office. 'Please sit down.' He gestured towards a cream leather sofa. 'My assistants will bring our latest creations. May I offer you a cup of coffee? Maybe a glass of champagne?'

'No, thanks,' Carlton answered, also on behalf of Amanda. 'Let's crack on.'

Soon, two assistants came in and placed a large casket in front of the two guests.

'Let me see,' Mr Gentry said, picking up a solitaire diamond ring, 'would you go for a classic diamond or do you feel other stones might be to your taste? Some latest celebrities' engagements have seen a rise in popularity for sapphires. Meghan Markle went for a yellow diamond...'

'What about a ruby?' Amanda suggested. 'She is a bloodsucking lawyer, that might be appropriate.'

Carlton turned his head in her direction, upset by the remark. Mr Gentry was still like a statue and didn't utter a word.

'What about this round-shaped diamond?' Carlton picked up a three-carat white-diamond ring.

'Boring,' Amanda whispered, 'or should I say, *too classic*. In line with your future wedding.'

'This will do,' Carlton said, giving a ring back to Mr Gentry. 'Do you have any necklaces?'

The store manager gave some quiet instructions to one of the sales assistants, who came back with another casket. As soon as Carlton saw a Bouton d'Or necklace, beautifully made in pink-and-white gold with diamonds, he placed it around Amanda's neck. The woman was breathless looking at herself in the mirror.

'This is by way of a thank you for putting up with me,' and then, addressing Mr Gentry, 'I'll take both.'

'Can I keep it on?' Amanda asked.

'Sure you can.'

When they finally exited the building and were in Carlton's car, Amanda kissed him passionately. 'Do you realise you spent more on me than on your new fiancée?'

He fixed his gaze the void ahead, without saying a word for a couple of minutes. 'It's time to go,' and then eventually, he started the car and drove into the lunchtime traffic.

CHAPTER 8

Ginger was still in the office that evening.

She didn't want to be a legal secretary, but she owed Mia, and she also needed a place she could call home. Too many changes in the past few years and not enough time to think about her future. She had to earn money, and fast, since she'd been thrown out of her parents' house. They were third-generation Irish and, in Ginger's opinion, they were still stuck with a two-hundred-year-old mentality brought across from the island. She'd opened up to them, and instead of having their support, as a result, she had to leave. Ginger swore not to open up again to anybody else. Not that it would be too difficult; she was shy by nature, although events had made her change; all her schemes required a dose of confidence she didn't have, but eventually she coped. For her, it was like acting, a role in a movie. It didn't matter who she was on the inside, the only thing that mattered was what she was showing to the people on the outside.

Mia could be tough at times, maybe much too focused on having a career, but she had been kind to her. Something that didn't happen too often.

Ginger didn't know what to do with her life, despite thinking about it every day. Conning people wasn't what she wanted. Her dream was to get involved in the fashion industry, although she lacked the right qualifications. She'd worked for a short period as a personal shopper, but that also wasn't exactly what she was looking for. She got a glimpse of the fashion world, but still, she didn't want to work for somebody else. Maybe the legal clinic was the closest thing to being independent she had come across. She doubted Mia saw her as a partner, despite bailing her out on a couple of occasions, but time would tell.

Ginger had a talent with people when she wanted, but what she was missing was the direction. All her little jobs were finalised to give her independence; being a fashion consultant was the best thing in town after being a food blogger or one of those YouTube celebrities who talked about nothing. It was the reason why she'd left a job as a waitress to try something that was ultimately her own. Almost.

Her mobile rang.

'Funeral Centre Enterprise, this is Ginger speaking, how can I help?'

It was one of her secondary jobs while she was waiting for a break that would change her life. She lived in New York, where people barely knew their next-door neighbours, and when someone died, Ginger came onto the scene. People didn't want to think about cultivating friendships; they were all far too busy trying to earn as much money as they could before they kicked the bucket. As an outcome, nobody was going to show up at their funeral, making them look like the miserable sods they had been their entire lives. So, Ginger had spotted a niche and opened a website offering her services as a professional mourner. She'd go to a perfect stranger's funeral, she'd weep, sob, and say a few gripping words about the poor departed, how good he was when alive and whatever came into her mind.

The professional mourner was a historical figure, the ancient Greeks used them, and Ginger even found a reference in Dickens' *Oliver Twist*. Unfortunately, it seemed it was less of a sought-after profession in the current century. But there was still room to make some money from the Chinese and the Italians.

'I see from your website you are a professional mourner,' the voice on the other end of the phone said.

'That's correct. What is your name and who was the departed?'

'I'm Charlie Huang, and the departed was my uncle. He was an old bastard, everybody in the family hated him. My father, his brother, used to work with him in the family laundry, but they hadn't spoken for the past twenty years. I barely know him, but he left me a few thousand dollars, and I think nobody deserves to be buried alone. My father won't budge, he will not go to the funeral even if that will disgrace us amongst the neighbours.'

'Okay, I got it. We have three kinds of service, as you can see from the website. With the "Basic" you will have myself attending the funeral. The standard weeping and sobbing plus some necessary interaction with other people, telling them how good your uncle was and things like that. The "Advanced" offering includes all the above mentioned in the basic one, plus a funeral speech. If you go for the "Premium Departed", then I can bring along a few other people who can do the same. The number depends on the budget, of course, and we can vary from five people to twenty.'

'He doesn't deserve a premium service, the bastard. How much would the "Advanced" service cost me?' Mr Huang asked.

'If it's a traditional Chinese funeral, let's see… one full wake for twelve hours, full interaction with guests, one ceremony and procession… that is two thousand five hundred dollars. Unless you also want me to attend *The Return of the Dead*, that will be another three hundred.'

'I think I will skip the *return*,' Mr Huang said.

'Perfect.' Ginger took some necessary information about the deceased and the funeral schedule. 'We accept Visa and Mastercard, or you can write me a cheque when I attend the funeral. I'm sorry for your loss, Mr Huang.'

'I'm not. I'll be glad when all this is over. He caused us so many troubles during our lives; hopefully, this is the last time we'll hear from Uncle Jim.'

'My condolences anyway, Mr Huang, have a great day.'

Ginger looked at her diary, and a "Jersey girl" was next in line. Thank God it was for her personal shopping business.

'Poor Jimmy,' Ginger cried, 'he was such a lovely man behind that tough skin. For those who took time to know him, he had a heart of gold.'

Jimmy was there, in his coffin, and if there was an afterlife, he was probably scratching his head wondering who the *black widow* was.

A few people were sitting behind her, and of those, only a couple were Chinese. Jimmy was old enough so, in theory, people should have been paying their respects. That was the custom.

'He was always willing to give good advice to the young in need, like me, and he was a generous man. AAAAAHHH, JIMMY, WHY DID YOU LEAVE US SO EARLY, YOU DIDN'T DESERVE THAT!' And then Ginger sobbed and cried. She could have emulated a trumpet in a jazz quartet by just blowing her nose; it was an acquired skill.

'Ohhh, Jimmy, Jimmy! You were a pillar in the community…' she continued.

'Am I at the wrong funeral?' a middle-aged man on her left asked.

'I don't know, this is Jimmy Huang, he used to have a laundry shop between Seventy-Fourth Street and Seventeenth Avenue,' she said, looking as miserable as she could manage.

'Then I'm at the right funeral, but that is the wrong Huang. The guy was an asshole!'

'I don't know about that, I mean, maybe you caught him in a bad mood. He was grumpy, but to those who listened he could be very compassionate,' Ginger said tentatively.

'Hey, Tony? Lady here says the old Huang was a good person, what do you make of that?'

'You mean the loan shark?' another man a few rows behind answered. 'I could not care less. I'm here because I'm waiting for the betting shop to open. Still, ten minutes to go. But I heard he was a bastard!'

'Sure,' the first man remarked, 'I'm here to pay my due because when he kicked the bucket, my debt was cancelled. Not that that had anything to do with him, I guess his relatives are decent people.'

'That cannot possibly be true.' A tone of indignation was clearly audible in Ginger's voice. 'Certainly, he lent some money to me, too, but the rates were quite affordable…'

'I'm surprised nobody thought of killing the old shark,' Tony said.

Few *pings* came from the phone the man was handling. Surely, he was playing some online betting game.

'Well, that is not a nice thing to say at a funeral,' she asserted.

'Lady, I don't know where you lived all these years, but I can assure you the only good thing you can say about Huang is that he's in a coffin.'

She wasn't ready to give up yet. 'Mr Huang saved my grandfather's life during the war! They were surrounded by Japanese, and Mr Huang carried my wounded father for twenty miles while keeping the Japs at bay. He was a hero!'

Fortunately, Mr Huang, the guy who'd hired Ginger in the first place, entered the room at that moment. Plainly enough, he could see what a good job Ginger was doing trying to fend off those insensitive people and defending his family honour.

'Ah, there you are, Charlie. This young lady was just saying how good your uncle was.' Tony pointed his thumb towards Ginger.

'He was a bastard!' Mr Huang said.

Hang on a minute, he hired me a few days ago to come here and weep, and now he's saying the old man wasn't a nice person? Well, he never said otherwise, but I thought he'd at least keep up appearances.

'Mr Huang,' she whispered, 'this is not helping.'

'You know, chaps? For *The Return of the Dead*, I got a pleasant surprise for Uncle Jimmy. I've rented his apartment to a bunch of rappers. It'd be interesting seeing his bloody ghostly face when he returns,' and then, turning to Ginger, 'you can stop crying. He deserved a bit of a weep because of tradition, but not too much. You will be paid as agreed.'

Ginger was without words. 'Mr Huang, are you drunk by any chance?'

'Just a bit, do you want a beer?'

'No, thanks.'

Back at the office, Ginger found Mia doing some tidying up despite it being Saturday.

'Hi there.'

'How was the funeral?' Mia asked.

'A shambles. Mr Huang turned up drunk as a skunk. He said the old man deserved to die, and all this after I cried for almost an hour. I thought I had to stay the whole day, but he dismissed me.'

'So, he might return later and ask for his money back?' Mia asked.

'No refunds on funerals. The poor soul has departed, and so has the money they paid.'

'Ginger, you have to stop this nonsense! You almost went to jail last time. I do appreciate you are doing it off hours, but I don't want to get associated with these side businesses of yours. Not now that I'm getting engaged to Carlton!'

'That asshole? Mia, you deserve better than someone who keeps screwing around. I mean, when he's not screwing his customers,' Ginger retorted. She didn't know why she'd said that. Usually, she minded her own business, but after the disappointment of the afternoon, she felt she had to speak up. She didn't know much about Carlton, apart from what she read in the occasional gossip magazine she came across, but more than once she went to buy her shopping in one of Allerton's supermarkets. Due to necessity rather than choice.

'Now you're being nasty. That's how the press is depicting Carlton. There is nothing wrong with him!' Mia fired back. 'How dare you interfere in my private life!' She was furious.

'First Xander picked an argument with him the other day, now you're also making judgement. You simply don't know him in the same way as I do. He is a lovable man, although impulsive on occasions. Why is everybody suddenly against him?' Mia took a long breath. 'What are you doing here, anyway? It's Saturday.'

If disappointment could have a face, it would have resembled Ginger's expression at that very moment. 'I was registering the latest invoices we had for this week. I hadn't managed to do it before...' She opened her bag, fetched a pink purse, and took out a bundle of cheques, which she slammed on Mia's desk. Then, without saying another word, she picked up her coat and walked out of the door.

Mia was speechless. She took the bundle of cheques from Ginger and started looking through them. The first was from a Mr Huang, two thousand five hundred dollars; the second was from a Lucy Brown, nine hundred dollars. There were more for smaller amounts, which covered their salary, the rent and some. On her side, Mia was still waiting for a few payments from her own clients, which were now long overdue. She ran towards the door and even removed her shoes to run faster, but when she exited the building, Ginger was nowhere to be seen.

Mia cursed herself. How could she be so stupid? Ginger was the best thing that had happened to her, apart from Carlton, and if she was still in business, it was because of her extra lines of work. How could she allow her to continue with those barely ethical activities and keep her integrity?

She came to the conclusion that she couldn't, but nonetheless, she was grateful to her... employee? Was Ginger really an employee or was she more of a partner to her, despite her dodgy businesses? Mia needed to speak to someone, she needed to vent her frustration and possibly listen to some good advice. Not Carlton's, though, not on that occasion; Mia already knew he would have suggested the simple option, to get rid of her. She needed some friendly advice.

CHAPTER 9

When Amanda woke up that Monday, she had the mother of all headaches and knew straight away that a couple of paracetamol would not have been enough to do the job. God, she hated Mondays. In her bed, there was a man and a woman, profoundly asleep.

Waking barefoot on the cold floor to the kitchen, she turned the coffee percolator on and then changed her mind, opting for a beer.

She went back to the bedroom and sat on a beige suede armchair, her naked legs huddled against her body, and sipped directly from the bottle, observing the two sleeping guests. She knew the man all right, Richard; he was a talented but penniless photographer from Brooklyn. As a matter of fact, she was supposed to have a photo shoot that afternoon, if only she could get rid of the hangover and the man, Richard, woke up. The woman, though, was a mystery. She had vague memories of the party she'd gone to the previous night. People were coming and going at all hours, mostly belonging to the fashion industry: photographers, models, specialised journalists.

That was it, she works for a magazine.

Richard had introduced her to Amanda. He was badly in need of a more stable source of income and, *Keeley, that was the name,* could have helped to open the doors to one of the most influential fashion magazines in the country, if not in the world.

Her phone vibrated, and a quick glance revealed it was Carlton. She ignored the text message.

Richard stirred and then carefully removed his arm from under the woman's head. He messed his hair up even further by passing a hand through it and then looked in the general direction of Amanda.

'Good morning,' he said with a complicit grin.

'Good morning,' Amanda replied in a raspy voice.

'Sitting like that, you make me wish we had time to go back to bed. Is it coffee what I'm smelling?'

'There is a pot brewing if you like.' Amanda pointed her head in the kitchen's direction.

Richard grunted but nonetheless got up and, barefoot, walked towards the much-needed coffee.

Amanda read Carlton's message. He wanted to meet that day, most likely to vent his frustration at work through sex.

'Are you still wasting time with that guy?' Richard was standing by the bedroom door and peeking at Amanda's phone from behind.

She shrugged. 'You're right, being with Carlton doesn't get me anywhere.'

'Well, now that he has announced his engagement, he'll keep the relationship undercover for sure,' and then after a pause, 'I don't think that going public or getting caught with him "accidentally" would do you any good. You might

81

be in the gossip columns for a couple of days and then disappear. There are other avenues, you know?' Richard pointed the coffee cups towards Keeley, who was still fast asleep.

'You reckon?'

'Nothing is certain in this world, babe, but Keeley is known to keep her part of the bargain. Not that I got any closer to her before last night, but that's the rumour.'

Slowly, Amanda's memory about the previous evening took shape. It was a party organised by a significant advertisement agency, the Milton and Revere Group in Manhattan. The major fashion labels were there as well as several specialised magazines. From what she knew, Richard, resourceful as ever, managed to get hold of an invitation by begging, twisting arms, and pleading within the photography community. Eventually, a more famous friend gave up and passed the necessary contacts to be added to the list. Being seen and creating a network in the right places was his way to get visibility and pick up the scraps, usually work that others weren't willing to take, but on that occasion, he'd hit the jackpot. Even getting closer to Milton and Revere's was a significant achievement.

Amanda had pawned a ring given to her by Carlton and had gone on a shopping spree. She needed only one dress, but things soon got fast out of hand and she ended up spending thousands of dollars to find the perfect outfit, a black Roberto Cavalli evening dress, semi-transparent, a pair of black Louboutin, a small purse and leather bag. But the top of the show was going to be the beautiful necklace Carlton had given her only a few days before. She didn't know what to expect, but she was utterly confident someone would notice her.

When Richard saw her in her outfit for the evening, his jaw almost dropped to the floor. 'Stay near me,' he told her. 'People are going to buzz around you like flies on honey. Get as many business cards as you can get in that purse of yours,' he advised.

'When did we meet her?' Amanda asked, depositing her mobile on the coffee table to her side.

'Who, Keeley?' Richard enquired. 'It was already eleven in the evening, and you were pissed as a parrot. She approached you, and you were as bitchy as you can be when you've had a few too many. Luckily enough, I was close by and saved the situation.'

'Keeley was the one hitting on me? The one in the red Valentino dress?'

'The one and the same. She plays both ways. I think she liked what she saw, despite your bad attitude. At some point she was so turned on she wanted to take you to the lady's bathroom, but you didn't want any of it.'

'I have foggy memories,' Amanda said. 'Here was this lady making compliments, and I didn't know who she was and what she wanted. I got upset because she was all touchy-feely. Did I rant about Carlton?'

'You did indeed. Fortunate enough, nobody cared or knew who you were talking about.' Richard laughed.

'Oh my gosh!' she exclaimed, putting her hand in front of her mouth.

'Yeah. Glad I was around to keep an eye on you. I got chatting with her, and she had all sorts of questions about you. It was clear what her intentions were.'

Amanda began to remember. Keeley was sitting on the sofa near her. She was commenting on her transparent dress and her figure; most of the time, though, she was peeking into her décolletage. Keeley casually put her arm around Amanda's waist, blabbing her way and getting closer and closer. She could remember her pungent perfume filling her nostrils. She was too drunk to realise what her intentions were.

'So, what did you say to her?'

'Simply, if she wanted to get into your pants, there was no way that would happen during the party. You needed to be in a much quieter place.'

'You bastard! I sort of have memories of the drive back. She was like an octopus; she had her grubby hands all over me.'

Richard laughed. 'It looked like you enjoyed the attention, though.'

Amanda observed the woman still fast asleep. She was in her late thirties, maybe even early forties; toned legs were half covered by the sheets. Her dark-brown hair wrapping her shoulders. She was undoubtedly spending time in the gym. Amanda had been in bed with women before, but she had to admit Keeley knew what she was doing. She had a vague recollection of the three of them making love, bodies writhing across each other. Keeley knew what button to push to turn her on. She enjoyed it and she sort of called to mind Keeley being more than satisfied with her performance. She was only hoping something came out of that experience.

'So, what now?' Amanda asked.

'Now we shoot some photos as planned, and then you pamper the lady there, for both of us. Come on, get ready.' Richard drank the last of his coffee and moved towards the bed. His clothes were still scattered all over the floor.

Amanda finished her beer and went to the bathroom. The warm water of the shower caressed her perfect body, and she got lost in her thoughts for several minutes. The shower door opened, and Keeley joined her. They kissed, and the guest caressed and soaped her body.

They made love again. This time without Richard.

CHAPTER 10

That evening, Mia was the first to arrive at Corrigan's; what she knew was that a beer wouldn't be enough to do the job while she was waiting for her friends.

She scrutinised the wine list on the blackboard, but there was nothing she fancied.

'JOE,' she said to grab the owner's attention. 'Do you have a moment?'

'Sure, Mia. The usual?' he asked. He stood right in front of her and passed a towel over some invisible mark on the table.

'No, that's the problem. I want something different tonight.'

'Sure, for a celebration or mourning?' he joked. Sometimes, barmen could read straight through their clients.

It should have been a celebration, but something was nagging away at her. She had a little voice in her ears telling her it wasn't going to be that simple.

Come on, Mia, you're getting married. You're going to marry the most eligible bachelor available in New York. You will have a fantastic career as a top lawyer in the city, an extravagant wedding ceremony, the most beautiful babies when you decide it's time... That was it.

Joe was waiting patiently, so she showed him her engagement ring.

'I could bring you a bottle of ninety-six Calon-Ségur.' Joe seemed to ponder what to say next. '*My heart is this vineyard*, Nicolas-Alexandre once said, Marquis de Ségur, despite also owning both the Lafite and the Latour. Hence the heart on the bottle. Love is ephemeral, but the love for a bottle of good wine is forever. It will serve you well.'

'You sound like a diamond advertisement. Deal.'

Joe went down to the cellar and came back with a dusty bottle. He uncorked it in front of Mia, poured a fair amount into a Bourgogne glass, and then placed the cork near it.

That was an old habit of his. If you picked up the cork and you sniffed it, you were automatically classified as a moron. Mia was not in the habit of sniffing corks—the only odour one could smell was that of the cork. One day, an occasional customer bought a cheap glass of wine. Joe asked him if he wanted to sniff the metal bottle screwing cap. They never saw that customer ever again. Well, Joe's place, Joe's rules.

Jennifer entered, strangely enough, on time. Xander was right behind her.

'Hey, you started without us, what... Oh my God, is that a Calon-Ségur?' Jennifer stared in disbelief at the bottle on the table. 'What is going on?'

Mia filled their glasses using her left hand and had a wicked grin on her face.

Jenny jumped on her feet, screaming, 'OH MY GOD! OH MY GOD! IS THAT WHAT I THINK IT IS?'

Xander kept looking at Mia and then at Jennifer and then back to Mia as if he was a spectator of the oddest verbal ping-pong match in the world. The women both gawked at him, and he raised his hands.

'Okay, I give up. What's going on here?'

'Fancy explaining?' Jennifer asked.

Mia laughed and then scratched her chin, trying to point her engagement ring in Xander's general direction. 'Let's see. This very bottle,' she said, stretching her hands across the table (still no reaction), 'and the wine you are going to drink tonight…' She was pointing straight at his glass.

'Oh, I got it! The ring,' he exclaimed. 'Are you getting engaged? Who's the…?' Xander stopped mid-sentence.

'Don't be an asshole, Xander,' Jennifer said, 'the right word to say is *congratulations*.'

'Yes, of course, of course. Congratulations. That explains why you're blowing a month of wine budget on a single bottle. My budget at least, not yours.'

'Shut up and enjoy the treat.' Mia laughed. 'Or I'll relegate you to a Zinfandel.'

'I shall abstain from any further comments,' he retorted, 'except on the subject of your husband-to-be.'

Mia told them about the previous days without sparing any details, and the reactions were as expected. Negative from Xander and enthusiastic from Jennifer. One big question was still troubling Mia, though.

'How am I going to tell my parents?' she asked.

'Send them a postcard after you get married.' Xander sipped his wine.

On the other side, Jennifer didn't take the troubling question as a joke. 'Do you want them at your wedding?'

That was the one-million-dollar question. Mia loved her parents but, knowing them, they would disagree with her marrying Carlton and hate him from their guts: in their eyes, he was the symbol of all the things that were wrong in America. Mia could already foresee some sarcastic comment from her dad during the ceremony. *If anyone can show just cause why this couple cannot lawfully be joined together in matrimony, let them speak now or forever hold their peace* and her father coughing loudly and announcing 'I'd say a word or two.'

'I don't know, I really don't.'

'Maybe you should not just call them. Go and visit your parents,' Xander said, who for once was being useful. 'Nothing better than explaining things face to face.'

'I know, but I have my business…'

'Bollocks,' he continued, 'it's not that you are making a fortune in that job anyway. You go back to

Maine and talk to your parents. I can keep an eye on the place.'

'Oh, that would be helpful.' Mia laughed. 'Let me guess, you want to write a legal novel and need inspiration.'

'Sort of, I need a place where I can take a break and write. Going to Starbucks costs me a fortune in coffee, and the time I spend at home is not enough.'

That prompted Mia to ask on how to deal with the situation which had been nagging at her. 'Actually, I need some advice on something that's going on with Ginger at the office.'

'Ah, the elusive Ginger. Is she cute?' Xander asked.

'Stop it, Xander,' Jennifer interjected. 'Don't you see it's not the right moment?'

Xander put the hoodie on his head and crossed his arms as a sign of protest.

Mia explained what bothered her and all the side businesses Ginger was involved in. Her primary concern was that she could cross the line and do something stupid that not only would put Ginger at risk but also damage Mia in the progress.

'From what you've said,' Jennifer continued, 'some of the things she's doing are okay. For example, the fashion consultancy. Even attending the funerals: it might sound odd, but she is not conning anybody, she gives service to adults who know exactly what they are paying her for.'

'I actually like the bit when she writes articles for incompetent bloggers. I should have come up with that idea, it's brilliant.'

Mia was taken aback by their reactions; she was secretly hoping they supported Carlton's view on the matter, hence relieving her of the guilt of firing Ginger. Instead, things had turned in the opposite direction.

'Come on, Mia, relax,' Xander said. 'If needs be, I can go to a funeral or two for a small fee and I'm definitely up to write some blog posts. Granted, I might not be the best person to give advice on what to wear.'

On that he was spot on. 'I'm glad you are aware that grubby jeans with cuts at the knees, a University of Wisconsin hoodie, and a beanie are not exactly the latest fashion.' *Why Wisconsin? He never moved from New York*, but she would not dare to ask. He could actually answer that question.

'It is, according to *Delivery Guy Fashion Magazine.*'

'I'll keep an eye on Ginger, so she stays on the straight and narrow while you're away,' Jennifer volunteered. 'I could help on the fashion front as well. I've picked up a trick or two, and then it would only be a matter of a few days. We promise not to ruin your business,' she said enthusiastically. 'We're not going to give legal advice, but if some clients turn up, we can schedule an appointment for when you're back. You know, keep the business afloat, or something like that.'

'For a week, I trust you guys to keep an eye on my empire.' Mia sipped the last of her wine. Joe definitely knew how to please his customers. 'Why don't you pop in by the office one of the next few days?'

'Sure,' they said at the same time.

For some reason, they seemed too eager. Maybe they were both thinking of having a week of fun, while Mia was sure it was going to be hard work.

There was another bombshell coming. 'Carlton asked me to work for him, taking over the legal department.'

'Wow!'

'For the whole of Allerton Groceries? That is a dream job, are you sure you are up for it?' Jennifer asked.

Mia didn't know how to respond. That was the reason she went to Harvard, to become one of the top lawyers in New York, although, in her imagination, it would have taken years of hard work and sacrifice. Another thing that would make breaking the news to her parents even more difficult.

'Well, it's a great opportunity, but it means closing the legal aid shop. I made it clear I have to close all my current legal aid cases, which can take a few months. I might have to start part-time.'

'Is that what you *really* want?' Xander asked. The guy didn't fluff around, he was always getting to the point using the least amount of words.

Mia bit her nails. 'I don't know, I don't think so. I wanted to build a career on my own; getting a position like that just because I'm his girlfriend, pardon, fiancée, doesn't seem right. I think that's the reason I didn't say yes immediately. I'm wondering if I should say no altogether.'

'As long as you're happy. Maybe a break is what you really need, to ponder things. Hey, can we come to your office on Monday? I finished a couple of night shifts so I'm owed a day off as compensation. I promise not to break anything, pleeeeaaaasssseee,' Jenny said.

'Deal,' Mia answered back. 'And you, Xander, come by whenever you want. You don't do Mondays, right? I'll figure out a master plan on how to split the work.'

'I'll make an effort for you, it's going to be fun,' he said.

Somewhere in the back of her mind, Mia hoped everything would go as expected. Things proved to be very different to her expectations as they unfolded.

CHAPTER 11

Sunday at work. In her previous job, Mia spent most of her Sundays at the office, at least ten hours of her own free time. Every single weekend there was some emergency to deal with, files to complete for the following Monday. She always liked working on a Sunday; in her opinion, it was a great way of bonding with colleagues, all driving towards the same objective. She missed the rush.

Now she had to bring forward as many cases as she could before she went away for a whole week. She couldn't remember the last time she'd had a vacation.

But in that new venue, it was only herself and Ginger, and their type of customers preferred by far the bar on the other side of the road rather than sticking around in her office. It was a new feeling. In the beginning, it felt odd, she was lost. Legal aid wasn't paying big money, the exact opposite of what she had gone to New York to do in the first place. She recalled the first Sunday after she'd been fired, at home in her apartment: restless as if she were a caged animal. Guilt was creeping up for not having enough to do, so she started cleaning the apartment. After a few hours of sweat, it could have been in one of those fancy architecture magazines. Still, Mia was not at peace, and she had to do something else.

She felt like the best years of her life were slipping away, being without a "proper" job. The dreams of having a successful career, to become a partner in a large firm, and later have one of her own, were precisely that, just a dream. All those visions were on ice, and she had to survive the crisis. She felt that the more she delayed, the more it would become difficult to get back into the game. She wouldn't be, for sure, the youngest partner in a firm, ever, if things kept going as they were. Jobs were hard to find, and that sowed the seed for having her own firm. Legal aid was a way of earning some money while waiting for the fortune to turn again in her direction. It was what bothered her most: she'd entered into a new career path because she needed the money, not because she believed in what she was doing. Of that, Mia was fully aware. The only thing that remained certain was her relationship with Carlton.

God, she missed the thrill of meetings with the most influential clients in New York, working with the top brands in the world, having to spend hours researching obscure quibbles that won the day in court.

She looked around at her small office. Ginger's desk was a mess, as usual, full of papers and folders, probably unrelated to the job. The sparse paintings on the wall had nothing to do with law, they remained from the previous tenant. The floor could have been suitable for a butcher, and it was on the opposite side of the opulence of the soft carpets in her last firm. And the smell that filled her nostrils. A mix of burgers and onions and Chinese food from the surrounding takeaways. The scent was a constant reminder of her failure; being there was the clear evidence she had failed. She was only an ordinary person trying to get by.

Inside, she knew she couldn't accept Carlton's offer. The measure of success for Mia was not in getting rich but in the journey. The how was more important, how she would gain that success she always yearned. She'd studied hard for her Harvard degree, she'd spent her life working an absurd number of hours to get where she wanted. How she could accept being handed her dream just because she had the right fiancé?

She exhaled, fully knowing she had to come up with a plan B. If accepting Carlton's offer was out of the question, that was something she was sure of, then she had to find another way to climb where she wanted to be.

The how was the big problem.

CHAPTER 12

When was the last time I visited my parents? She could not remember. She went home once, while she was still at Harvard, but that was it. After the "troubles" with her father, she hadn't informed them of her graduation date, although she'd sent a postcard to her mother when she'd passed the bar exam. Then, once in New York, she hadn't had time to take a vacation or, at least, that was how she justified to herself not being in touch with her parents anymore. She had started working around the clock, including weekends, and on the rare occasions she had time off, Mia spent it dozing off on her sofa trying to regain some energy.

If you work hard enough and long enough, granted you have talent, then the sky is your limit. She repeated that to herself like a mantra, while the reality was that she numbed herself to a point where thinking about her mum and dad was no longer painful.

Who am I kidding? I hadn't kept in touch with my parents, hadn't even spoken to or about them, because they were from Camden, Maine.

All her colleagues came from affluent families, and in their spare time they all went to their luxury country homes in Connecticut, and Mia was ashamed of her own parents. Camden was a beautiful resort, so on occasion, she mentioned it without risking odd looks, and when someone asked about her parents, she often said, 'Oh, you know, I think at this time of the year they're up there in Camden enjoying skiing, (or sailing, depending on the season)'. Mia never went into details of her father's boat, which was as small as her New York bathtub, or the fact that they couldn't actually ski. The matter was, they were just getting by; she grew up seeing tourists full of money coming and going to the town, winter and summer. Eventually, she promised herself she wasn't going to be poor, she wouldn't become like her parents, relaxed in an ordinary life. Whatever it took, she had the drive to succeed. What she hated most was to find herself with a family and letting the time pass by, day by day, always the same. Buying a secondhand car, owning the cheapest boat in the village; those were the things that made her cringe and, she realised, she never condoned her parents for not being more ambitious with their lives.

What infuriated her most was that her parents had the means and enough culture to build a better life for them and their family. Both had studied at university, and for some time, they had worked in Boston.

She was lost in thought when Jennifer entered the legal clinic.

'Hey there, nice place you have here.' She contemplated the surroundings like an estate agent would do, evaluating spaces, furniture, ambient light.

'Indeed. It's quiet in the morning; usually my customers spend the day in the bar on the other side of the street. They come here in the afternoon after they've had their fill. Not that I can blame them. I'd rather do the same than go back to Camden,' Mia said.

She got up from her desk and kissed her friend on the cheeks. It was a rainy day, and she helped Jennifer take her coat off. She put it on an empty chair near her desk.

'What a rubbish host I am. Do you want some coffee?' And without waiting for an answer, she went to the small kitchen and turned on the kettle, the only luxury she had allowed herself. 'I'm afraid it's going to be instant coffee.'

Jennifer examined the surroundings, and immediately Mia imagined what she was thinking. The place would have benefited from a lick of paint, and the furniture, purchased from a sort of yard sale, was battered and old. The kitchen was made of Formica and probably built in the fifties; it wouldn't have looked good even when it was new.

'I see you're into vintage furniture here; I like the style.'

In her mind, it was a temporary solution, not worth spending money and effort in making it prettier. Mia put her hot cup on the table. Jennifer wasn't going to accept a generic answer this time.

'Yes, that is exactly what I told the architect. *Vintage, please.*'

They both laughed. Mia passed a cup to her friend.

'Nice coffee.'

'It's Illy, and despite being an instant one, I think it's the best. Italians know their brews. I wondered about getting one of those fancy coffee machines and have a proper cup to wake me up, but it takes too much time to make.'

'Bullshit,' Jennifer said, 'there is always time to have a proper coffee. Have you booked your trip yet?'

'I was going to,' she lied.

'I bet you were. You never told me what went wrong with your parents.'

Mia took a deep breath and started explaining.

'I was thinking about them. After my birth, my parents moved to Camden, Maine, from Boston, where they bought an old colonial house and then spent the next umpteen years renovating it. I mean, what was wrong with an old-fashioned brick house? No, they wanted one all made of wood. Being by the sea meant they'd had to repaint it every few years. After that, they had to rewire the whole damn thing. Then it was the time to change the heating. A never-ending story. What was wrong with Boston? They had careers there.'

Jennifer kept quiet for a while. 'You know, at some point we all dream of a cottage in the countryside. Or on the seaside, in your parents' case. It's called getting older.'

'Yeah, I get it, but they were far too young for that. I still remember that period, I must have been eight or nine years old. My father spent the weekend chopping wood, making phone calls to those elusive guys who were supposed to install the heating and, in the meanwhile, we had the fireplace raging like mad during the whole period. And guess what? When the heating was finally installed, they wanted to change the floorboards, redo the fireplace, and I don't remember what else after that. I didn't have a dad; I had a carpenter living with us. When he wasn't working on our house, he went out and did some handiwork at someone else's place. You know, sometimes he went away for days.'

'If he worked on an oil rig, he would have spent weeks far from home,' Jennifer interjected.

Mia wasn't finished yet; she had opened up, and now the words came out of her mouth without interruption.

'A life spent being a carpenter, fixing things while he could have put his degree in Economics to good use. What a waste. And you know what, he worked for the *Boston Globe* when he was younger. He resorted to writing articles for the local newspaper. I never understood if moving to Maine was only due to my dad's lack of ambition or if my mother had any input at all. She also studied Economics at school, they actually met at university, but somehow I believe my father convinced her to give up on her dreams.'

Jennifer, without saying a word, picked her coffee cup up and sipped.

'Now she has a bakery in the centre of town. I mean, a ba-ke-ry. If you believe bread just happens, I have to tell you the truth: that is not the case. You have to prepare the dough and then wake up at silly hours to actually bake the stuff. And get up even earlier if you want cakes for sale, too. Day in, day out. No person with any amount of sense would do that. If you have to work hard, you want to be in New York, doing it for some top-notch company and make millions in the process; otherwise, it's simply not worth the effort.'

'Hmm. I see, so the issue is that they are ordinary people doing ordinary jobs? Like millions of others in this country,' Jennifer pressed.

Mia remained quiet for a few seconds, thinking about her friend's words. She wondered if there wasn't a more elaborate explanation than her being a snobby bitch.

'I don't know, Jenny. I swear, I don't.' She opened the computer and searched for flights. She could have asked Ginger, it was her job after all, but something stopped her. Asking her to book the trip meant she would actually do it, no room for procrastinating there.

Am I afraid to tell my parents? She wondered for how long she should stay at their place.

'How long does it take to say *I'm getting married*? Five minutes?' Mia asked.

Jennifer sighed profoundly and went to the kitchen for a second helping of coffee.

When she came back with two filled cups, Mia was still pondering the question. *What should I say? I'm getting married, don't bother to attend my wedding; that requires tact and diplomacy. Maybe I should book an entire week.*

Oh gosh, a full week of interrogation, about my life, Carlton's and my lifestyle. Come on, Mia, you have to do it.

Delta was offering a reasonably priced ticket to Bangor International Airport. From there she could either hire a car or use a limousine service to Camden. With a rented vehicle, she had the chance to run away anytime if the atmosphere became too tense, but with a limousine service she'd be pampered, avoid driving narrow roads, and could relax throughout the entire journey.

Right at that moment, Ginger entered the office.

'Jenny, this is my secretary, Ginger. Well, she is more than that, she keeps the sanity in my chaotic world. She organises pretty much everything here, I would be lost without her. Ginger, this is Jenny, a good friend of mine. She is a surgeon at Mount Sinai Hospital, but she's agreed to lend a hand for a few days. I have an urgent family matter to attend to.'

'Hello there.' Jennifer jumped to her feet and walked towards the newcomer. 'So is Ginger your real name?'

'No, my name is Magdalene, but they usually call me Maggie. I guess Ginger is because of the colour of my hair,' Ginger said, 'although, sometimes I introduce myself as Ginger. I've gotten used to it.'

'Hello, Maggie. Yes, I see why the nickname stuck. It's a gorgeous name, by the way, it reminds me of romantic walks by the Seine in Paris, hand in hand in the sunset,' Jennifer lifted her hand and stroke the secretary's hair.

She blushed. Ginger's cheeks went from a pale white to a deep burgundy in a matter of milliseconds. For sure she was not used to compliments as direct as Jennifer's.

Great, precisely what I need, my best friend hitting on my secretary while I'm going away. 'Hands off the merchandise,' Mia said. 'We have business to discuss. Do you know where Xander is? He also promised to come.'

'Most likely is still asleep. Hang on a second,' Jennifer said, looking at her phone. 'He'll be here in a couple of minutes. He said *do not go in without me, wait for me outside*. I guess it's a bit too late for that.' She made the most resounding laugh, showing a line of perfect white teeth. 'So, shall we wait a few minutes?'

'Indeed.'

'I'll prepare something to drink. Coffee or tea?' Ginger-Maggie asked.

'I'll have a coffee, please, lots of cream, lots of sugar, lots of love in making it,' Jennifer said. 'I might give you a hand, actually,' and then she followed her into the kitchen in the same way a puppy followed its owner who held a treat in their hand.

Xander arrived a few minutes later, and he hadn't made any effort to look professional. His dark-grey leather biker jacket had clearly seen better days. No point in putting him in charge of the personal shopping, even if it was only for a week. No hope there.

'Wow!' he said after he noticed Ginger in the kitchen, and then, almost like a whisper, 'You didn't mention your secretary was THAT HOT. I mean, how am I supposed to work here with her going around in that bodycon? Does she have a boyfriend? I'm up for reconsidering my entire lifestyle. Mia, please, please tell her that I'm a good guy, or a bad one if she prefers, I don't mind. I'm in love.'

'Hold your horses, cowboy.' Mia showed the palm of her hand. 'We're here for a specific task, let's try to keep it professional, shall we?'

'Aye, aye, Captain.'

Ginger arrived with a tray full of cookies and cups, which she distributed to those present and was ready to go back to her own desk when Mia said, 'Hang on, we need you, too. You've been here since the beginning, and it's only fair you're part of this discussion.'

'Me? I... I don't know how I could...' Ginger looked around as to find an escape route.

'Sit down, please,' Mia said.

Both Jennifer and Xander stood and hurried to grab a chair for the newcomer. Jennifer was first, and she went to the right of her seat, to the disappointment of her companion.

'Of course you can. You were here since the beginning and you'll have a say. No discussion, take a seat.' Mia knew she was being too bossy, but she also knew she still had to rely on the firm staying afloat for the time being, until she found something better. She needed all the help she could get.

'I will be away for a week or two, and although none of you can carry out legal work, we will be in a situation where the firm will earn no money. I, we, cannot afford that. So, I've reconsidered some of those funny businesses of yours, Ginger…'

'I've seen a lot of *Perry Mason*, *The Good Wife* and *Suits* on the telly,' Xander said.

'Not a chance in hell,' Mia replied, pointing directly towards Xander, 'and be quiet.'

Ginger-Maggie tried to say something, but she was interrupted straight away by Mia.

'Please let me finish. Although some of the things you've done might be considered unethical, other side jobs you have are legitimate. You've helped me greatly, Ginger, I recognise that. So, if you agree, for the next week or so, Jenny and Xander will help you out. It's not acceptable that whilst working for me I won't be able to pay you, so I think it'd be fair if we are in this firm fifty-fifty, as partners.'

Ginger-Maggie was taken aback from what Mia had just said. She opened her mouth as if to say something and then changed her mind. She stared at Jennifer and Xander, who were smiling in her direction. 'What's the trick?' she finally managed to say.

'No tricks, Ginger, believe me, it's not an intervention. So, what kind of side businesses do you have currently?'

Ginger fidgeted with the rings on her fingers, then looked at the floor and started talking. 'Quite a few. The most revenue-generating are the fashion consultancy and the funerals.'

'I'll do it, I can help with fashion,' said a far too eager to please Xander, unleashing a general laugh. 'Okay, I understand I might not appear as an expert in that sector, but if you team me up with Gin... Sorry, Maggie, I'm sure I'll do an excellent job.'

'Nice try, buster!' Mia said. 'No, Jennifer can help Ginger on the personal shopping front. The last thing I want is to be taken to court for sexual harassment in the workplace.'

'You're missing the point here, Mia, I could have brought a different, fresher perspective to the world of fashion.'

'Yeah, I'm sure of it. Baggy trousers, hoodie, and cut-up t-shirts, the *real* Manhattan attire. That is if you deliver parcels.'

'That's nasty. Okay, I give up,' he said, raising his hands to the ceiling. 'So, what am I gonna do?'

'Funerals. Some weeping will do you good. Thinking about the meaning of life will give you a fresh perspective for your writing.' Mia laughed.

Xander nodded and let out a big sigh. 'That's unfair.'

'No, Xander. And then you'll be amazed on how easy it is to pull at a funeral. All those widows in need of a sensible soul who could comfort them. Believe me, that is right up your alley,' Jennifer joked.

'Not to mention all those stories you'll be told by the older generation, which might even give you ideas for your books,' Mia chimed in.

'So, you are a writer?' Ginger asked in awe.

Jennifer and Mia coughed.

'Okay, I suppose I could do that. What's next.'

They all looked at Ginger.

'Fake referrals for job applicants who are actually unemployable,' Ginger whispered.

'That will have to go!' The tone in Mia's voice didn't leave any room for negotiation. 'What else?'

'I have a small erotic phone line.'

'Mine! No discussion. Hey, I write erotic books,' Xander said, all excited, 'I'm good with words, I had years of experience exploring the world of Domination, submission…'

'Xander, watching porn online doesn't make you an expert,' Jennifer interjected, 'and there is a slight problem with you managing the hotline.'

'Which is?'

'You're a man. If a woman wants to get excited, she doesn't phone an erotic line. Men, on the other hand… Unless you're interested in a gay hotline.'

'Hmmm, I'll pass on that.' Xander was clearly disappointed.

'Wait, wait, wait. Ginger, are you saying you were running an erotic phone line from these premises?' Mia couldn't comprehend to what extent her secretary had gone to in order to raise money.

Ginger was suddenly very interested in her shoes and didn't answer at first. Eventually, she came clean. 'It generates almost six hundred dollars a month. I do it mostly in the evening.'

'That explains you working until late! No, that will have to go, unfortunately,' Mia announced.

'Oh, come on, Mia,' Jennifer pleaded. 'That sounds fun. What if we promise not to use the office for it?' Now she was on a roll. 'But I think we should make some small addition. I suggest a lesbian hotline? It's my ballpark, and if it happens that I get a date out of it, so be it, I will sacrifice myself for the cause.'

Yeah, sure. My business is going to be used for personal purposes, a dating agency exclusive to Jennifer. Damn, it's only going to be for a week, she can't do any harm. 'But Ginger will monitor your calls, I don't want to find myself, or you for that matter, in any kind of trouble.'

Jennifer made her best attempt to pull an offended face. 'I wouldn't dare put your business at risk. Here we are, questioning my professionalism and integrity, but I accept having to work under supervision.'

Mia exhaled. She was hoping they wouldn't put her future at risk in exchange for a week of what seemed to be shaping up as fun, at least in the eyes of her friends.

There was another line of business. 'What else have you got, Ginger?'

'Writing articles for incompetent bloggers,' Ginger continued.

'Xander, I think you should also take the blogging tasks.'

'How exactly does it work?'

Ginger-Maggie explained to him that the job was quite eclectic. It was a matter of writing articles for bloggers—sometimes it was about cookery, others on literature, fashion, and so on. She had more requests than she could cope with. 'It's listed on Fiverr,' she said. 'Of course, it has a more resounding name, but that is the essence. I write articles for someone else. Reviews are not great because I do it when I can; mostly they complain about the delivery time.'

'No problem. Hey, I'm a bloody writer, I can cook up a few thousand words in a matter of minutes. Have you ever considered outsourcing that line of business to me? I could actually make some serious money with it.'

'So, when do we start?' Jennifer asked.

'What about next week? Or is that too soon?' Mia was running out of excuses to delay her visit to her parents any further.

'My diary looks free,' Xander said, scrutinising his phone and making his best business-like face.

It was Jennifer's turn. 'I guess I could take vacation.'

'I'm here all the time anyway.' Ginger shrugged.

Damn! But they needed the money for the time being. All that was left to do was for her to book that flight.

CHAPTER 13

Her two friends left for the day, and Mia was alone with Ginger. They sat there in silence, sipping coffee from their mugs.

'You have wonderful friends.' A note of sadness was clearly present in Ginger's voice.

'Indeed. I guess on a few occasions, they made the difference between getting completely lost and keeping my sanity. They bring you down to earth right when you need it.' Mia didn't know why she was telling Ginger that. In all their time together, they'd never shared personal information. Mia attributed that to being her own fault, though. She hadn't considered the clinic job as a permanent one, a way of getting by while she was waiting for her chance. *Perhaps Ginger felt the same. Maybe she knew all this was just a temporary arrangement.*

'Where are you from, Ginger?' she asked.

'I'm from right here, Marine Park. I always wondered what makes people come to New York in search of their fortunes. I've been here all my life and never received an ounce of it.'

Mia could relate to what she was saying. For most people, that was precisely the case. To live and work in an over-expensive city, which had a lot to offer, but usually, people were too busy following their dreams to even realise that. For those who didn't buy into the idea, it was hard.

'So, I guess you're of Irish descent. You don't strike me as Italian or Greek.'

'Yeah, what gave that away, my red hair?' She laughed.

Mia usually saw her secretary all business-like and focused on what she was doing, most of the time unrelated to the job she was paid for. Not a grin or a joke, just work, work, work.

'I come from a Catholic family. I lived with my parents until recently when they kicked me out. No, I don't want to talk about that. It felt like I was in jail, or worse, on parole. That's it: I did not have parents, I had parole officers. They kept organising blind dates for me, hoping I would finally find the love of my life. Which never happened. If you were wondering why I spend so much time in the office, I actually prefer being here than home. I feel too lonely there.'

That was something Mia could relate to. She never found herself comfortable at home either, although for different reasons. Her father's lack of ambition being the first. She knew she had something to prove, and for a few years, Mia thought she was on the right track. She couldn't understand why people wanted to live in places other than New York.

She looked around at her poorly organised office and realised her dream of being successful was half-baked. Sure, there was Carlton and, sooner or later, especially after the engagement announcement, she'd crack on at finding that elusive job. She was missing the thrill of being part of something bigger; in her previous post, they had Fortune 500 clients. She could go to the supermarket, find products on the shelves and say 'those are my clients'. The sense of achievement was immense, and she often dreamed of going back to that life. She went through the folder on her desk: two DUIs to take care of, and she had to be in court the following morning. She flicked through the pages but already knew their story; they were all the same.

She wrote a few notes in regards to a Mr Fresnel, arrested on the spot by the NYPD after failing the breathalyser test. At least he wasn't speeding when the police caught him. The report said, though, that his car was swaying dangerously across the traffic lines and it was by sheer luck the driver hadn't caused a major accident. Mia had no empathy whatsoever for her client.

She raised her head and saw Ginger who, as usual, was on the phone. For a moment, she wondered if she was resenting her. The reality was that without Ginger's extra work, she'd have struggled in keeping the place alive. Failure was not in Mia's vocabulary, but the truth was sitting right in front of her: Ginger had paid most of the bills recently. No, she did not resent her. In some strange way, she was grateful, although she didn't like getting help. For her, asking for help was the equivalent of admitting defeat, but she was not going to give up on her dream. She was in New York to stay; it was a matter of how and when.

An old man entered the office. Mia raised her head, and she recognised the face, although she couldn't place a name of the individual. Unquestionably not a client, given the elegant dark-blue pinstriped suit. Ginger got up from her chair and asked a few questions that Mia couldn't hear. The secretary pointed him in her direction.

The old man walked towards her as if he owned the place. When he was right in front of Mia's desk, he glanced around at her office, the contempt evident on his face. 'I'm Jason Allerton,' he said eventually.

'Of course.' Mia blushed, jumping to her feet. 'Carlton's grandfather. You're welcome to my humble office. I've discussed many times with him about a formal introduction, but somehow we always missed the opportunity...'

Jason Allerton showed the palm of his hand to Mia, stopping her mid-sentence. 'I'm not here for chitchat,' he said. Then he sat on an armchair, uninvited. 'What does it take to stop this nonsense?' he eventually spat out.

Mia was without words. The man was clearly not in her office seeking legal advice, he could hire the best lawyers in the city. And he definitely was upset. She sat again on her chair and said, 'I'm not sure what you're talking about. Would you mind elaborating?'

'Of course I will. What is it going to take to stop this silly idea of a wedding with my grandson? I know the lot of you, always after money.' He put his hand in the internal pocket of his jacket and took out a cheque book. 'Just give me a number, and we can close the deal here and now. One million dollars? It appears you badly need some cash, given the shithole you have as an office.'

Mia couldn't believe her ears. There, in front of her was her future relative, and on first meeting, he was offering her money to go away.

'EXCUSE ME?' was the only thing her lips managed to let out. Inside, a whirl of emotions was taking the best part of her. She was outraged, she wanted to slap the old man in the face and tell him exactly what she was thinking. But, also maybe there was some sort of misunderstanding she wasn't aware of.

'You heard me well, young lady, but I'm going to spell it out for you one more time. One million dollars, damn, let's say one and a half; I can sign the cheque straight away, and you can crawl back to that pothole you come from as a rich woman. Think about it, you can open a decent shop somewhere in the Midwest, make your parents proud; you will be the only lawyer in town and breed some other scoundrels like yourself. A million and a half would be a good jumpstart for anybody. You wouldn't be the first.'

Is he testing me? Her cheeks were hot with anger. *Who in the hell is this guy, and how dare he offer me money?*

'Mr Allerton,' she eventually decided for the polite way to answer—he was, after all, the grandfather of her beloved future husband, 'I'd like you to leave immediately. And you can take your money back with you.'

'Very well, I see you play hard.' Jason Allerton stood from his chair. 'The offer is valid for a week, then I will start playing dirty.'

'LEAVE!'

Ginger reached the office at the exact moment the old man was leaving it. She stopped for a second and then rushed towards Mia. 'What the hell was that all about?'

'I cannot believe it! That was my fiancé's grandfather, and he offered me a million and a half dollars to break off the engagement.'

'Did you take it?' Ginger asked eagerly. 'Am I getting a bonus this year?'

'Of course not!' Now that Jason Allerton was gone, her hands shook. She regretted not having slapped him or throwing a glass of water in his face. Her heart was beating fast; adrenaline and anger flowed through her veins.

'I cannot believe he came in here and threw his money in your face,' Ginger said, 'but now you have a bigger problem.'

Mia was looking at the empty seat in front of her, mulling over what had just happened. 'I know,' she eventually answered. 'If I tell Carlton he will surely confront his grandfather, and if I don't tell him anything... Damn! I'll have to go to their Thanksgiving dinner and smile as if nothing happened. Either way, I am in trouble.'

117

Ginger got closer to her employer and hugged her warmly. 'Mia, things are happening too fast, and you need a break to collect your thoughts.'

That was the first time she'd thought of Ginger as more than an employee. Ginger was a nice girl, and she had to admit to herself that without her, her life would be much messier.

Eventually, Mia recomposed herself, glad she wasn't alone in that squalid office. 'I think you're right; I should go home and prepare the luggage. My clients are all sorted out for next week anyway. Please, please, please don't get up to any mischief during my leave.'

Ginger laughed. 'I won't, and then you've got your friends policing me anyway.'

Mia nodded. Too many things were rushing in her head at that moment: what happened minutes before, the wedding, having to meet her parents. There was enough there to drive anyone crazy.

CHAPTER 14

Gareth Szymansky exited the elevator at the twenty-second floor of a building on 3rd Street, one of the several storeys belonging to the law firm Myerscough, Nibley, and Holton.

He was a tall man in his late forties, despite a large amount of grey in his hair. That was from his mother's DNA, he kept repeating as if he was innocent of his older-looking appearance and someone else needed to be blamed. He was slightly overweight. When he walked, his upper body swung from left to right, making him resemble a retired rodeo cowboy rather than a New York City top lawyer.

He hardly set foot on the twenty-second floor, his domain was usually two levels above, where all the other top lawyers resided. The twenty-second floor was just a cost. Nobody there brought any revenue or billable hours. Like the IT department. A bunch of nerds only good at spending money, always asking for new servers and other expensive items nobody else knew what for. Szymansky, as a senior partner, had to sign off their shopping list, and every time he asked what "exactly" all that money was used for and for what benefit, he always received foggy answers in return. When they were not technical. That bunch of people spoke a different language altogether. Szymansky thought they probably knew what they were talking about, they hired the best of the best, but damn! Those people could not articulate their demand in a simple language. He should have sent them all in the clouds, as some consultants suggested. Not that he fully understood what that meant, but the idea of kicking out all the non-revenue-generating IT guys out of the window amused him.

He was head of litigation, at that point the most profitable sector in the firm with a profit margin of sixty-five percent, but the department working in Intellectual Property was catching up. In an era where technology was moving fast, the opportunity to get revenue from misappropriation of IP was growing more quickly than ever.

He disliked the IP guys with all his guts. Mostly because they rarely went to court and instead preferred a quiet license agreement among the parties. No, to be a "real" lawyer, one had to set foot in a courtroom. To walk in front of a judge and a jury and make a case heard. That was lawmanship, and he needed fresh blood to throw into his department.

They were the fourth revenue-generating law firm in the US, making around two point three billion dollars a year and a profit per lawyer of four hundred and fifty thousand dollars. Szymansky wanted the third spot. Their lawyers were among the highest paid in the country and, in exchange for the privilege, they required total dedication from their employees. Which often translated into working day and night. It wasn't unheard of people sleeping on the floor for a few hours to avoid losing time with the commute. Some offices had wardrobes.

The twenty-second floor also hosted the HR department, and that was the reason for his visit.

As he walked through the corridors in his impeccable Alan David suit, the employees were moving aside, like the waters of the Red Sea in front of Moses. People avoided eye contact, fearing Szymansky might ask them a question, or ask them to repeat by memory the company vision statement. The bravest mumbled a 'Good morning, Mr Szymansky.'

He didn't bother to wait for the secretary to announce his presence and entered the office of Peter Higgins, head of the HR department.

'What you got for me, Pete?'

Higgins looked at the imposing man in front of him and nodded, half as a salute and half to acknowledge his presence. He was in his early sixties and the oldest partner in the firm. By age. Being on the twenty-second floor, Szymansky knew the partner would never have a pivotal role in deciding the direction of the company. Undeterred by his age, he still clocked over eighty hours a week; it wasn't a requirement, given his hours were hardly billable, but nonetheless, partners had to set an example by not going home too soon. Not that anybody was waiting for him there. His wife left several years before, after he got caught with his pants down with another woman. Szymansky took care of it. The irony was that the older lawyer had the affair with a younger secretary, despite it being Higgins who wrote the company policy of "no fraternisation" among employees.

'I think I got five sure and another four probables.'

Szymansky sat on the large black leather armchair in front of Higgins' desk; he made a beckoning gesture, and Higgins turned the pile of folders towards the senior partner. He chose one randomly.

'Paul Montgomery, a fifth-year associate at DLG; three years in litigation.' Szymansky flipped through the CV. 'Yale.' There was a hint of disgust in his voice.

'I thought you might say that.' There was nothing wrong with the candidate. If two people had a similar experience, the choice inevitably went to the Harvard one.

'This was a "maybe", right?'

Higgins sighed. He was indeed a "maybe".

They spent over an hour going through the other candidates, debating the pros and cons, Higgins pleading for some, explaining his hiring thought process. There were only two spots in Szymansky's team, and the partner wasn't keen on spending billable hours in recruiting and interviewing. That was a job for the twenty-second floor. He wanted the right choice the first time.

'Mia Crawford,' he said, picking up the last folder. The CV was neat and to the point. Harvard. Good for her. Several years at Carnegie, Stephens, and Honeycomb. A steady career but in the wrong field, corporate finance. CSH slimmed down, trying to keep the focus on squeezing the wealthier clients and lost the bet—they were nowhere to be seen among the top firms now. Not in the top twenty at least. Szymansky read between the lines that Mia Crawford got the chop just before becoming a partner and then she moved to open her own legal aid clinic.

'Are you kidding me?' Szymansky looked Higgins straight in the eyes.

'Not one bit. It takes guts. Miss Crawford could have settled for another less paid job; she could have moved to the Midwest. She could have done the same as she is doing now, but in one of the other legal aid firms already in place. They are all short of people. On the contrary, she stuck around and took her chances.'

'Not much experience in litigation.'

'True. But Miss Crawford kicked the ass of one of your junior partners a couple of months back. Do you remember the MCH case, the developers?'

Szymansky frowned. 'That was her?' He perfectly remembered the eviction case. Instead of going through the negotiation rule, as most would have thought wise, she fought them in court and won. MCH had to delay demolishing the building and had a setback of several months on building a new skyscraper in downtown Manhattan. A two-point-two billion dollar project; not the most expensive tower in the whole US but close. He couldn't recollect the details but he well remembered the bollocking he'd received by the MCH rep for what was supposed to be a slam-dunk.

'The very one. And she's from Harvard,' Higgins added. If you can't lick 'em, join 'em.

'The name rings a bell.' Szymansky tried hard to recall where he'd heard it before. It could not have been another case; he would have marked the lawyer's name in his book.

'She's Carlton Allerton's new fiancée.'

'Who, Mr Fifty Percent Discount Guaranteed?'

'That's the one. Miss Crawford cannot be perfect in every aspect, can she?'

They both laughed.

'Will she be able to cope with the pressure? Our profit per lawyer has to go up significantly this year.'

'I think she will.' Higgins was clearly eager on the candidate. 'And the fact she applied for the opening means she wants something more than what she is doing right now.'

'She better be. Okay, bring the three in next week, and we'll have a chat with them. Maybe we should give them a knife and see who survives.'

The selection was harsh, and Szymansky was going to put pressure on all of them to perform. He didn't envy the candidates. After twenty years, he hadn't decided yet if working for Myerscough, Nibley, and Holton was a blessing or a nightmare. Probably both.

I DON'T DO MONDAYS!

CHAPTER 15

The Delta flight to Bangor was uneventful and, as soon as she collected her luggage, Mia went straight away towards the car rental booths. She checked her bank account for the last time, knowing very well she could not afford a limo service, and then she hunted the best price for a rental. Bangor Airport was more in line with her bank balance. Sober. With little choice. Millions of miles away from the temptations of La Guardia Airport. Perfumes, jewellery; expensive clothes belonged to New York. Not here. Mia exhaled in relief, not sure if it was because her bank account would be much safer for the following week or because she was already getting accustomed to the local way of doing things.

She realised she had forgotten to call her parents and let them know of her arrival.

Damn! How could I have been so careless?

She tried to justify herself with everything that was going on in her life. The firm was making far less money than she needed to survive in New York, the wedding, Carlton's grandfather. She sat on a bench staring at her phone, angry with herself for forgetting to make the call. After a minute or so, she took a deep breath and dialled the number.

Her mother answered at the third ring. 'Hello?'

'Hi, Mom, this is Mia,' she said in a sheepish voice.

125

'Hello, darling, how are you? It has been ages.'

'I know. Listen, I was thinking… ehm… maybe I should come and visit you. I have some news to share.' She hated lying so bluntly to her mother, but she thought she had no choice.

'About the wedding? It's a week now that we've done nothing but talk about it. We'd love to have you here, when are you planning to come?'

They knew already. Of course, it had been plastered in several tabloids.

'How is Dad?' That was the question she wanted to avoid. She knew how he thought, he'd have snarled at her choice, saying people like Carlton represented everything wrong in this country. People who didn't think twice to fire employees to keep the shareholders happy. On that front, she would have lost the argument, as Carlton was right in the middle of a reorganisation, but that was not the point. Companies had to grow and deliver value to the shareholders, that was the basic idea of any profitable company, people who invested their own savings in shares expected that, but…

'Your dad is fine,' Mia's mother said, 'always the same. At our age we change little. By the way, let us know when you're coming. He would love to collect you from the airport.'

Yeah, two hours driving with my father, my personal idea of hell, apart from the fact that she was already in Bangor.

'No, Mom, don't worry. I still have to check if I can find a ticket, but would today be too soon?'

'Absolutely not. Are you spending the weekend here?' There was a tremble in her mother's voice, her anticipation after years of almost silence evident.

'If it's okay with you, I might spend the whole week.' Since she had been in New York, Mia had never taken a single day of vacation. She didn't even know what a vacation looked like. At first, because she was working a hundred hours a week for a demanding law firm, and lately when she had her own clinic, she was working as hard just to scrape enough money together to survive in one of the most expensive cities in the States.

'Great! I will prepare the meatloaf then,' her mother said, 'and the apple pie that you always adored. Or the lobster lasagne...'

'Mom! I'm only coming for a week, please, don't go mad cooking.' If she wasn't careful, considering her mother's overeager attitude towards food, she'd end up gaining ten kilos. It was the same every time she went home from college, her mother would launch into a food frenzy, preparing two or three of her favourite dishes a day. Whenever she objected or asked if they were usually eating all that stuff regularly, her mother shrugged and said a simple 'at least you have a choice'. Feeding her was her favourite sport.

'Okay, no worries. Give us a ring when you're on your way, and if you want your dad to come and collect you, just ask.'

'I will. See you later.'

Mia had a few hours to kill. The smallest and cheapest car she could rent cost as much as her flight to Bangor, and she struggled to fit her two large suitcases into it. Eventually, one had to be placed on the back seat. *Why in the hell did I take two bags and all these shoes?* She regretted bringing so much luggage while probably most of the time she was going to wear jeans and a jumper. A pair of boxing gloves to fight her father would have been useful, she mused.

Mia drove slowly towards Bangor downtown and finally arrived on Main Street, where she found a parking space. She got out of the car, and the crisp, cold air filled her lungs. The sun warmed her skin slightly and reverberated over the thin dust of snow that was still present on the side of the street. She had landed in a different world. The first thing that struck her was the pace at which things were moving. The little traffic was flowing, slowly and uneventful. Far different from New York where there were only two speeds: stuck in a queue or in the mad rush.

On the opposite side of the road, there was an art gallery and a wedding dress shop. She smiled, thinking that soon she would have to hunt for her own, but she decided not to go in. Bangor was hardly the place to go for a wedding dress, especially if you were marrying the heir of the Allerton empire. Farther down, there was a cafeteria and a restaurant, and that was where she headed. A delicious, rustic lunch, plenty of coffee, and time to kill reading her emails and making plans. The first one on the agenda was how to convince her parents they shouldn't bother to come to the wedding and make it look like it was their own idea. She was a lawyer, after all. Mia thought she'd figure something out, and with a week ahead, there would be plenty of occasions to cover the matter.

The restaurant was warm and cosy. When Mia entered, she could feel the friendly atmosphere, the same one she was used to when she was still in her teens.

It was a place for locals. A Jim and Jinny would drive their pickup truck to meet the rest of their family in town, have an essential meal, and a chat and then drive home. They'd know the waitress by name, and the waitress would know theirs. Probably neighbours.

A waitress rushed towards her and directed Mia to a wooden table by the window. On the walls of dull brick, old pictures of the town intermixed with some more modern ones. The waiter working behind the bar was busy cleaning glasses. Everybody seemed jovial and down to earth. She put her bag under the table and looked at the menu. It was a difficult choice between the pork belly and a mix of scallops and monkfish. She didn't dare to ask for the wine list for fear of disappointment and also because she still had a long drive ahead of her to reach Camden. The restaurant was more oriented towards local brews than high-end wine anyway.

She was definitely overdressed for the place, in her pumps and navy-blue suit. What she was thinking?

Mia grew impatient when she closed the menu as none of the waitresses ran towards her to take her order. But then she realised she was no longer in New York, where things happened at a hectic pace. Here it was different. The waitresses had time to chat with each other and the customers, who most of the time were friends and neighbours. Nobody was pushing her to eat in a hurry and leave the table for the next client, so she relaxed.

When the waitress finally came to her table, she was friendly with her as if Mia had dined there for the past twenty years. She settled for a portion of pork belly and a local ale, which was suggested to her.

She was not used to all of this anymore, but she forced herself to calm down and take things as they happened. She had to stay in the place for a few hours more anyway. On a nearby table, six people were celebrating a birthday. For a moment, she thought of opening her computer but then considered otherwise. She was on vacation. Vacation, the sound of that word sounded alien to her ears.

She enjoyed the meal and passed the time crowd-watching out of the window.

This was Maine.

CHAPTER 16

Once in Camden, Mia drove another mile north on the 105 towards her parents' home. The infrequent houses had the lights on, and Mia recognised a few of them as belonging to long-lost childhood friends. People were getting ready for dinner. She felt the need for a home-cooked meal.

Her parents' house was on the right side of the 105 in a corner plot delimited by a white, short wooden fence. The main building connected to the separate guest house, a project that was discussed in the family for years. There were two young pine trees on the well-maintained lawn on the front, recently planted, and an apple tree.

As soon as she parked, her mother appeared at the front door.

'Hello, Mom.'

'Oh, look at you!' Mia's mother rushed from the porch and ran to hug her, the emotion clearly visible in her eyes.

Mia felt uncomfortable for a second, but then she let go and felt happy to be home again, despite only for a week.

'Here, let me help with the luggage.' Her eager mother opened the car door and lifted one of the suitcases as if it was empty.

Mia tried to stop her, but she already knew it was a futile attempt. She opened the trunk and took

131

the second suitcase. Her mother was leading the way, turning towards Mia at every step so as to ensure she wasn't dreaming and her daughter was really there.

They deposited the luggage near the wooden stairs leading to the upper floor; a flood of memories came to her mind. Coming down that staircase for her prom, playing hide and seek with her friends when she was a kid. Everything was exactly as when Mia had left, including a painting she did when she was at school. She wondered if her mother still kept her drawing from elementary school stuck on the fridge door. She probably had.

'Where is Dad?' Mia asked, looking around. She had played in her mind all sorts of arguments that might happen when they met. Had imagined sarcastic comments on her New York life, to which she had already prepared a couple of retorts. She'd have made a comment on his lack of ambition, and soon they'd have started shouting at each other. At least that was what she imagined all the way during the trip to Camden.

'Oh, he's out for a job. He should be back tomorrow as he's promised the Johnsons to clear their guttering.'

'Is he still doing handyman work? Shouldn't he be retired or something by now?'

Her mother shrugged. 'You know how he is. He likes to be active and be part of the community. But don't stand there, come on, let's go in the kitchen. I'm sure you're starving.'

Mia could smell something delicious was cooking, and several hours had already passed since her lunch, so she followed.

'What's the nice smell?'

'A lobster pie is in the oven, almost ready, and I was finishing off some Maine potato chips cooked in duck fat.'

A bit of cholesterol wouldn't kill her straight away.

'I brought some wine.' Mia looked back towards the general direction of her suitcases, unsure if her mother would appreciate, or even recognise, a hundred-and-fifty-dollar bottle. What a silly thing to do. She was strapped for money, bought an expensive wine, and she had nobody to impress. Things were really different in Maine.

'Excellent. The corkscrew is in the first drawer,' her mother said.

Mia went in search of her luggage. When she walked back to the kitchen, she realised how noisy her high-heeled shoes were against the wooden floor. It was an unnatural sound echoing through the hallway. She felt she didn't belong in that place anymore.

'And what about you? Still working in the bakery?' Mia asked, sitting at the kitchen table. She managed to remove the cork from the bottle and poured the wine into two crystal glasses.

Her mother started serving dinner. 'Of course I am. What else should I do?'

'I mean, it's gruesome work, waking up at silly hours and all that sort of thing,' Mia said.

'Your father and I don't do that anymore. Do you remember little David Allen, the one you used to babysit? He's now doing most of the work, although he follows my recipes. I still make some cakes, though; I won't give that up. And we added an Italian coffee machine, so people can get their brew before going to work. And a few tables. You should come along one of those days.'

Mia tucked into the lobster pie as if it were her last meal, not leaving a scrap on her plate. She told her mother what happened in the past few years, her high-paid job in Manhattan, her current one at the clinic, and her aspirations in getting back to corporate law.

Her mother, sitting in front of her, was sipping the expensive wine and nodding at every word. Eventually, she said, 'I like that Ginger lady. She seems... how should I say, determined. She has a vision, although maybe it's still a bit foggy for her. I'm sure she'll go somewhere in life.'

Mia couldn't believe her ears. What about her? Was her mother even listening to what she was saying? That was an aspect of her parents she never understood: they were always focused on the wrong thing. Who'd be so silly to swap a journalist job in Boston to become a handyman? And her mother, she had a degree in economics, and now she was making cakes and serving coffee as if she had little education at all. Mia felt that with the years, the gap between them grew even more prominent. This was an alien world, light years away from hers. Sure, they were doing okay, they made refurbishments to the house, but who wanted to do okay when they could have done great?

'And what about that boyfriend of yours? You hardly spoke about him,' her mother enquired.

The question took Mia by surprise. Her wedding and Carlton were the essence of her visit. She blamed herself for that. She was too concentrated on trying to defend her way of living, her ideals, that she totally forgot the reason she had to come to Maine. Mia pondered where to start. The last thing she wanted was to also try to defend her wedding and her marital choices.

'Carlton? You'd like him, actually. He is not at all as they depict him in the papers. Yes, he works hard for the groceries, and at times it can be tough to meet, we both are swamped, but he actually is a very caring person. And we share lots of interests.'

Her mother laughed. 'I wonder if Gregg agrees with your opinion of him.'

'Dad has his own way of dealing with life, and I guess he disagrees.'

'You can bet the farm on that. When your father read about the engagement in the newspaper, he stayed grumpy for a couple of days,' her mother said, but she didn't go further.

Throughout the years, Mia had learnt that it was better if the two bickered on their own without having to share her point of view. They were both adults after all.

'So where is he now?'

'Down to Wiscasset for a roofing job. He's helping an old friend.'

'And he won't get paid,' Mia added matter-of-factly.

'You should know your dad by now. Not everything is done for money.'

Mia knew that argument very well. Cutting Mrs Jenkins' grass for free, helping another neighbour building a cabin. He never had the guts to ask for what was due. She remembered when she was a kid and they had a boat. It was the smallest, most pathetic boat in the whole harbour, a derelict that probably needed to be sold as scrap and that her father bought as a restoration project. He spent hours and hours fixing it, and at some point, he also involved her in the project. They spent time together, that was true, but sanding down wood wasn't precisely Mia's idea of fun. She eventually joined a pottery course at the end of that summer under her father's suggestion. That also didn't end well eventually. She liked it and she had a talent, but who really bought pottery nowadays?

Mia felt the toll of the long trip and soon afterwards went to bed, taking leave of her mother's company. Her bedroom was untouched; she fell asleep almost immediately in that silent, peaceful night.

CHAPTER 17

Mia woke up at ten in the morning feeling like she'd had the best sleep in her life. Around her, it wasn't completely quiet, apart the occasional bird and the wind passing through the trees, but it was a sort of light, pleasant noise. No traffic, horns, neighbours shouting at each other, doorbells ringing or postmen receiving abuse.

She got up and, after a long, warm shower, went downstairs for her breakfast. She took her computer with her to catch up on emails and a few other pending matters. Her father was reading the newspaper at the kitchen table. A large, hot mug of coffee sat in front of him, and the smell was filling the room.

'Hello, Gregg.' Mia had always called her father Gregg or occasionally Crow. The family name was Crawford, and it seemed to fit with the dark hair she'd inherited from him. It was cool being part of the Crow bunch, at least at that time. Not anymore. Despite his age, Gregg wasn't going grey anytime soon. On that, she hoped to have received part of his genes.

'Come here and give me a hug.' Gregg opened his arms and moved a step closer.

He was much taller than her and still fit as a fiddle. Since she was a kid, she always had the impression of having to deal with a giant. His arms were strong from a lifetime spent doing manual labour, and his eyes were sharp, like those of someone who still had an ace up his sleeve.

'Sit down. Your mother prepared for you some lobster pancakes with a samphire and celeriac mash. She learnt the recipe from one of those fancy culinary shows on television.'

'She did WHAT?'

'Just kidding. These are regular pancakes with blueberries. Do you remember the time when you hated lobster? Until we figured out the reason was that you didn't know how to open them?' Gregg went to the oven, took a plate with a gigantic portion of pancakes, and put it on the table. Then poured a coffee in a second cup. No milk, no sugar.

'Yeah, I remember that. So, what are you up to these days?' Mia asked.

'The usual. In an hour or so I'll have to repair Mrs Jenkins' porch, and then we're putting up a new barn at Joe's. Do you remember Joe? The one with the farm near Appleton?'

'Uncle Joe? Of course I do. Does he still have that Lamborghini tractor?'

'He does indeed.' Gregg laughed. 'He thinks it's a vintage one. He had it repainted blue and orange and hopes one day it will skyrocket in value. He is often on the receiving end of banter, but he likes it that way. I don't think he will ever sell it if you ask me.'

Mia knew they were both avoiding the big question. Her wedding.

'Tell him I might go and visit him. It has been ages.' Mia dug into the pancakes, realising she was hungrier than she thought. She'd burn off the extra calories with a hike to the lake.

'You still working for that firm of crooks?' her father asked suddenly.

'No, they let me go. I'm doing legal aid work now.'

Mia pondered the sentence 'let someone go'. It was a ridiculous phrase, used by every company when they decided to fire people. Let someone go. As if it was their decision to leave in the first place and the company made every possible effort to keep the employee. What sounded odd was that employees also started using the same sentence. They were probably ashamed of saying 'I've been made redundant.'

'Sounds like an excellent job. Helping people in need who cannot afford to pay a lawyer to exercise their rights. Right up there in the Constitution.'

'It's far less glamorous than it sounds. Quite often I'm dealing with rental issues, evictions, DUIs.'

'Most of the jobs that make a difference in society are,' her father said matter-of-factly. He always disapproved of her career choice in corporate law and wasn't afraid to voice his opinion.

'It's a rubbish job, and it pays peanuts,' Mia retorted.

'Well, money isn't everything in life, and believe me, it's far better helping people in need than making the rich richer. Wealth is never created, it's

139

transferred, so the more money the corporations make, the poorer the general population is.'

'And what about the American dream?' Mia asked. Her body tensed, knowing very well they'd never agree on anything.

'The American dream is rigged, my dear. Nowadays, if you work hard enough, you earn a misery, and if you don't, they move your job somewhere else. As long as the next quarter shows a profit... You should know something about that, right? You've been on the receiving end of the stick and still, you haven't learnt the lesson.' Gregg poured another cup of coffee. He was moving slowly, and his voice was assertive.

'You can be so cynical when you want! Of course there are hiccups and things can go wrong, but it's not always like that all the time. When I was in corporate law, I was on the fast track to becoming a partner. I'll be back there in no time at all. Companies have to be profitable and on occasion, to be flexible, they need to get rid of employees. Nothing new there. It has been like that since forever.' Mia knew trying to convince her father was a lost cause, but she wasn't going to stand there and keep quiet.

'Okay, I hear you, but the fact that it's yesterday's news doesn't necessarily mean it's right. Listen to yourself, kiddo, you talk like those people but you are not one of them. They fired you, and still you defend a system that doesn't give a damn about you. You might be able to enter that world, you are smart enough, but don't come here and tell me that is what you really want. Come off it, which kid has a dream of becoming a corporate lawyer? "Daddy, Daddy, when I grow up, I want to help rich people save money, avoid paying their taxes, and shifting jobs to Mexico."'

Her father had a point, Mia recognised, but she was too upset to even consider discussing the matter with him. It was his fault if she decided to go to Harvard and then to New York. He could have earned big money and gave it all up without a fight to live in that town. What an idiot. 'Well, sorry if you don't approve, but I still believe I can make a difference with my job.'

'You can make a difference in your current job, helping people in need, of that, I'm sure of it,' Gregg retorted. 'Come on, kiddo, did I make such a lousy job as a father that I even failed to teach you what is good and what is wrong?'

'Dad, that is where we disagree. There is nothing wrong in making money, and just because you decided otherwise, it doesn't mean I have to follow your path.' Mia tried to remain calm, but her voice was trembling. It was always like that. Every time they met, they clashed on something.

'Sure there isn't. Make all the money you want, but at least be honest with yourself. Say it out loud that there is no enjoyment in what you've done as a corporate lawyer. There's nothing wrong with making money, but do it in a way that makes you happy. Don't choose a career because of the salary they pay. You're smart enough to find something that fulfils you, and if you do that, you'll learn that whatever it pays, it might just be enough.'

Mia thought about it. She always wanted to be a ceramist, but there was no way she could make a living out of it. There were dreams and then there was the harsh reality. To have a decent job that paid rent and a few other bits. She feared bringing that up would prolong the debate with her father indefinitely. She looked at her cup of coffee, now cold, and then turned away from him. *Pretending to be busy might work.* It did.

'Okay, I think I'm gonna get ready for Mrs Jenkins' porch. You take care of yourself, and if you're getting bored, go to town and visit your mother's shop. She added a cafeteria now, you'll love it.'

Mia doubted she'd be impressed. She couldn't possibly imagine what could be so unusual in a bakery with a coffee machine. Near her office, there were more bars than anyone could possibly desire. Some better than others, of course. She was living in a city with seventy-two Michelin-star restaurants. There was a reason why millions of tourists visited New York every year and only a fraction went to Camden, Maine.

'I will, no doubt.'

Her father drove away, and suddenly the house was entirely surrounded by quiet. It was like a silent dream. She opened the computer and went on *The*

New York Times website to catch up on the news, whilst still sipping her cold coffee.

What caught her attention was an article about a new Kowalski street art painting that appeared the previous night on a side street in Boston. It depicted a few women, bent on a sewing machine and clearly overworked and deprived. Near them there was Carlton Allerton throwing pennies at them; behind him, one of their grocery stores and their catchphrase "Fifty Percent Off Guaranteed" written on an advertisement panel. What made Mia fume was the word on top of it: Payday. The reference to Allerton's underpaid employees and vendors was evident.

A few weeks previous, there was a controversial article in a newspaper about Allerton Groceries. The journalists visited, under false pretences, a sweatshop factory in India, where people were forced to work eighteen hours a day and lived and slept on the factory floor. Their salaries were miserable and the conditions inhumane; one of the journalists took a picture of a dress, and it was labelled 'La Gioia', Allerton's own brand of clothes. The company soon issued a statement where they were planning a review of all their vendors, and that they already eliminated many sweatshops from their list of providers, but the damage was done. People didn't like that they took jobs out of the country for sheer profit, and for a while their shares went on a roller-coaster ride. Eventually, all was settled, according to Carlton, but this new Kowalski wall art would stay around forever. On the web at least, if not on the actual wall. People would share it on Twitter, take a selfie in front of it. Carlton was marked forever.

Mia thought that this time Kowalski had gone too far. He had hardly attacked individuals directly in his over twenty-year career, and this was a first. People would talk about it. But most of all, she was annoyed because Kowalski was her favourite artist and she thought they had a sort of connection. During all these years he showed her what was right and what was wrong. Which battle to choose. Of course, she wasn't always in agreement with the statements of the mysterious artist, but even in her disagreement, she admired his clarity of thought and directness. Not this time.

She slammed closed the computer and went for a walk in the woods. The air was brisk and filled her lungs. She pushed the hat down on her head and walked at a fast pace towards the lake. What a start for her first vacation in years.

CHAPTER 18

'Hello?'

Cleopatra tentatively entered the legal clinic or, at least that was what Jennifer thought. The woman was in her thirties, with dark hair arranged in braids. At the bottom of each one, she had blue lapis lazuli jewels. Her white dress could have been an Egyptian tunic; a leather belt with a golden buckle the size of Central Park was reflecting the morning light into the office. She was almost glowing. Around her neck more gold and lapis lazuli. No slaves holding fans were in sight.

'I'm looking for Maggie?' she asked in a tiny, squeaky voice. The woman kept gazing around the same way people did when they were sure they'd entered the wrong place.

'That'd be me,' Ginger answered from her desk. 'Are you Georgina? I was waiting for you.'

Georgina approached the desk and looked quizzically at Jennifer, who sat opposite Ginger.

'This is my new assistant, Jenny, she will work with us today. You know, I have to show her the ropes.' Ginger pointed in the general direction of her companion.

'I was unsure if this was the right place. It says legal clinic outside.'

'We specialise in crimes against fashion,' Ginger said.

Jennifer suppressed a giggle.

'What was that? I didn't catch it,' Cleopatra asked.

Ginger didn't repeat her sentence, therefore avoiding hurting the regal ears of her new customer.

'Never mind.' Ginger opened a drawer on the side of her desk and picked up a folder, which she then carefully deposited in front of her.

To Jennifer, the scene resembled a policewoman studying a dossier in search of a missing clue.

Ginger mumbled, 'Let's see. One change of wardrobe, complete makeover, redesign of a new style from scratch. Main motivations: lack of interest from the male counterparts on Tinder, difficulty in socialising at events. Education, master's degree in mathematics. Budget four thousand.' She fixed her eyes on her client's and asked, 'Is that correct?'

Cleopatra searched for an escape route.

Jennifer had read the online form with all that information previously, but after hearing them repeated like that, she shivered.

'I guess so,' Cleopatra said.

'Anything else I should be aware of?' Ginger pressed.

'Like what?'

'I don't know, having twenty cats at home, a past as an axe murderer, thoughts of world domination. Things like that might prevent me from doing my job properly.' Ginger had a poker face.

Cleopatra looked at Jennifer, searching for a comforting word, but she received none. She was too busy biting her tongue and doing mental calculations. Anything to prevent her from bursting out with a hearty laugh.

'No, I don't think so,' Cleopatra said eventually.

'Very well.' Ginger slammed the dossier closed and got on her feet.

Jennifer, surprised by the sudden move, did the same, jumping up like a sleeping soldier caught in the act by a general. She was still pondering about Ginger and how different she could be when fully involved in one of her schemes. By talking to her, she understood she was vulnerable, full of uncertainties about her own life and her future. Sweet, on occasion. And then there was this other version she presented to the world. A woman without fear of anything, assertive, entirely in control of her capabilities. Which was the real Ginger? She reserved judgement and delayed the answer for a later stage. The truth was that the more she learnt about this woman the more she was fascinated. She was like a magnet, and perhaps that was partially why people innately trusted her. As opposed to Jennifer's first impression, Ginger wasn't really scamming anybody; most of the time she was saying what people wanted to hear and brought some relief, if not joy into their lives. She had to ensure she wouldn't cross the line, as Mia had instructed. Jennifer examined Ginger's outfit: high-heeled black pumps, a pair of skinny dark-blue jeans, which enhanced her toned legs, and a white turtleneck jumper. The jumper wasn't one of those baggy outfits that were often seen in winter; on the contrary, it seemed extraordinarily light and adherent. Jennifer's gaze lingered for a second too long on the ample cleavage. Over that, Ginger had a rust-coloured Zara coat reaching just above her knees; the overcoat was left open.

A small black Gucci bag with a long golden chain completed the outfit. Jennifer couldn't decide if the bag was a real one or one of those cheap fakes you could buy on the internet, but it didn't make any difference to her. The result was astounding, and she salivated. She could understand why people accepted advice from her. She toyed with the idea of inviting Ginger to her den and spending the afternoon trying different outfits. Lingerie, in particular. She shook her head, pushing away the thought of it, as she already felt excited. She was there to be a guardian, not to pick up ladies.

Outside, they grabbed a cab that was passing by. Cleopatra entered on one side of the back seat. Ginger sat in the middle, and Jennifer squeezed in on the other side. Her legs touched Ginger's. She felt excited. Ginger didn't retract herself from the connection, and that sent Jennifer's fantasies spinning again. It was going to be an exciting morning.

CHAPTER 19

One hour later, Xander arrived at the legal clinic. He sat in Mia's chair, and the first thing he did was put his feet on the cheap desk. He wished he had a cigar. 'I tell you what! I'll see you in court!' he said. Pleased with his performance, he composed himself and opened the files Ginger had left him. The office was silent, apart from the occasional car passing by.

In the printed emails, there were all sorts of requests. The first was for a funeral to be hosted that afternoon and needed confirmation. Xander was not in the mood and put it aside. Maybe later.

He moved on to the pile containing requests for articles. Fashion, fashion, fashion. Home interiors. *Why in hell have they prevented me from dealing with style?* He was no expert, but Xander was convinced he could cook something up through browsing the internet. *This is not about me*, he reminded himself, *this is about Mia*. And Ginger. His thoughts went to the redhead, and he wondered how he could manage to invite her out without jeopardising the whole operation. She was single, no doubt there. Not that she wouldn't have a swarm of men hovering around all the time, but something inside him gleaned that she was definitely not seeing anybody. A hunch.

He picked up another email. Bingo, this was about books. The blogger, Donna Smith, wanted an article on Faceblip advertisements, and if it was an effective way of reaching further potential readers. The piece needed to give some explanations on how ads worked without boring the public. She was also an independent author, albeit in chick-lit. *Hello, Donna, welcome to the club.*

He opened the computer and searched for the blog. It was a nice one and with good content and many reviews. Fair ones. He didn't understand why Ginger called them incompetent. It was just a matter of subjects that maybe, in this case, the blogger didn't know in-depth.

He had some experience around it, so he started writing.

When he finally finished the article, a while later, he smiled, proud of himself. Everything was factual and based on his own experience. No tricks. Xander pressed the send button. One done, two thousand to go.

Next one was from a post-atomic blog. Preppers waiting for the end of the world, a Russian or Chinese invasion (it didn't matter), an asteroid hitting the earth. They needed recipes for the potential survivors. That got him thinking. The easy route was to say 'Open a can of tuna. Eat it!' but they might have not appreciated the irony, and those people carried guns. He looked on the web in search of ideas. He needed to give them a *proper* article.

A few hours and several articles later, the office door opened, and Jennifer and Ginger, giggling.

Mostly Jennifer. Ginger was singing 'Cleopatra, comin' atcha!'

'What's going on here? Isn't that an eighties song?' he asked, amused by seeing the two women singing and dancing.

'We hit the jackpot!' Jennifer said.

'Cleopatra, comin' atcha!' Ginger sang, mimicking an Egyptian profile.

'Care to explain?'

'Today, we earned six hundred dollars. By going around shops and spending someone else's money,' Ginger said.

'It was more than that!' an eager Jennifer added. 'Today we transformed an ancient Egyptian into a modern, fashionable, attractive twenty-first-century woman. And we had fun. Xander, you should write a story on it. After we were done, every man on the street was looking at her.'

'They did it before, but for the wrong reasons.' Ginger was full of enthusiasm.

She and Jennifer did a high five.

'Ah, you mean the fashion thing?' Xander was still trying to understand.

'Yeah, the fashion thing.' Jennifer was ecstatic, still full of energy from the experience. 'We saved a woman from herself, restored her confidence, gave her direction for the future. For a mere fifteen percent of her budget. Six hundred dollars! And you should have seen the transformation. Ginger was brilliant giving advice; I only followed her lead. The woman was so happy she couldn't stop thanking us.

Now that I think of it, six hundred for half a day makes a thousand two hundred a day. Twenty days, eleven months, it's a whopping two hundred sixty-four thousand a year before taxes. I wonder why I keep going to the hospital and sawing bones, cutting out appendixes and tonsils when the *El Dorado* is just here.'

Xander sighed. No way he could invite Ginger out. Not until part of the excitement was gone. If he was lucky, it would be a celebration involving the three of them.

'And what have you been up to, Xander?' Jennifer asked.

Ginger was still walking around like an Egyptian. Punching the air occasionally.

'Writing. I wasn't in the mood for funerals, but I might change my mind.'

'Let's see?' Ginger picked up the printout of Xander's work. 'Wow! You did all this in one day?' She kept reading. 'Hey, this is good stuff. It might have taken me days.'

'Yeah, it took me a while to hit my stride, but then everything came easy. I like this stuff.'

Jennifer peeked from behind Ginger's shoulders. A bit too close for Xander's liking.

'I think we should go to Corrigan's and celebrate,' Jennifer proposed. 'We can share our stories with a glass of wine in front of us.'

Bang goes my potential date, but nonetheless he stood and deposited his laptop in the bag. It had

been a good day of work; a glass of wine was
surely overdue.

CHAPTER 20

Corrigan's had more customers than usual that evening, but nonetheless, Jennifer, Ginger, and Xander managed to get a table. A well-placed phone call to Joe ensured that.

Despite being mostly a winery, Corrigan's also served food, and the trio thought it was excellent to have both in the same place, given they were later than their usual hour.

Ginger looked around to get her bearings, and Xander led the way to their table after a few gestures exchanged with Joe. It wasn't noisy enough that they couldn't hear each other, but the two had apparently developed a sign language of their own.

The table was round and made of dark wood. Some of it was patina, some of it was due to years of spillages, but whoever went to Corrigan's didn't pay any particular attention to the ambience. The wine list was all that mattered.

'Red or white?' Jennifer asked.

Ginger looked at both; she panicked.

'I... Don't drink. I mean, a lager once in a while, but that's that,' Ginger said tentatively.

'Well, that's something we have to rectify then.' Xander scanned the chalkboard listing the "specials" of the day.

'Indeed. Shall we do red?' Jennifer asked again.

'Shouldn't we first check at the menu?' Ginger seemed out of her comfort zone.

'Nah, that is a common misconception,' Xander said, dismissing the question. 'The wine is the most important thing, then we pick some food that doesn't clash too much with it.'

'I'm tempted by the Beringer private reserve,' Jennifer muttered. She adjusted a lock of hair that was blocking her view.

Ginger twisted her head to the chalkboard and squeaked. 'A hundred and fifty dollars a bottle?'

'Don't worry, it's my treat,' Jennifer said, 'and then if we have to initiate you to the art of wine tasting, we better start on the right foot. You don't want to have a cheap wine from a box as your first experience.'

Ginger shrugged. 'I'll go with the flow.'

It had been a good day. Leaving the hospital for a while turned out to be a pleasant novelty. Ginger had been brilliant all along, full of energy and enthusiasm. For once, Jennifer felt less lonely, maybe with the beginning of a friendship. She couldn't remember the last time she spoke to someone as freely as she did today.

And then, there was Ginger's laugh. Sound, carefree, as if nothing in the world could bother her. Her contagious smile made Jennifer wonder that maybe out there, there was a chance to be happy. Ginger also opened up to her, though just a little. Since "the incident", the redhead only spent her time working, trying to get by and earn as much as possible. She told her she saw the first glimpse of friendship in her relationship with Mia, who recognised her for what she was. Jennifer never pressed her for answers she wasn't ready to give and, within limits, she accepted her way of living. She realised a new hope lay in Ginger's heart, that maybe there was another way, an honest way of getting where she wanted to be.

Xander took care of ordering the wine, then they looked at the menu.

'I go for a *burrata campana,*' Jennifer said, scrutinising the paper in front of her. 'Mind sharing?'

'I'll have a burger,' Xander added. 'The abundant aromas of burning embers, charcoal, purplish-toned fruit, cedar, and tobacco notes from the Beringer well suits a classical homemade burger.'

'I didn't know you were a smoker.' Jennifer laughed. 'Oh well, the arteries are yours, you can clog them with whatever you want. That is my professional opinion.'

After flicking through the menu and much deliberation, finally it was Ginger's turn. 'I'll go for pigeon and peas.'

'What?' they both asked to her in unison as if they were one. 'Where did you see that?'

'It's on the specials.'

'Corrigan's never had anything similar before,' pronounced Xander, and then he opened the menu again, just to find a yellow Post-it with them. 'I'll have to have a serious word with Joe.' Having said that, he caught the owner's attention and then united his thumbs and, with open hands made the gesture of a flying bird, followed by a question mark.

Joe smiled and shrugged. Jennifer eye-rolled.

'To hell with the burger, I'll go for the pigeon as well.' Xander had made his mind up.

His phone rang. He showed the display; Mia's name was on it.

'Hello, darling?' he said and then mouthed *she is okay.* 'Corrigan's. Yeah, I thought you recognised the sound. Can you believe it? They have pigeon on the menu.'

Silence, then Xander nodded, followed by a long series of 'hm, hmm.'

'Here we did brilliantly,' he eventually managed to say. He then gave Mia a summary of the day, his own version, much more embellished than the reality.

Jennifer was eager to step in, but it was evident Xander didn't want to pass the phone over.

'Okay, love, have a great time there,' and he hung up.

'It's not always that good.' Ginger opened her arms so as to show defeat. 'Sometimes it takes weeks to get another decent customer. It's a lot of fishing.'

Xander reported the conversation he had with Mia. She had managed to clash a couple of times with her father, but so far, nothing too serious to allow her to reach the point of not inviting them. She was enjoying long walks in the woods and having a rest. '… And she sends her love.'

'I never understood why she doesn't want her parents at the wedding,' Ginger said. There was true concern transpiring from her face.

Joe arrived with the wine, which was poured into three crystal glasses, but the question wasn't forgotten.

It was Jennifer who spoke first. 'Maybe she doesn't either. Mia has always been reluctant to talk about it, but from what I've gathered during these years, she's afraid of not succeeding in life. Her parents made the choice of leaving Boston for Maine, a simpler way of living, which many of us don't dare to pursue. Somehow Mia is in search of self-realisation, she wants more, whatever that is, and she is not able to forgive her parents, who have settled for *enough*.'

'That was very well put,' Xander added. 'Don't worry, Ginger, we love her nonetheless.'

That sparked smiles at the table.

'Yeah, I've understood that. But it's Mia's wedding, she's going to regret it for the rest of her life if she doesn't invite them.' Ginger tentatively put her lips on the glass and sipped the wine. 'Delicious.'

'Yeah,' Jennifer got closer to her, 'welcome to the brain cell killers' club.'

'I hope everything goes well for Mia. I've grown to like her despite her being a sergeant major in disguise,' Ginger said.

The food arrived, and the three went quiet, none of them a believer of eating and talking at the same time, a behaviour that in recent years had seemed to become, strangely enough, less popular.

They resumed chatting after they'd finished their main course, and a new bottle of wine arrived. This time a Riesling Auslese, well below the one hundred dollars mark. As there wasn't another personal shopping client lined up, Jennifer asked how the erotic line worked.

Ginger explained that it was on-demand, nothing she could deal with regularly, because of her job. An advertisement was posted online, specifying the firm's name and times, and then it was a waiting game.

'You should do it in the office,' a too-eager Xander said. 'I might use some of the material in one of my books.'

Jennifer punched him in the shoulder. 'Nice try, buster, as if I'm going to expose my sexual fantasies to anybody. It has to be a stranger or not at all. Anyway, haven't you got any funerals lined up for tomorrow?'

'I hate funerals. I might write some other blog posts. By the way, how much do they fetch per piece?'

Ginger shrugged. 'The easy ones ten, twenty dollars, but for some others, when the blog is much bigger, they might give up to two hundred dollars.'

Xander whistled. 'Let me get this straight. For each book I sell at two ninety-nine dollars I got a seventy percent revenue. That means than a single top article at two-fifty is just short of a hundred and twenty books sold. In one day. I could make that my primary career and ditch...'

'A career change?'

'That's the question. Which one is my first career, writing or delivering packages?'

Jennifer already knew the answer. The pen was mightier than the bicycle. 'Maybe you should do a joint venture,' she proposed. 'Fifty-fifty. Or maybe sixty-forty.'

The third bottle of wine was well underway, and she found it challenging to think straight. 'But it's something for tomorrow. Shall we call it a day? Midnight has come and gone.'

'I think I'm ready for bed, too.' Xander's voice trembled, the word slurred out of his mouth. 'At this point, I couldn't tell the difference between wine in a cardboard box and a Brunello.'

'Oh my gosh,' Ginger replied, 'I've never drank so much in my life, and tomorrow I have work to do.'

'Don't worry, babe, I'll take you home.'

Jennifer laughed. 'Yeah, and tomorrow morning you both will still be wandering around Brooklyn trying to figure out the way home. No way, we get a cab. Joe can take care of your bicycle. I'll go with Maggie as she is on the way.'

'Roger that.' Xander caught Joe's attention, then he made the phone gesture, stretching the thumb and the little finger, followed by the steering wheel one. Eventually, he showed two fingers and then pointed at the three of them.

'What is the story with all those gestures?'
Ginger asked.

'What gestures?'

'Never mind.'

Joe signalled back to wait for five minutes.

After sorting out the bill with a waiter, they
staggered towards the entrance. Jennifer helped an
unbalanced Ginger by the arm. They made solemn
promises to each other to be in the office at a
reasonable time, and the two women took the first
taxi to arrive.

On the back seat of the cab, exhausted by the
long day walking and the wine, Jennifer exhaled.

'I really enjoyed the day. You're both
wonderful,' Ginger said.

'Me, too. I thought today might have been a
good diversion from my job, but actually, it was
fantastic. I think we made a difference with that
woman today. She seemed so happy. I didn't realise
how gratifying it would be. Thank you.'

They were sitting close to each other in the back
of the cab; Jennifer felt Ginger's body against her
every time the car turned. She enjoyed the feeling.
Her gaze stopped for a second too long on Ginger's
legs when she crossed them. The dark-beige coat was
covering her, but she well remembered the
burgundy bodycon her companion was wearing,
having changed at the office. And her well-
proportioned curves. She positioned her hand on
Ginger's, who didn't flinch. It was soft and warm to
the touch. Ginger-Maggie made a few comments on

the neighbouring area, she said she always liked Brooklyn and she'd never move away, no matter what. Everything she wanted was right there, it was only a matter of grasping it.

I wouldn't move from this cab, as long as you sit near me.

The cab stopped, and Ginger retracted her hand from Jennifer's to take care of her share of the fee. She didn't want to hear complaints, what was fair was fair. She gave twenty dollars to the driver and said to keep the change.

'Thank you for the lovely evening.' Ginger played with the purse in her hand for a moment and then placed it in her bag. 'I hope we can do it again soon.'

'Me, too, Maggie. I felt very comfortable with you.'

'Likewise.'

There was an embarrassing silence between the two. Neither of them knew what to say next, and for a few seconds, they looked each other in the eye. They smiled, but nobody talked.

'Okay then, I'm off,' Ginger said eventually.

She moved towards Jennifer to kiss her on a cheek, but they both went in the same direction, and their lips touched in a warm kiss. Jennifer lingered a moment too long on Ginger's full lips and then she pressed a little further.

Ginger extricated herself, her eyes on stalks. 'I… Sorry… I have to go!'

In the dim light of the cab, Ginger's cheeks reddened.

Ginger abruptly exited the cab and ran to the main entrance of her building. She fiddled with the keys and then she turned quickly towards the taxi. The cab moved on.

Oh my God, what I have done? All sorts of doubts came to her mind. The possibility she had misinterpreted all the signs Ginger had been giving her. She thought about them holding hands and realised it could have been considered as a friendly gesture, nothing more. *How can I show my face tomorrow at Mia's office?*

Mia.

She was going to put Mia's business at risk. She couldn't afford that; their friendship was too important. She knew already she wouldn't be able to sleep. Tomorrow she'd have to act professionally, despite what she was feeling. Things could crumble without notice if she didn't act rationally.

CHAPTER 21

Mia woke up again in a silent house. She looked at her clock and learnt it was still seven in the morning, despite feeling totally rested. Outside, it was snowing.

She'd always liked the snow, it brought joy to her, mostly because it made her think about Christmas when she was a child. How many times she had gone down the road and had a snowball fight with her friends?

She had a quick shower and dressed casually as she had promised her mother to help her in the shop. Not that her mother needed any assistance; she had managed well for all those years, but doing something different, for once, was going to be refreshing.

With all that snow, Mia decided not to go into the woods by herself, despite having grown up in the area. She had been reluctant to visit the bakery, at least for the past couple of days, but she couldn't delay any further and risk upsetting her mother to boot: she was the only gate preventing Mia and her father from arguing all the time. There was some sort of mutual, silent agreement that they didn't bicker with each other in her presence. Not much, at least.

She also avoided going to the shop for another reason. Neighbours and her parents' friends would have bombarded her with questions. 'Look at little

Mia, I remember when you were this tall,' pinning their hand at hip level, 'Oh, now she's a full-grown woman, isn't she?'

And the worst question of all, 'Are you married yet?'

That opened a totally different can of worms. But it was the lesser of two evils, far better than going fixing roofs with her dad while it was snowing. Or whatever handyman job he could come across, and in Camden, apparently there were plenty. Something didn't add up. Camden was beautiful; people took pride in what was considered one of the jewel towns in Maine. Everybody was looking after the place. It wasn't as if they were in a deserted village, and yet despite that, her father managed to keep busy every single day.

The bakery, now also a cafeteria, was on Main Street, about a hundred feet from the National Bank. Mia parked near the harbour and stopped in front of one of the art galleries. Opening time was two hours later, but she nonetheless peeked through the window. A few landscape paintings, mostly in oil depicting the countryside and sea views were on display in the main window. She couldn't fathom the name of the artists, but those canvases were lovely. One was from Vermont, at least that was what she could read. Even trying to shade the glare of light on the window, she couldn't learn much more. It was definitely somewhere worth visiting later on during the day. And the prices were reasonable.

Mia walked the few hundred feet to the bakery. She entered and looked around. A few customers were sitting at the tables, chatting. Her parents had done an excellent job, and the first impression was outstanding. A large unit of dark wood was holding the different types of bread, all labelled with her mother's handwriting. On the front, there was a cabinet display with several cakes and sweets, all homemade. There was an oven in the back of the shop, Mia remembered that, but recently, with the employment of "little" David Allen, all the work was done in a small building outside town. Despite that, she could smell the freshly baked products and she felt hungry all of a sudden.

Her mother was busy preparing a coffee on her new, fancy Italian La Cimbali, and hadn't spotted her yet. That gave Mia the opportunity to inspect the cafeteria further. It was elegant although rustic. On the wall, paintings of the marina, the harbour, the mountains in the autumn. Some seemed familiar, but she couldn't place where she'd seen them. She suddenly remembered walking with her father in the countryside, and that was a view of Megunticook Lake. If Mia were a writer, she would have loved working on a novel at that table by the window. Sipping hot coffee and eating pastries.

'Hello, dear. I'm glad you made it,' her mother said, awakening Mia from a daydream. 'Come on this side, I've got an apron and a shirt for you.'

She reluctantly went to the back of the shop to wear the uniform. They had a little boat as the company logo. Fair enough, the harbour was the main attraction.

'I'm not sure what I'm supposed to do.' Mia reached her mother behind the counter.

'Nothing to worry about, just smile. I'll show you how the register works after lunch.'

A squeaky voice interrupted them. 'Oh my gosh, is that little Mia?' Mrs Clark was one of her teachers at elementary school. She did look old then, but time seemed not to have passed by for her. Maybe she was slightly more stooped than before. She was using a walking stick, something Mia didn't recall her having previously. 'Did you come back?'

'Mrs. Clark? It's so nice to see you!' Mia slipped away from the counter and hurried up to hug the old lady. This time the roles were reversed, she stood tall in front of her. 'I thought you lived in Rockport.'

'I did. I moved here with my son and the grandchildren a few years back. You know, I cannot drive anymore, and we thought, after the departure of Tom, it would be better if we all stay together. I still have the house, although it now lies empty. I think all the time I should sell it, now that I don't need it anymore, but I never wanted to face it. Too many memories, and I'd hate seeing it used as a holiday home. Closed all the time except for summer. A house needs to be lived in or not at all.'

Mia remembered the house. It was a lovely building in dark wood with a view of the Marine Park and the harbour, walking distance from the town centre. Inside it was nothing special but it had three bedrooms, a large separate garage, and a secondary building that Mia didn't know what it was used for. Maybe a little guest house, although she'd never set foot inside. She had never been an admirer of country houses, but she had in her memory an image of the building in the winter snow, Mrs Clark standing on the doorstep and Mia and her father outside. Her dad had to do, as usual, some work to the property, and she spent half of the day playing with Mrs Clark's dog, chasing each other in the snow. For a moment, she thought of asking about Bessie, a mongrel that had some resemblance with an Alsatian. Too many years had passed, and the dog had surely died.

'Well, at least with the family around you have some help, especially in winter,' Mia said.

'That is true. Paul still takes me there once in a while, you know, to let the house breathe and remove some dust. But I'm getting older. So, what are you up to these days? Did you come back permanently?'

'Mia is a lawyer in New York,' her mother interjected, with a sense of pride in her voice, 'she helps people in need, and she recently won a big case against a corporation.'

'How do you know that?' Mia asked. It wasn't a *big* case, but the other side was indeed a significant company. A slam-dunk in court, but it took her a substantial amount of time to prepare and study. She was sure she hadn't mentioned it to her parents.

'It was reported in the local gazette, quite an article if you ask me,' Mia's mother said.

'Why didn't you say anything?' Mia asked, almost whispering, but her mother ignored her and kept talking to the customer.

'Such a clever girl,' Mrs Clark continued. 'I could tell she'd do great even from when she was at school. And she has a good heart, exactly like her father.'

The comment didn't go down well, and Mia excused herself and went to the rear of the shop. She was fuming, but at the same time she couldn't start an argument in front of the customers. She sat on a chair and exhaled. Coming to Maine was a big mistake. She and Carlton should have organised the wedding in some remote location, such as Bali, or New Guinea, on the opposite side of the world, hoping her parents didn't show up. As soon as the thought presented itself in her mind, she discarded it. They'd have made every possible attempt to be present and ruin her wedding day.

The oven beeped, and that was enough to wake her up from her musings. One of her mother's cakes was ready. She carefully took it out of the oven and placed it on a tray. The smell took her back for a moment to her early teens, when she used to help her mother cooking. She loved to knead the dough, there was something therapeutic in working with her hands, shaping things. Being that a cake or ceramic. She started that because of the film *Ghost* if she had to be honest with herself, but then, the more

169

she progressed, the more she felt a growing sense of peace inside her when she was working with her hands.

Mia returned to the shop bearing the cake. There was quite a queue of people, and things were doing well for the bakery. Now all the tables were also full.

'Mia, a latte and an apple pie for the table in the corner, if you don't mind.' Her mother walked around as if she were on wheels.

How remote was this work from what she was doing in New York. Her feet hurt, she wasn't used to walking up and down and standing for long periods like that. She wished for a pair of tennis shoes, like the ones her mother had on her feet. The table in the corner was occupied by a lone male. His face was buried in the newspaper, but he was wearing a squared red lumberjack shirt and a pair of jeans. He had toned, muscular arms, and scruffy hair, the sort that never found shape even after a good combing session. It looked like the result of a troubled night's sleep.

'Here we are, latte and pie.'

'Mia?' the man asked, 'is that you?' His voice was deep and warm.

Her heart skipped a beat, and she let the plate with the cake slip through her fingers. When it fell to the floor, a few people turned in her direction. Her cheeks heated, and a shiver ran down her spine. 'Sorry,' was the only word she managed to say for a few long seconds. She bent to pick up what remained of the splattered cake and the plate, and now she was half-covered by the table. 'I didn't know you were back in town.'

Mia's mother came to help with a dustpan and a cloth in her hands. 'Here, let me help you. Hello, Ethan.'

The man nodded a salute and smiled. Mia cringed even further. She remembered that smile too well. There were only a couple more wrinkles around the eyes, but she never had forgotten. How could she?

'I've been back in town for the past five years,' he answered nonchalantly. 'What about you?'

'I'm just passing through.' Mia stood, and she felt the same way as she had during their first date. Nervous. Memories flashed through her mind without interruption. When they were kids playing hide and seek in the woods. Her first crush on him. Dreaming of being Demi Moore in *Ghost*, doing pottery and having him behind her. Their first kiss. She wanted to run.

'Why don't you pass by our house this evening,' Mia's mother said. 'I'm cooking meatloaf, it's one of your favourites, right? And you two can catch up.'

'It is indeed, Mrs Crawford. I have few errands to do with Gregg today, we won't be late.'

'Excellent. I'll prepare the guest room, so you can have a couple of beers and not worry about driving home.'

Mia assessed the whole scene, and she couldn't believe her ears. *His* favourite food? The fact that Ethan worked with her father added a totally new dimension to the whole story. Gregg hadn't said a word, nor had her mother, and they knew what past she shared with Ethan. Mia also knew the bakery wasn't the place to start making enquiries; she felt too vulnerable there. She managed a 'See you later, Ethan,' and stormed back behind the counter. Getting busy with the customers was always the right way of not overthinking her private life. She had learnt that lesson well before.

CHAPTER 22

'You did what?' Xander asked.

'I kissed her,' Jennifer replied sheepishly. She looked down at the floor.

'Hang on a second, I left you two in a cab going home, at least that is what I half remember. When did you kiss her?'

'I'm embarrassed, because the only reason I'm here is to help Mia. I failed her and I don't know what I'm going to do when Maggie enters that door.' Jennifer took a long breath. 'We reached her home, and before she exited the cab, that's when it happened.'

'Yeah, I got that part. It's the *how* which is not clear. Was it like Clark Gable and Vivien Leigh in *Gone with the Wind* when he leaves for battle? An Argentinian tango sort of kiss? Mind you, I'm struggling to imagine you with a rose between your teeth. Or was it a sneaky kiss? You know, when one is going for the cheek and the other one goes for full lips. For sure you weren't eating the same spaghetti and one of you got greedy.'

Jennifer laughed nervously. She seemed relaxed in the armchair, her cup of coffee in hand, trying to analyse what went wrong the previous evening, but Xander knew better. She was struggling. Jennifer wasn't the type of person who sought advice in the love field. She always had clear ideas about pretty much anything. It was not the case that morning.

'Xander, you're not helping. It was definitely a sneaky kiss. From my side. God, what was I thinking? Although I must say, all the signs were there, she was leaning towards me. Her laughter, she teased me. I could have bet the farm she was lesbian.'

Xander's knowledge on the matter was limited to what he wrote in his erotic novels, and he felt he couldn't really give any advice. As usual, when nothing came to mind, he joked, 'Maybe we can find a technician to recalibrate your gaydar.'

'It worked fine until yesterday, thank you very much, and I have a headache as if I had drunk Romulan beer the whole night. I don't know, maybe talking will solve the matter.'

Xander doubted that; Jennifer was a woman of action, not a talker. He could well understand why she'd made a move on Ginger. She was beautiful and smart, although on occasion she seemed to have a dark side. He couldn't explain to himself the duality in her persona. On occasion she was shy and introverted, and then all of a sudden, she came up with ideas on how to make money that were at the very least bizarre. Some were so strange that they were on the boundary between being a huge success or an utter delusional failure. Xander understood Ginger was talented. From what he had seen, the blogger posts service could have been a goldmine, but it was not scalable. Ginger had the right ideas, but she wasn't focused, too many things on her plate and not enough time to develop a winning strategy on one of them. He knew that very well because of his writing—he jumped from science fiction, to erotica, to dystopia. All good fun, but there wasn't a focus. Great authors wrote in a genre, not in twenty different ones. In that, they were similar. He also remembered his "grumpy" period. Several years back, he could barely speak to people, he grunted. It took time and forcing himself to be more social to actually have some friendships. His problem was that he could *read* people. Understand their motivation at a glance, and often he didn't like what he saw. With the years, he learnt to ignore the feeling and concentrate on the few friends who were really worth his time. Maybe it was the same for Ginger; lots of unexploited potential. No wonder Jennifer was fascinated by her, he was, too. Most of all, it kept his hopes high for a date, although he felt sorry for Jennifer. She seemed to have fallen hook, line, and sinker.

'Maybe she's going to talk to Mia and take you to court for harassment in the workplace.'

'Xander! Not helping!'

'Take it easy, Jenny, everything is going to be fine. What have you lined up for today?'

'We were supposed to have the erotic phone calls, but somehow I doubt it would be appropriate.'

'Given the mood you are in,' Xander caressed his two-day stubble, 'you're perfect for attending a funeral. Here, there is one that seems suitable. A car

175

crash. I'm already on my third article today, and guess what? I'm having the time of my life. It's like a drug, I cannot stop writing, and it's so much fun. It's even put me in the mood to start a new novel.'

Ginger entered the office, bringing the chat to a halt.

'Good morning,' Xander said, followed by a much quieter hello from Jennifer.

'Hello to you two.' Ginger removed her coat and sat at her desk, showing her back to them. She got immediately busy reading emails and making phone calls.

'Righty-ho,' Xander announced, 'I'm off to do some deliveries, see you later. Don't do anything I wouldn't do in the first place, okay, ladies?'

Imploring looks towards Xander from both of them resulted in nothing.

'Bastard!' Jennifer muttered in a barely audible voice.

He returned a couple of hours later. 'All good here?'

'Yep,' was the reply from the two women.

The tension in the room was palpable; it was if all the winter cold had suddenly decided to pop into the office and rest there for a while.

Xander fired up his laptop. 'Listen up, ladies, I need some advice.'

'You,' Jennifer voiced, 'without an opinion about something? That might be a first.'

Ginger giggled.

'I know, I know, but I'm taking my job seriously, and this time I'm struggling. Only the most capable mind can recognise when they are stuck and they need help.'

Both the women turned towards him, Jennifer from her desk on the right and Ginger from her seat.

'Fire away,' Ginger said.

'Come on, ladies, gather around, I don't want to shout all the time.' He invited them to get closer to his desk.

Ginger rolled on her chair whilst Jennifer stood and moved her seat.

'Okay, I've got this article to write for a Lauren Kermode's website; she's got some personal stuff to deal with and she doesn't want to drop the number of followers. I'd usually go wild or use a bit of humour, but this is not about me. It's about Mia's and Ginger's business, so…'

'Come on, get to the point. What kind of advice do you need?' Ginger asked.

'As I was saying, this Kermode lady manages the *Lesbian Today* website and needs a piece on lesbian dating. It's just a seventy-five bucks' article, but I've procrastinated for too long; bottom line, I think I'm stuck.'

'Use your common sense,' Jennifer said. She relaxed in her chair.

'Sure. I mean, I went on a speed-dating event a while back,' Xander explained, 'you know, where you sit at a table and every two minutes you have to interact with a potential new date? Well, my strategy was to ask each one of them if they wanted to go to bed with me. No chitchat. I thought, I might get ninety-nine rejections but I just need to get lucky once.'

'And how did it turn out?'

'Badly. One woman even threw a glass of water in my face, but the law of great numbers is with me. Well, you see why *my* advice might not be really suitable?'

Everybody laughed.

'You got a point there.' Ginger, fortunately, was eager to help. 'But maybe you should take a step back. You're already thinking about the actual date, but before that comes the flirting. It's not easy to spot someone else's sexuality.'

'Of course it is,' Jennifer exclaimed, the passion evident in her voice, 'they send out all sorts of signals, the way they look at you, how they talk to you, when they go touchy-feely and demonstrate an interest. More explicit than that and you have to have a sticker with "I'm a lesbian" written on it.'

Xander took out his block notes and scribbled on it. 'Carry on, ladies.'

'I disagree,' Ginger retorted. 'Smiling and being friendly is the polite thing to do, and maybe someone might misinterpret it as more than friendship. And you have to consider that *someone* might still struggle with her own sexuality. Not everybody has clear ideas right from the beginning.'

'True,' Jennifer replied, 'but isn't life too short to waste time with the ifs and the buts?'

'That poses another problem,' Ginger continued, this time talking directly to Jennifer, 'how is *someone* supposed to know if *the counterpart* is only interested in a one-night stand or a relationship? Something more serious? If *someone* is already struggling, going full tongue at the first occasion doesn't help. The *someone* might be still worrying about how her family took the news. Too little time to think about the consequences.'

'This is good stuff,' Xander said, who at that point had almost a page of notes. 'Carry on.'

'So, what would be the ideal flirting approach that might work for *someone* in that situation?' Jennifer asked.

'I don't know, I think the *subject* might appreciate the initial attentions, like sitting across from each other and gently putting their hand on hers, some compliments. But I think it's also important letting them know she is attractive, invite her for dinner, just the two of them. I'd even push it to the point of sending flowers with a handwritten note. A slow pace flirting would go a long way for *someone*.'

'Isn't that too old-fashioned?'

'Maybe it is, but *someone* might still appreciate the attentions, and that will give some breathing space to think about what's coming next.'

Jennifer nodded, clearly pondering something else to say, but Xander interrupted her train of thought.

'Okay, ladies, thank you. I think I have enough material to write the article. Really appreciated.' He turned towards his laptop and started typing.

Ginger and Jennifer looked each other in the eye.

'So, what task do we have today?' Jennifer asked.

'Nothing much. There is a potential client who needs a new wardrobe, and then the erotic calls, later in the evening.'

'I assume those type of phone calls requires quiet, so a restaurant might not be suitable.'

'Right.'

'What about this,' Jennifer said. 'Maybe we could go for lunch now, meeting the client in the afternoon, and then I could invite you for dinner this evening at my place. I'm actually a decent cook, and we could chat and get to know each other better whilst I prepare dinner, that is if you like Italian; I have a secret recipe for aubergine rolls with spinach and ricotta that one of my patients gave me as a thank you.'

'Sounds fantastic.'

'Xander, are you coming?'

'Nah, I'm tangled with a few more articles and I'm on a roll. I already have something planned for this evening anyway. Sorry.'

'No problem, your loss. Shall we, Maggie?'

The two women put their coats on and went out onto the street in search of a taxi. As soon as they left, Xander crumpled up his notes and threw them in the bin. A perfect slam-dunk.

There wasn't any article to be written for an alleged *Lesbian Today* website.

CHAPTER 23

'So, meatloaf is one of Ethan's favourite dishes now, right?' Mia asked. The bitterness in her voice was evident. It was almost seven in the evening, and her feet were hurting like hell after only half a day working at the bakery. Not even a long, warm shower gave her relief. How her mother could manage to work there, day in and day out was a mystery.

Mia's mother was intent on putting dishes onto the dining table. They were the same ones they'd used years back, when Mia was still a kid. She tried to remember if anybody in her family ever broke anything, or they changed something for the sake of it. The house was pretty much the same as she always remembered. The same furniture, the same identical colour scheme, even most of the paintings on the wall were the same, apart from a couple of notable exceptions.

'Sorry, dear, nowadays Ethan is more around here than you are. Sometimes he works with your father, you know. He's like a son to us.'

'I guess some things have changed and others haven't,' she said. 'How come you still use these old plates? I mean, they might be older than I am.'

'What's wrong with them? Did you spot a chip?' Mia's mother asked, carefully examining the one she still had in her hand.

'No, nothing like that. They are just old.'

'If they are not broken, why change… Oh, here is your father,' Mia's mother said, looking out of the window.

The car headlamps briefly illuminated the dining room.

Gregg entered a few minutes later with a bunch of flowers in his hand. 'For my lovely ladies of the house.'

'I'll take care of them.' Mia walked towards her father, but in that very moment, her phone rang. 'Hang on a second. This is Mia Crawford speaking.'

'Oh, hello, my name is Peter Higgins from Myerscough, Nibley, and Holton. Sorry for calling you at this late hour. Is it a good moment to talk?'

'Yes, sure, please give me one second…' Mia mouthed the words *work, important, five minutes* towards her parents and went outside to the porch. The gust of frozen air enveloped her. She shivered. 'Sorry, yes, Myerscough, Nibley, and Holton, you were saying; how can I help?' She knew that name, one of the best firms in New York.

'We're refreshing our roster and we came across your CV. We have an opening for a fourth-year associate in the litigation department, and I was wondering if you would be available for an interview tomorrow morning.'

'You said litigation? Not Corporate Finance?'

'You heard me right. Is that a problem?' the deep voice on the other end of the phone asked.

'No, not at all. I'm currently in Maine, though…'

183

'Let me see…'

The man tapped on a keyboard.

'Next free appointment slot is in two weeks' time according to my calendar, but we might have already filled the position by then. It's a nice opportunity; it comes with a salary of two hundred thousand per annum plus the 401K. Litigation also gets a marginal profit share. Are you sure you cannot make it? We came to appreciate your skills in litigation recently.'

Mia remembered that case very well, and how they'd almost brought her to the verge of giving up law altogether. They were the best. 'I'll be there, don't worry. At what time is the appointment?'

'Nine o'clock?'

'Perfect, see you there.'

'Excellent news. Please ask for me at reception. Peter Higgins.'

'Peter Higgins,' she replied, to fix the name in her memory, 'see you tomorrow.'

They both hung up, and Mia sat on the porch steps, speechless. *Damn, tomorrow morning.* She did a quick search, and the first available option was a direct flight from Bangor to Newark, arriving at 8.35 AM, for a whopping nine hundred dollars. Which she didn't have. No way she could reach Manhattan in time. The other option was to drive during the night. Asleep at the most important interview in her career. 'Hang on a second,' she said. Boston was on the way to New York. She fired up her phone once again, and bingo! A flight from Boston departing at silly o'clock but arriving at JFK at half past six. Five hundred dollars she still didn't have but she could nap at the airport and during the journey to New York. *I have to bite the bullet,* and she booked the flight.

Now the problem is to let them know I have to go back to New York. I haven't even touched the wedding subject.

Mia put the phone in her back pocket and walked a few steps towards the old barn to collect some ideas. As usual, it was unlocked. She flicked the lights on and, as expected, nothing had changed much in there. Tins of paint, half used, various pieces of timber, a tarpaulin covering the old Bristol Roadster, a pet project that her father carried on for many years. Apparently, it was still an unfinished one, judging by the dust. She looked around, and at the bottom was the huge kiln her father had built when she was in her teens. A monster almost thirteen feet long. She stepped forward and touched the cold bricks. It was in the exact same condition as when she'd left. On its side lay the other one, the electric kiln she desired, now completely rusted.

'I remember the day it arrived. You were so happy,' a voice said behind her.

'Ethan.' Mia didn't turn. She tried to open the kiln, and the handle broke off.

'You were so proud of it,' the man said. 'I still remember the day. It was summer and strangely warm. I was on my way here, and the UPS van driver asked me for directions. The next thing I see is you unwrapping it.'

'It was a nice piece of equipment, it served me well for several years.'

'We built the other one with your father, secretly. He was so proud of what you'd done so far. "She deserves the best", he kept repeating. I spent weeks in the library trying to figure out what your father wanted and almost broke my neck when we installed the ventilation system.' Ethan walked closer and took the rusty handle from Mia. 'Let me get this. The seaside mist is hard on metal in this place.'

'He said the Ancient Greeks and the Romans used something like that. That I could have learnt the essence of pottery, controlling the temperature, being in charge of the process from start to finish. Built on a slope and based on an Anagama Japanese kiln.'

'I had to do all the research, the measurement, the refractory arch and so on.'

'And I had a tantrum, worrying that my friends at school would call me *the Stone Age girl*.'

'I remember that also.'

'What a bitch I was,' Mia said.

'No, you weren't. You know, we fired it once, after you left, only to see if it worked.' He pointed at the massive kiln.

Mia turned towards him. 'Really? And?'

He walked past her and picked up a piece of dusty pottery. 'Here. Our first and last attempt.'

She passed her fingers over the rugged surface of a wonky vase. 'You didn't cook it enough. This monster had to be on for days.'

'We didn't know what to do, it was just curiosity.'

'So, what are you up to now?' Mia asked.

The Ethan in front of her was a more mature version of the young, beautiful boy she'd fallen in love with. They were inseparable, at first as school friends and later as a couple, always planning how to make the world a better place to live.

'I'm busy with social care here in Camden and the surrounding area. Sometimes I tag along with your father and do some work with him.'

'Still trying to save the world?'

'A bit at the time, nothing too complicated. We have a nice community here, and I do my part. Not sure about saving the world, but if more people were involved in their communities it could make some difference.'

Nothing much changed in Ethan, the lack of ambition was what drove them apart, as the more she spent time with him the more she saw her father in him. 'Do you still paint?'

'As a matter of fact, I do, in my spare time, but not very successfully. I have a couple of pieces in the art gallery in town, the one in front of your mother's shop. Your parents have a couple on the wall.'

'I saw those!' Mia said, remembering peeking through the gallery window. 'They're not half bad. Maybe you should try Boston, or New York. A much greater audience. The taste is different and more refined than here…'

'No, thanks. I'm happy as things stand.'

No ambition. Which was what eventually broke their relationship. *Being in love with Ethan is not enough if he decides… oh my gosh, did I just think "is" instead of "was"?*

'Maybe we should go back.' Mia hurried towards the barn door.

The dinner was uneventful, and nobody discussed touchy subjects until after dessert, when Mia announced she had to go back to New York.

'You only just arrived. Are you sure?' her mother said.

'I have an interview tomorrow morning at nine, Mom. I cannot miss it.'

'Either they are not organised enough,' Gregg said, 'or they're assholes. Who sets up an interview for the day after when you're in Maine? If you ask me, they're assholes.'

'Dad, this is with one of the most important firms in New York. I cannot let this opportunity slip,' she pleaded. She already knew what was coming next, an argument for sure, so she changed tactic. 'I'll send you the invite to the wedding, okay? I don't know the date yet, but hopefully it will be soon.'

Gregg grunted, and Ethan stood.

'I think it's time for me to go. Lilly, thank you for the lovely dinner; Gregg, see you around.'

'One second, I'll walk you to the door.' Mia stood and followed him to the entrance and then on the patio outside. 'I'm sorry to see you leaving.'

'We both have an early start.'

'You are still angry with me because I went to Harvard.'

'Harvard was never the problem and you know it. I could have waited,' Ethan snapped.

'What's the point in going to Harvard and then coming back to Camden? All the jobs that can make a difference are in New York, in Washington, not here.'

'And how did that work out for you? Corporate law? You're making a difference now, in your clinic, but you're prepared to throw that away in a heartbeat. At least be honest with yourself and say you're doing all this for the money,' Ethan retorted.

'What's wrong in making some bucks in the process? And what have you done on your side?' Mia crossed her arms; the air was freezing, but she knew that was not the reason, she was being defensive.

'Tell whatever lie makes you feel better and sleep at night, okay?' Ethan climbed in his car and stormed away into the night, leaving her on the cold porch, barely illuminated by the light coming from the hall.

Damn!

CHAPTER 24

'You're back early,' Xander said when Mia entered the clinic. 'What's with that fancy dress?'

She looked around the office. Everything was as she'd left it. Unfortunately. She'd just came back from Myerscough, Nibley, and Holton's interview, and the difference was right in front of her eyes. Instead of a view of the Manhattan skyline, her office faced a betting shop, cars illegally parked, and a Chinese takeaway. No fancy paintings on the wall, no secretaries buzzing around, none of the opulence she'd witnessed half an hour earlier.

'I had a job interview.' There was no point in keeping that quiet. Everybody knew the clinic was a way to get by; sooner or later, this moment would have arrived.

'Wow. Just like that, out of the blue?'

Mia took a chair and sat in front of him. For the first time, she sat where her clients usually were. 'They called me yesterday evening. It's one of the best firms in the country, and I couldn't say no. It's my first interview in ages, I couldn't miss this opportunity.' She explained how she'd driven down to Boston and took a flight back.

'You must be knackered.'

'Indeed. The interview started at nine and went on till almost one hour ago. They grilled me. After that, we had to make a mock trial with other candidates; on the spot, with minutes to prepare. Then more grilling. I'm exhausted.'

'Talking about grilling, do you want to go out and get a bite?' Xander asked.

Mia looked at her watch and realised how late it was. She'd come back to the office on automatic pilot, not even thinking about the time.

'Sure. Where are Ginger and Jenny?'

'They went a couple of hours ago. I stayed here because I was having fun with an article, but I guess it can wait until tomorrow. Shall we?'

'Corrigan's?'

'There is a B&B under the Brooklyn Bridge that opened recently, and friends are swearing by it. I happen to have made the acquaintance of a fellow author who is working there as a waitress, so maybe we could sneak in without a reservation.'

'A B&B?'

'Yes, Barbecue and Beers. Unless your social status doesn't allow you to lick your fingers anymore.'

They both laughed. Xander took his phone from one of his pockets, flicked through the contacts, and dialled. Mia observed him flirting with the woman on the other end of the line, joked, and agreed for a table in half an hour's time.

'Won't she think that I'm competition?' she asked.

'No. Come on, you and I have been friends forever.'

'Still, though, if she sees you going there alone with another woman, she might think it's a date.'

'Damn, that hadn't crossed my mind. I've messed up, haven't I?'

'Not necessarily. I'll make sure I let her know I'm engaged. To someone else, obviously. I don't want anybody spitting on my plate because they're jealous.'

'Ahaha. Come on, that's an urban myth. Nobody would risk their reputation. Shall we?'

They took a taxi, and halfway towards the restaurant she received a call. 'Mia Crawford speaking.' She put a finger on the other ear to block the traffic noise.

'Yes, good evening.' A pause. 'Sure… excellent.' A longer pause. 'I still have some clients at the clinic…' Another pause. 'Okay, then, thank you very much.'

Mia hung up and exhaled.

'What was that?' Xander asked.

'I got the job. Two hundred and ten thousand dollars a year. Plus bonus, plus all sorts of benefits. They want me to start next week.'

'Two hundred and ten? Mia, I've always been in love with you, would you marry me instead of that Carlton? I'll make you happy. No pre-nup agreement, of course, in case I become a bestselling author.'

'Ahaha! You wish. Hey, that is our restaurant.'

'It is indeed.'

They shared the taxi fare and entered the fairly large building by the riverside. Xander looked around until he spotted his fellow author and waved. She was a dark-haired woman in her thirties, attractive and with an athletic build. A pair of black trousers, sneakers, and a candid white shirt enhanced her figure.

'Hi, Xander, I'm glad you came, the opening has been spectacular, and the place is getting good reviews already.' The waitress squared off Mia from head to toe.

'Oh, yes, this is Mia, an old friend of mine. Mia, this is Pauline Bailey.'

'A friend? Now I'm just a friend,' Mia interjected. 'Only two minutes ago you asked me to marry you...'

'Mia!'

'And no prenuptial agreement, in case you become famous. Now we are back to friendship?'

'Mia, please...'

'Just messing with you. Nice to meet you, Pauline, Xander here speaks highly of you, and he said you're a fellow author?'

'I am indeed, although no success at the moment.' Pauline looked over her shoulder. 'I better take you to your table, we're getting busy,' and she led the way into the restaurant. 'Do we know each other?' she asked when they reached the table.

'You probably saw my face plastered on a few magazines recently. I'm engaged to Carlton Allerton, the one of Allerton Groceries.'

'Of course you are; engaged, right? Good. I mean, good for you.'

They sat at the table, and Mia read the menu nonchalantly.

'What the bloody hell was that? I almost freaked out!' Xander hissed.

'Don't worry, she likes you. You should make a move, she's pretty. How did you meet her?'

'Faceblip,' he said, as if that explained everything. 'So, what are you having?'

'I'll go for the spicy chicken wings, mind sharing? And the pork ribs. And you?'

Xander pondered his choice. 'Brisket and whatever comes as a side. And beer.'

'I love the menu,' she said, 'straight to the point.' It was a one-page sheet of paper, four mains and three starters. No fancy names or lists of ingredients and how they were cooked or foraged. In certain matters, simplicity was the best option.

Pauline came around a few minutes after and took their order. She spent more than the necessary time smiling and chatting with Xander.

'So, you accepted this new job, right?' he asked.

'I had to. It's a once-in-a-lifetime opportunity. That's why I sacrificed my years studying hard at school, to be in the best place I could possibly be. It's my own ticket to success, Xander, as it would be if one of your books climbed the charts suddenly. You wouldn't stop and think, and you'd grab it with both hands.'

'I do get that,' he nodded, 'but what about the clinic, what about Ginger?'

'They said I can take the few clients I have with me as pro bono. I don't know about the clinic. I'll have to close it, although I still have about two years left on the lease. Ginger will have to find something else, I suppose, but that is life.'

He remained quiet for a moment, playing with his fork.

Pauline arrived with their orders. 'Here is a brisket for you, Xander, and the ribs for… Mia, right?'

'Yes.'

'So how did the two of you meet?' Pauline asked.

'We live in the same road,' he explained. 'She moved there a while back. How long has it been now, almost a year?'

'Sounds about right.' Mia pondered those words. Suddenly, she remembered when she'd first moved to her apartment. It was one of the most depressing days in her entire life; the deep feeling of having failed permeated the whole street. She was standing there, in front of her trunk, looking at her few possessions, when Xander, on his racing bike, said, 'Do you need a hand with those?' He didn't seem dangerous in his sporty outfit, the large delivery bag on his shoulder. At that time, he had long hair arranged in a ponytail and a scruffy blond beard. A sort of Viking on wheels. 'Why not,' she'd answered back. From that point, they'd become friends. He introduced her to Jennifer, a friend of his from high school, and since then the three of them had become inseparable. They shared their struggle, Jennifer being an intern at Mt. Sinai, Xander with his writing, and Mia with no hope in finding another decent paid job. The idea of the clinic came during a boozy night at Corrigan's.

'Enjoy your dinner,' Pauline said, and off she went.

'So, what would you do?' Mia asked.

'About Ginger? Not a clue; I never wanted to work in an office because I hate those sorts of things. I guess I'd do the decent thing.'

'Which is?' she pressed.

'No idea, babe. I knew the clinic was temporary. Ginger knows it, too, I'm sure of it, it's just that this change is coming too suddenly. I got fond of her and her schemes, to be honest.'

'And her curves, and her long, sexy red hair.'

'Yeah, those, too, but that train has gone, I'm afraid,' Xander answered. He smiled and waved at Pauline.

'I hate these sorts of things; they're not right. I don't even know what I could tell her.'

'Leave it for today. Sleep it over, and maybe we can discuss it tomorrow, with a fresh mind.'

'I'll drink to that.'

At the same time, Kowalski was in Buffalo, in a small alley behind Central Terminal. He'd parked a few streets away and walked with a large tube under his arm. He inspected at the surrounding area. Just a couple of houses from the wall he chose for his next work, none of them overlooked his designated spot. It was dark and cold. He opened the tube and fixed the stencils on the wall with Sellotape. He worked fast and meticulously; he'd done it several times before. He touched the cold wall, his hands covered by a pair of surgical gloves. He started working with the sprays.

As soon as he finished, he removed the stencils, rolled them up, and carefully placed them back in the tube. He walked away at a fast pace. He never spent time in checking his work, he didn't want to get caught in the process. There was plenty of time to see the result the day after, once the drawing was discovered. He'd mix with the few admirers and take a picture for his website. Nobody would pay attention to him.

CHAPTER 25

"Allerton acquires King General" was the title on *The Wall Street Journal* front page that morning.

The merge of Allerton with the Dutch groceries company was not the biggest seen in the most recent years, but it was indeed one of the largest in the sector, worth tens of billions of dollars. The article carefully avoided using the term "acquisition" and always referred to it as a merger, quoting the initial statement issued by Allerton.

Mia read it avidly, but she knew it was a surprise for the whole market. Carlton had always been cagey about that part of the business, not sharing even with her who the target was. From what she knew, Allerton was planning to buy some small to medium company in the Midwest.

The article gave a brief highlight on King General: founded ten years previously, the company had incredible success in the Netherlands, France, and Germany. Soon afterwards they acquired Superdiscount in the southern states and Kevin's, giving them a foothold in the US market. It was one of the fastest growing companies, and the merger opened all sort of possibilities, including Allerton having a foothold in the European market.

She closed the newspaper and opened the clinic front door. It was very early in the morning, and she felt exhausted; too much emotion from the previous day prevented her from having any sleep, spending the night tossing and turning. She needed a strong coffee.

Xander entered a few minutes later.

'Hey, Mia, did you see the news?'

'Indeed. Totally unexpected, but I think sooner or later it was bound to happen,' Mia said without turning. 'Hey, do you want a coffee?'

'I'd murder for one. Black, please. Any reactions from Carlton?'

'I haven't called him yet. Yesterday it was hectic and, by the time I went home, I was too knackered. I'll call him later; he'll be busy with the press this morning for sure.'

Xander went quiet for a spell. 'Wow, I didn't think it was that bad to require a meeting with the press, but what do I know?'

'Xander, it's the biggest event in his career, what are you talking about?'

'What am I talking about?' Xander picked up a tabloid from his backpack and gave it to Mia.

A blurred picture of her and a man in a restaurant was on the front page. *Troubles in the Allerton's Paradise?* was the title. She flicked through the pages and reached the article. There wasn't much, except a few pictures of her and Xander at the restaurant the night before. The article quoted "sources", which swore there were difficulties in Carlton's relationship with Mia; they were wondering who the mysterious man in the picture was and if the public should wait for an announcement that the wedding was off. Most infuriating of all, they never mentioned Mia by name, referring to her with a generic "Carlton's girlfriend".

'I cannot believe it!' She dialled Carlton's number on her mobile. It went to voicemail. 'Hi, first of all, congratulations on the merger. Wow, that was unexpected. Secondly, I wanted to let you know there is a picture of me and Xander in the tabloid. It's Xander, for fuck's sake, we just went out for dinner, I don't know how we got plastered in the news. Please call me.'

Mia sat back at her desk and turned on the laptop. She had to decide which of her clients to take over to the new firm. Unfortunately, dumping a client was not a straightforward matter, and the rules of professional responsibility were quite clear on that point. She could have found a few subterfuges if she really wanted, but her clients were mostly desperate cases. A judge might not agree to her withdrawal. She decided to take over most of them and test the water. She'd ask the remaining clients if they were willing to switch to someone else, given she was closing the clinic. If she worded the letter correctly, the clients might decide to employ a new lawyer rather than making further trouble. Nobody wanted a less-than-motivated attorney.

Ginger entered. 'Hello, did you read the news today?'

'Which one?' replied both Mia and Xander at the same time.

'The merge of Allerton's and King General,' she said, matter-of-factly.

'Ah, that one? Sure we did,' Xander replied, the disappointment on his face was clearly visible.

'Okay, no problem. I see, a multi-billion takeover is no longer something to be impressed about. We did dozens ourselves in the past few months…'

Mia looked at Ginger. She was radiant, jovial, the exact opposite of the cagey, conspiratorial woman she was just weeks before. Her heart shrank, given the news she had to deliver that same day.

She went back to her list, only to be interrupted by her phone ringing.

'Hi, Carlton.'

'I'm extremely busy today, as you can imagine. What's this story with Xander?'

Mia closed the office door to have more privacy. 'It's actually a non-story. We went out for dinner, and someone must have taken those pictures. How they even remember who I was is a mystery.'

'I thought you were in Maine.'

His voice was tense; if it was a hint of jealousy or it was because of the merger, she couldn't tell.

'I had to cut my trip short, I had a job interview.'

'What? What interview? I haven't organised anything yet, what are you talking about?'

Mia recalled her conversation with Carlton. She'd decided not to accept his offer to work for him, but somehow, she'd forgotten to mention it; she was too worried about breaking the news about her wedding to her parents, her financial constraints. 'This opportunity came out of the blue two days ago, I had to come back in a hurry. I'll work for Myerscough, Nibley, and Holton.'

'Nice firm. So why didn't you tell me?'

'I don't know, I've been busy and out of sync for a couple of days now. It's a great opportunity for me to go back to the big league.'

'You had time to go out for dinner with Xander…'

Mia grimaced. When Carlton was in a foul mood, the only option was to let him steam out. She changed tactic. 'What about dinner tonight? I can tell you the whole story.'

'Tonight I'm busy. We still have a lot of work to do here with the acquisition,' he said. 'What about tomorrow? My place?'

Acquisition then, not a merger. 'I'd love to.'

'Maybe we should discuss something else. We still haven't set a date for the wedding, and if you're going to work here in Manhattan, maybe you should move in with me. I hate coming to Brooklyn to that apartment of yours.'

She went quiet for a moment. Moving in, just like that. Her life was going to change in the future, she was aware of that. Too many things were happening at the same time. 'Sure, why not,' she said eventually.

'Okay, got to go. See you tomorrow, then,' and he hung up.

She exhaled. She wondered about moving to Carlton's apartment and how much that decision was driven by a hint of jealousy towards Xander. It didn't really matter. They were going to get married, and sooner or later that would have happened. If Xander was the catalyst that made it possible, so be it. Her rental contract was also due soon, one less complication.

Shit, it's happening. She was right where she wanted to be. A fantastic new job, a future husband like Carlton, moving to Manhattan, and the potential for a brilliant career. Who could desire more? Mia thought she had all the reasons to be the happiest woman on the planet. So why did she have the sensation of her stomach churning?

CHAPTER 26

Carlton placed the phone on the desk and stared at the empty space in front of him. It was done. The acquisition was received positively by the market, and the share price held. Things were going much better than he'd anticipated.

His secretary's voice interrupted his daydreaming. 'Mr Allerton, your grandfather is here.'

'Let him in.'

Jason Allerton opened the glass office door and stormed in. 'What the bloody hell is this?' He threw *The Wall Street Journal* on Carlton's desk.

'Hello, Granddad, how are you today?'

'Don't give me the granddad bullshit! I thought you were buying Roddy's Market in the Midwest, not King General.'

Carlton rubbed his eyes. He could feel in his body the tension accumulated in the past weeks. 'A devious plan, I admit, but it went well. Nobody suspected the acquisition until it was in the paper this morning. Don't worry, the shares are holding, and the market is responding favourably. I spent the morning talking to the analysts, and all have positive feedback. We are doing great.'

'Where in the name of God did we get the money to even consider biting into King General?

This is total madness!' The old man was raging, and his face reddened.

'We did a leveraged buyout.'

'You did what? Are you out of your mind?' He opened the door and shouted to Carlton's secretary, 'Get me Bill Ross here, IMMEDIATELY!'

Before he could say anything, Carlton preceded him, 'Bill is gone, I fired him.' He smiled.

'You're beyond insane. We don't have enough operating cash flow to maintain both companies and pay the debt. You idiot, you're going to put us under.'

'I've had enough of you, coming in here and barking orders at me. The rest of the board of directors are with me, and there is nothing you can do about it. Go and retire to Florida, it's about time, and let younger people manage the business. Don't you understand? We grow or we die, that is the reality. You're stuck in a world that doesn't exist anymore, and if you don't understand this move in the current economy, you should really give up. You didn't even bother to attend the board of director meetings in the past six months, you were too busy playing golf with your pals and enjoying the dividends. So, now it's your time to shut the fuck up.'

The great Jason Allerton was beaten. The old snake gave him the CEO position, and now there was little he could do. He couldn't certainly disagree publicly about the merger; the stock price would collapse right in the moment they needed even more stability. He watched him turn his back and walk towards the door.

'We shall see about that,' he said on his way out of the office.

Bastard.

But this was the end of it, he was sure. He'd spent years under the yoke of his grandfather, but this time he was free. He didn't resent him, he was the one who made the choice of skipping one generation, giving him full responsibility of the company. Carlton's father was useless, as far as possible from being a chip off the old block. His sister couldn't care less about the business side of the family. As long as she received her monthly cheque, a substantial amount, to keep her in a continuous spending spree, she wouldn't dare challenge him. Not that she had any idea on how to run a company that size anyway.

No, this time, Jason Allerton was out for good despite him still owning shares. His ideas were antiquated, and nobody on the board of directors would listen to the old fool, not now everybody was going to make a hefty profit from the acquisition.

Carlton needed to let off steam, release some of the pressure, and picked up the phone. Amanda's number was still in his contact list.

He tried once, twice, each time going to voicemail. She was probably fast asleep at that time of the day.

She wasn't too far away, and he still paid for the flat, so he decided to pay her a visit; he hadn't heard from her in weeks.

Carlton took the elevator to the garage and opted for the low-profile Mercedes with tinted glass. No driver this time.

He parked on 35th Street near St Vartan Park and walked back to 34th Street where Amanda's apartment was. It was a modern, tall building, and she was in a two-bedroom apartment on the top floor. The doorman nodded when he saw him entering. In the past several months, he gave him enough tips to send his children to university. Discretion was often bought in his case, otherwise the risk was to have a storm of paparazzi waiting for him outside.

CHAPTER 27

The doorbell woke Amanda.

What the heck? She gave a glimpse at the clock and turned on the opposite side, but the damn thing kept ringing.

'One moment,' she managed to say and then got up, catching herself reflected in the mirror. Her blonde hair was a mess, and she looked tired, as if the only thing she'd done in the past week was party until early in the morning. She opened the door.

'Oh, it's you,' a half asleep, half naked Amanda said. 'What do you want, Carlton?'

'May I come in?'

'Be my guest.' Amanda reluctantly stepped aside. She pushed the door closed behind her, and whilst Carlton nosed around at the apartment, she went into the kitchen to pour a coffee for herself.

'I've seen you got a stunning photo shoot recently,' Carlton said.

If it was up to you, I'd still be here begging for work.

Keeley was a senior editor for a top magazine, and she had the power to decide pretty much which model could become the next celebrity in the world of fashion. That time, Keeley made good on her promises, and she lined up a series of five shoots. The first was in the central section of the magazine. She also got busy boosting her image on Twitter.

Amanda was determined to keep her happy in bed for a while longer, despite her kinky side. The second time they made love she was sober and a bit more reluctant, given the amount of false promises she had heard over the years, but Keeley had been good to her. She bossed her way around, and in no time, Amanda was in headquarters, taking directions from one of the most influential resident photographers. Richard also got some side work for the introduction.

After that, everything came easy. Teasing Keeley, feeding her constant desire for sex and satisfying her at every possible occasion. It didn't matter if she had to crawl under her office desk or slip a hand between her legs during a gala dinner. She was keen on getting her wet every time she even thought about her. Keeley needed the promise of constant orgasms at her fingertips, and forget about any other possible models in the world who had a wish for a career. She was Amanda's most treasured possession.

'Checking me out on Twitter?' she replied. The coffee was a day old. She poured it down the sink and made a fresh batch.

'You know I do care about you.' Carlton got closer to her. He pushed his hips against her back, making her feel how excited he was.

Amanda wriggled free and moved away from him.

'Yeah, sure. I saw how much you care about me. All false promises. I'm good when you have your needs, but every time I ask you for something, you shy away. It doesn't work like this, Carlton. I'm not your dumb girlfriend who adores everything you do, and I'm sick of listening to your voice.'

Carlton grasped one of Amanda's arms and pulled her towards him.

'LET ME GO!'

'Do I have to remind you who is paying for this place?' he shouted. 'If it wasn't for me, you'd be back in Nebraska working as a waitress instead of being here in Manhattan, partying all night. That will count for something.'

Carlton clung to her with both arms and tried to kiss her.

'LET. ME. GO!'

'Too easy, babe, you owe me…'

The doorbell rang again, and Carlton composed himself. He combed his hair with his hand. She ran towards the door.

'Amanda, is everything okay?' In front of her was Keeley, dressed in a Gucci velvet-trimmed black coat. A floppy hat on her head partially covered the blonde, almost white hair.

'Come in, please,' Amanda urged, her voice shaken.

Keeley walked in as if she owned the place and looked around. Her eyes met Carlton's.

'This is…' Amanda said, apologetic.

'I know who he is. Mr Allerton, rumour has it you're extremely busy with a merger; nonetheless, here you are.'

'Who the hell are you?'

'Keeley Williams, chief editor of *Style Magazine*. It's sheer luck to find you here. Maybe you'll allow a quick interview? Our readers and your shareholders would be most interested in learning how the CEO of Allerton Groceries spends his time.' The forty-year-old woman moved a step closer to Carlton, as an experienced cage fighter would do before the beginning of a match, then she opened her bag and started a tape recorder after placing it five inches from the man's mouth.

Carlton's face stiffened. 'I just passed by to say hello to an old friend, that's it. I was in the area.'

'I'm sure you have a busy schedule,' Keeley pressed without losing eye contact.

'Indeed. I have to go.'

She escorted him to the door and, once he was outside, she said, 'I trust now that there will not be a repeat anytime soon? We don't want your pretty face plastered on the *National Enquirer*, them making conjectures on your friendly visit here. Their assumptions sometimes run wild, and they'd love to spend the next few weeks writing all sort of lies about you.'

Carlton didn't answer and walked out of sight whilst she closed the door behind her.

'What the hell happened here?' Keeley asked.

Amanda threw her arms around Keeley's neck and cried. The two women remained like that for a few minutes until the sobbing became subdued.

'Come on, let's sit on the sofa, and tell me, what was he doing here?'

Amanda nodded and followed her into the lounge. She told Keeley about her relationship with Carlton. She exaggerated on their breakup and told her exactly what happened few minutes before.

'Carlton is paying for this place. I don't know what would have happened if you didn't show up. I fear he'll return sooner or later.'

'That's not going to happen,' Keeley replied. 'You pack your things, all of them, and you come to my place. Today. And if he bothers you again, I'll take care of him.'

'I have a lot of stuff to pack; are you okay on waiting?'

'Of course I am, I'm not going anywhere without you.'

'Okay. Thank you. Maybe you can take your coat off whilst you wait. It's quite warm in here.' She stood and walked towards her bedroom.

Keeley chuckled. 'I'm not sure that's a good idea this very moment.'

Amanda peeked out of the bedroom in Keeley's direction. 'How come?'

'That's why.' Keeley unbuttoned the coat and showed that underneath she wasn't wearing anything, except for a sexy set of gold-and-red lingerie and stockings.

'Oh! You did that for me?' Amanda approached Keeley and kissed her on the lips. 'I'll hurry in packing my stuff. I'll want to have a very good look at this outfit.'

'You will, my dear.'

CHAPTER 28

Mia could not procrastinate any further. She had to do something but she didn't really know what. And when the *what* came, she'd have to face the *how*.

The best place to discuss the matter at hand regarding her new job was at Corrigan's. The relaxed atmosphere of the wine bar was better suited for an "informal exchange of ideas" rather than an announcement in the office.

She was delaying, she knew that far too well.

She reached Corrigan's at 8.00 PM on the dot, after going home for a change of clothes. Xander, Ginger, and Jennifer were already at their usual table. A bottle was passing hands.

'So, what's the choice this evening?'

'There is a Rossese di Dolceacqua on offer, so we thought of going for it. We saved some for you, but I see people are restless tonight.' Jennifer pointed at Xander. 'So we might well do a second round.'

He is not the only one who is restless. Both knew what was coming.

She gave a brief account of her visit to Maine, but it was clear to her she was avoiding the big matter of her new employment. She filled her glass and didn't delay any further.

'I got some news that I wanted to share.' She paused, and the others looked at her with curiosity. Xander checked emails on his phone. 'I have been offered a job in the litigation department of one of the most important firms in the city.'

Nobody spoke. Mia was waiting for a barrage of questions, which didn't come. *What was I expecting? Congratulations? Of course, they might be happy for me, but the implications about Ginger's future are palpable. Xander himself got more involved; how can I do this to them?*

'Did you accept it?' Ginger asked eventually.

Jennifer placed a hand on her forearm. Whether the gesture was for her to wait or to comfort her, was unclear.

'I did,' Mia answered. 'It's what I aspired for my entire career, a fantastic opportunity. Working for them is what every lawyer dreams of at night. Think about the TV series *Suits* on steroids.' There was no point in delaying any further, she had to explain what she had in mind. Better a bullet to the head than three to the chest and bleeding to death. 'I know this is going to put you, Ginger, in an awkward position. I'll not have time to keep the clinic open and I don't know if there's a secretarial job available there.' As if the latter was a real opportunity. The firm wouldn't have hired her, there was a long list of paralegals, all with far more experience than Ginger and a cleaner past, who would have murdered for a position at Myerscough, Nibley, and Holton. It didn't matter if it was for a job washing the floor. Just setting foot in that firm would have been enough for them.

'I didn't ask for a job,' Ginger retorted.

215

'I know. I'm sorry because I've grown fond of the clinic and the type of work I do. The problem is that I barely make a living out of it. I haven't forgotten you helped me out when the rent was due and I didn't have any money to pay you. In some respects, it seems you'd have been better without me than with me around.'

Ginger gazed at the floor. 'I'd probably be in jail by now if you didn't help me out. I mean, that stunt I pulled up in Queens was pretty bad.'

'It was. But nonetheless, I don't feel I'm on the giving end here. We've helped each other when we needed.'

'So that long speech you gave about being in fifty-fifty? That was bull then.'

Mia didn't have an answer. She felt she was betraying her; as soon as she had her opportunity, she was ready to jump ship whilst Ginger, on the contrary, stayed even when there was no money in the bank.

'How long have you left on your lease?' Xander asked.

'The one on the clinic? Two years, why?'

'Can you transfer it?'

'No, I don't think so, it's pretty ironclad. Why, are you planning on becoming a lawyer? You need a degree and to pass the bar for that,' Mia joked, halfhearted.

'I'm not kidding, I think I could make some money out of those articles I'm writing, more than I'm earning delivering parcels. And I'm writing

216

every single day, which is what I love to do. Ginger might be up to something with that fashion consultancy thing. I don't know, there might be a solution in it, somewhere.'

'Would you really do that?' Jennifer asked him. 'I mean, helping out with the blog articles?'

Xander shrugged. 'Why not? It's hard work, but so is delivering parcels across the city. Without the risk of an accident. And I can expand, by doing some editing, proofreading. I'll get paid for working on literature. A dream job.'

Mia, quiet for a spell and in search for a solution, interjected, 'I surely can afford the lease with my new salary and I still have two years of rent to pay no matter what. If things don't work out, the clinic might be my safety net. We could do it like this, if you agree: I keep paying the rent, and if you two want to continue using the office, I have no objections. What you earn is what you get. Carlton has also asked me if I wanted to move to his place. I won't have rent for the apartment to pay either.'

'Sounds reasonable.' Xander scratched his stubble as he always did when he was up to something. 'Apart from the bit when you move to Carlton's, I mean.' Everybody laughed. 'Ginger, what do you think?'

'I'd love that. I also have a few other ideas that I might want to explore as part of the business.'

'Nothing weird,' Jennifer said, 'you promised.'

'All legit.' Ginger's mood had changed, and the mixed expression of sadness and anger she had few minutes before had vanished.

'I can draft a legal agreement between the parties, if you want,' a reinvigorated Mia said. 'No charge.'

Jennifer, the sensible one, appeared yet to be convinced. 'Do you think you can make a living out of that?'

Ginger picked up her phone and did some calculations, and then some more. She started scribbling numbers on a napkin. The response arrived a few minutes after, when everybody got anxious and fidgeted in their chairs. 'I don't know. I removed the rental, the fashion business is profitable but erratic, so are the funerals. The articles are steady but generate less revenue. The other things I cannot do anymore, well, that is a loss. We might make it, we might not, it's close.'

It was Xander's turn to digit furiously on his mobile. 'I can throw in my books' revenue. It's not much but it will be some steady hundreds of dollars each month. I might write more erotics, those sell like hotcakes.'

'Deal,' Ginger said, 'and if you become a bestseller, you throw the money in the pot.'

'And if you become the queen of fashion or funerals, you do the same.'

Mia was relieved. She knew she had let her friends down, but the arrangement seemed satisfactory for all of them.

'Hey, there is a new Kowalski,' Xander announced, still with the phone in his hands.

'Where?'

'Buffalo.'

'Let me see…'

Mia did a quick search on her phone, and her face reddened. Damn Kowalski. He had indirectly spoken to her through the years, she even let herself be guided by him on occasion. She also disagreed with some of his messages, but he still was the most influential artist around. Not this time.

She wasn't selling her soul to the highest bidder, as the picture was going to suggest. Mia understood the message far too well. Just minutes ago, she almost threw her friends under the bus. But maybe she had also redeemed herself by offering the use of the office to Xander and Ginger.

Who are you kidding, other than yourself; that is who you are, who you always wanted to be. Looking at the picture, she put a hand on her mouth and started crying, unable to prevent the tears falling

Jennifer was the first to spot it. 'Mia, what is going on?'

Unable to speak, she ran towards the bathroom.

CHAPTER 29

'We need a business plan,' Xander said, lifting his head from his laptop.

'I thought we had one. Make as much money as we can, as fast as we can, and don't overspend in the process,' Ginger answered.

There was an uncomfortable atmosphere in the room, as if something wasn't right. Everything was still in place like the old furniture, the ghastly wallpaper, and the few paintings on the walls, but the place was not the same.

They knew they were on their own.

Mia brought an aura of legitimacy to the place. It didn't matter if the office was in need of complete refurbishment. A lawyer with a Harvard degree was working there. It was like entering a derelict church. It might be old and tatty, but whether you liked or not, it was still a holy place. Without Mia, something had changed. It returned to being one of the many non-notable shops in the surrounding area.

'Yeah, I was thinking about something less generic than that. Sort of, how much money we need to make each month in order to pay the bills and survive and what are the low-hanging fruits. I mean, I don't mind working hard, but we need to be clever, otherwise we find ourselves in a year's time in the same position as today.'

'I can do clever,' Ginger said.

'Okay, let's do clever. What are we talking about here, Ginger?' Xander asked.

'I don't know, making money. You started the whole business-plan discussion. '

He exhaled and invited Ginger to come closer. He turned the laptop so she could see the screen. 'See? These are my entries on books. I know that each book has a peak at the beginning, and if it's half decent it keeps selling afterwards. Less, of course, but steadily. Are you with me?'

Ginger looked at the graphs on the dashboard and nodded. 'You wrote that stuff? *Confessions from the Cotton Fields? The Countess' Orgies? The Black Masses of Sex?* Seriously?'

'That's not the point, Ginger.' His face reddened. He knew it was dime literature; he should have aimed to write something different. But he also knew he had to make a living, and apparently erotic books were what most of his public wanted. What was the point of spending a year in writing a novel that would sell little when in a month and a half he could write a decent raunchy book? Ten a year, a hundred in ten years' time. 'What I mean is that after the initial bang they keep selling. The more books I have, the more of a steady income I get.'

She nodded, and Xander took it as an invite to continue.

'Additional books equate to a stable, regular income.'

'Mind if I ask a question?'

'Fire away.'

'How many of those books are likely to become a bestseller?'

He pushed back on the chair. His first instinct was to show her the snapshots of when some of his erotic novels entered the Amazon charts, but he thought better. Ginger was right, and he knew it. Those books never appeared on the *NY Times* bestsellers' chart. Not because of the genre but because they were hurried works. Good enough to read in the evening after a long day of work and spice up the bedroom. Good enough to have a bit of excitement reading them, unknowingly by the others, on the busy underground train. But would anybody say that Xander was doing great literature? Not a chance in hell.

'Probably none. Scrap that, none for sure.'

'So, what are we talking about, Xander? We aim at making money or we aim at surviving. We have to try different things until we nail the path of least resistance. That is what I was doing with my schemes, as Mia…'

Xander knew what she was trying to say. A*s Mia would say*, but she stopped mid-sentence.

She was no longer there, not to protect Ginger nor to guide her. He understood why Mia had left. It was her occasion to shine. The two women weren't too dissimilar; the only difference was that Ginger still hadn't found what she was looking for. Would she have stayed if one of her *schemes* had suddenly taken off?

'I was saying, I tried different things exactly for that reason. You don't get rich by doing a regular job, you have to do something out of the ordinary, something that any other Joe in this city cannot do. That's how you make money. I don't mean to scrap that part, the erotic books. Keep writing them, but by all means use them to prepare for the real deal. Test some characters you'll use in a bestselling novel. Or in a series: I always want to buy the next book.'

It was Xander's time to nod. She was right; he was stuck in doing something for quick and fast gratification rather than writing an outstanding novel. Ginger was pushing him towards a cliff. Fly or die. Towards what he was most afraid of, to understand and prove if he was the good writer he always hoped he was, of if reality would hit him in the face, clearly proving that he wasn't. Xander was reluctant. If he failed, he was going to be left with nothing.

'A series needs a strong character, someone who can survive more than one book. Same world but new adventures. Not an easy task,' Xander said, so as to justify to himself on the why.

'Well, you are a writer, right? Invent one. It's not that you are lacking imagination, I've read some of the articles and blogs you send out. They are good.'

'You have a point there, although I don't think I like it. Maybe I could use the morning for the articles. By the afternoon I should be warm enough to write a novel, a proper one, and dedicate some hours in the evening for the sexy bits. Let's see how it goes.'

'Atta boy! Hey,' Ginger looked at her watch, 'I've got a client in need of a new wardrobe, mind tagging along?'

Xander considered his creased jeans; he passed a hand through his scruffy hair, making it worse, and said, 'Are you sure? I mean, I'm not exactly dressed for the occasion.'

'I'm not expecting you to give advice. Just tag along, you could do with some fresh air.'

He nodded and closed the laptop. In the worst-case scenario he would take some notes. He liked to use real people as characters, and meeting new people was exactly what he needed. Ginger stood and picked up her beige coat. Xander couldn't stop himself from admiring how beautiful his partner was.

They met the client at the corner between Court Street and Carrol Street. A woman called Madison, no surname, in her early forties, with mousy hair reaching her shoulders. She seemed a bit cagey when Ginger introduced herself and explained the plan for the afternoon. Her work was still a word-of-mouth business. If a woman suddenly changed her appearance and look, friends and family complimented her and asked in awe how she managed to appear so stunning, and she eventually spilled the beans: this personal shopper helped me out. Sometimes people shrugged, sometimes someone asked for a phone number.

She didn't seem to be in need of advice on what to wear, and she only had a budget of few hundred dollars.

He pondered about going back to the office to write. He could write five decent articles or two or three good ones in an afternoon, but Ginger thought otherwise.

'This is Xander, by the way. He knows Brooklyn inside out in case we get lost, and he can help carry the goods. He works with me.'

The woman nodded and seemed to accept the unusual presence for an afternoon of shopping.

'So, what are you most dissatisfied with concerning your current look?' Ginger asked whilst texting a message on her mobile.

'I don't know,' Madison answered, 'I think I have good taste in clothes, but nothing really satisfies me when I'm wearing it. I don't know how to explain it. If I knew that, I wouldn't be here today.'

Ginger nodded. 'Do you mind taking your coat off for a minute? I'd like to see what you are wearing.'

Madison thought about it for a second, and then she complied. She had a pair of dark trousers and a white shirt under a horizontal blue-and-white-striped jersey.

'Okay, you can put your coat back on,' Ginger said, 'it's quite cold today. I think I have a couple of ideas if you don't mind walking. It's five minutes from here.'

Their destination was a mid-sized shop farther down on Court Street, named Roberta's.

Xander sat on an armchair near the entrance, and Ginger went on looking at clothes, followed by her client.

'This is what I was hoping to find. You should try this shirt first.' In her hands, Ginger had a nice cream-coloured one. She put it in front of her client, guessing the size and, satisfied, sent her into the changing room.

The woman came out few minutes after.

'Maybe I should wear a belt with it?' Madison asked.

'No,' Ginger answered categorically. She found a belt, then placed it around Madison's waist. 'You're tall but you have, how should I say, ample hips. Nothing wrong in that, but if you place a belt around it you intensify the effect. Without it, the shirt just flows, comes down from your shoulders and hides your hips. That's why I think you're unsatisfied with what you're wearing. If you prefer trousers, you need these sort of shirts, left hanging outside. They have slits on their side which is great for moving around, and they slim your overall figure.'

Madison nodded, pondering Ginger's words.

'You see? You could also wear skinny jeans underneath, and the effect will enhance your figure. Here,' she passed a cardigan to Madison, 'try this. For a moment ignore the colour, we'll get one somewhere else, but you see how it splits your bust,

226

almost minimising it. The stripes you're wearing were shouting *look at my breasts*, whilst this type of cardigan tones that down.'

'I think I understand what you are saying... covering, but in the right way.'

Ginger nodded, and Madison bought the shirt. The three of them moved to a new shop farther down the street. The cardigan was bought there in addition to a large red tartan scarf that Ginger took pride in sorting out around Madison's neck. On a whim, she took her to another street. A red floppy hat completed the shopping experience, but Ginger wasn't yet done.

'Do you trust me?' she asked Madison.

They took a taxi to Kingston Avenue where Ginger had a last surprise. A hairdressing salon. Madison planted her feet—she probably wasn't expecting a haircut to be part of the service, although they were still well within the budget she'd set. 'It's going to make a lot of difference,' Ginger had promised, and Madison seemed committed to seeing the day through, for better or for worse. She talked to what appeared to be the owner, explaining what she had in mind, and they both nodded after a brief but concentrated exchange of opinions.

'I think we should go for a coffee or something,' Ginger said to Xander, who all that time had followed the two women like a faithful puppy. 'It might take an hour. Bruno will call me when he's done.'

Xander settled for a beer whilst Ginger took a black coffee, no sugar, no cream.

'Do you have a website for this sort of service?' he asked.

'Yeah, but it's a basic static page. You know, phone number and a brief description, why?'

'I think you should take a picture of that woman and ask if you could post it on it. We could write a blog on this. What a day out looks like.'

'The website is useless. The totality of the work comes from referral.'

'And still, I think we should do something about it. Do you have Instagram?' he pressed.

'Who, me? No way.'

'How come?'

'Well, from a privacy point of view. I mean, I had some dodgy businesses and I thought the less I was in the system the better it would be.'

Xander pondered the answer for a second. 'Listen, here is what I think. The dodgy businesses are gone. It's obvious that you have great taste in clothes, and maybe if we could add a blog to your website, with pictures of what you're doing et cetera, there will be people out there willing to read it. You cannot believe the crap I have to write sometimes.'

'I trust you. Been there, done that.'

'Right. I mean, this woman is a perfect example. Low budget, excellent choice of clothes. She already looks like a million dollars, and you spent what, three hundred on clothes? And you are stunning... no, let me finish... Your Instagram is going to be about fashion. You wearing different combinations, maybe a picture of some of your customers if they agree. It's going to be a hit.'

Ginger didn't know what to say, so Xander took a picture with his phone of her in front of her coffee. Then he started to digit on his mobile. A couple of minutes after came the announcement. 'You are now the proud owner of an Instagram account. I can share it later when we're back to the office. I seriously think we should do this.'

She nodded, although still in doubt. They passed the rest of the time in silence, Xander thinking about the wonders of the internet and Ginger lost in her thoughts. They woke up from their dream when her phone rang. Madison was ready, according to Bruno.

They walked out of the coffee shop, and the client was already on the street, a radiant smile on her face.

'Oh my gosh, I cannot believe it!' she said, hugging Ginger.

'You look amazing.'

Madison turned around and checked her reflection in the shop's window. She was stunned by the results. 'Do we need to buy other things? I'm super-excited,' she asked, eager to continue with the shopping event.

'We could, but you set a budget, and we should stick to it. I know how these things play out, and it's like gambling. You get addicted, and without even noticing, your cards are maxed out. I suppose this concludes our day out, a deal is a deal. Maybe you could give me a call next month,' Ginger said. 'Do you mind if I take a picture? I might consider putting it on my website, with your consent, of course.'

Madison agreed, and then they discussed fees, which came at a meagre seventy dollars. They exchanged private numbers, and Madison took note of the website on her phone.

'It's under construction at the moment,' Ginger justified herself.

The two women kissed on the cheeks and promised to stay in touch, then Madison called for a taxi.

'Sorry,' Ginger said to Xander, 'I was hoping she had a bit more spending power. It's sheer luck— sometimes it happens, sometimes it doesn't. I had the gut feeling it wasn't right to push her into spending more money.'

'Are you kidding? Don't worry about our earnings at the moment. I think you're onto something here. We need to crack on with that website. And Instagram.'

They took a taxi themselves back to the office in complete silence. Xander's head was spinning with ideas. He was convinced he'd stumbled upon something important that day but he couldn't figure out yet what it was.

As soon as they reached the office, he knew what needed to be done.

'Ginger, bring your clothes here on Monday. I mean, all of them.'

He finally understood what they should do next and explained it to her.

Ginger grinned. 'I've done a lot of stupid things, one more won't make matters worse.'

CHAPTER 30

It wasn't the first time Jennifer had invited Ginger for dinner, but it felt that way.

She looked at the table, and everything seemed perfect. The plates were aligned, forks and knives in the right position, no fingerprint marks on the crystal glasses. She had a bottle of Gewürztraminer, and fresh flowers were in a vase by the window not far away. She needed to light the candles as soon as she buzzed. She knew it would take Ginger at least thirty seconds from the main entrance to the apartment, and Jennifer had timed the procedure twice already.

She also had a bottle of champagne in the fridge as a backup option in case Ginger didn't like the Traminer. Or in the event things went according to her expectation. She thought about adding some Barry White music in the background but then dismissed the idea as overkill and opted for a Gabrielle album. Sometimes dreams could come true.

Damn! I've never been this nervous about a date.

The menu was designed with the intention of giving a hint to her guest, starting with the raspberry and *passion*fruit Martini. The main was a lobster and potato salad dish for which she struggled to find an appropriate name, but she had a *passion* layer torte as a dessert, followed, as a backup, by some Valentine biscuits, with pink heart patterns. More explicit than that was placing an advertisement on a billboard in Times Square. Everything was ready and prepared with surgical precision.

Ginger rang the bell at exactly eight o'clock, and Jennifer went into overdrive.

'Oh, that is beautiful,' Ginger said when she entered the apartment, 'you did all this for me?'

'The best of the best for you, obviously.'

She kissed her on the cheek and stepped backwards to let her in. Ginger seemed even taller in those crystal-embellished suede stiletto sandals and silhouette blush evening dress with asymmetric sleeves.

'You look beautiful, and I love the new hairstyle.' Jennifer touched the silky long red hair, and her hand lingered for a moment on Ginger's shoulder.

'You look beautiful as well.'

Jennifer blushed and invited her to sit down.

'If you don't mind, I'd prefer coming with you to the kitchen. I'd hate sitting in here, knowing you're busy in another room. At least we could talk.'

Jennifer was in need of wine and opened the Traminer. She filled two glasses and passed one to her guest. She put an arm around Ginger's waist and, proudly, marched her to the kitchen. The stiletto sandals on the floor sounded like a light *ticktock*, an imaginary clock that marked the passing time.

'How was your day?' Jennifer asked.

'By now you pretty much know everything about me. Even things that I didn't share with anybody, so maybe this time we'll talk a bit more about you.'

'Fire away. What do you want to know?' Jennifer asked. She had opened the lobster and was making a bisque with the carcass.

'When did you know?'

Jennifer turned the heat down under the pan and looked at her from over her shoulder. 'You mean when I realised I was lesbian? I think I always knew that. I actually came out when I was sixteen, and my mother didn't make any drama. On the contrary, she was very understanding and explained to me that what I felt was normal and I shouldn't let anybody tell me otherwise.'

'What about your father?'

'I don't know my father well. He had money and a mid-life crisis and he left when I was ten for a floozy from Tennessee. I never bothered letting him know. He wasn't there where I needed him, I definitely don't want him in my life now.'

Jennifer filled her glass a bit more.

'Tell me something about you that nobody else knows?'

'Sometimes I have panic attacks, usually at the beginning of my shift at work. Being a resident is not an easy job, and we have to deal with a lot of pressure. So I go to the hospital an hour earlier and watch episodes of *ER* and *House*.'

'You what?'

'Yeah,' Jennifer continued, 'we have a room for venting down, and I sit there and watch the series. Not that I could learn anything, but they always seem so in control, even during a crisis, and I find it reassuring. Life throws difficult cases at them, and they soldier on. With perseverance, they solve the medical mystery.'

Jennifer stepped forward and caressed Ginger's hair. Her hand stopped on the pale neck of her companion. She felt the pulse under the skin of her fingers. She leaned in closer and kissed her on the lips. Then they stood there for a period that seemed eternal. Ginger's perfume filled her nostrils, and her hair caressed her cheeks.

'I better crack on with this lobster,' Jennifer said eventually, breaking the spell, 'or we'll never eat.'

After dinner, they sat on a sofa that was too large for the small lounge. Jennifer was slightly turned in the direction of her guest, and she was sitting on her legs. Her arm was on the back of the sofa, and she was leaning towards her companion. It had been a pleasant dinner, they joked like old friends, they studied each other as potential lovers do, hinting, complimenting each other without breaking the barrier of discussing what the future might hold for them. Jennifer sought a second kiss. Ginger got closer, having had the same idea.

A phone rang.

'Sorry about that,' Ginger said apologetically, whilst the ringtone was playing *Business Time* from *Flight of the Conchords*, 'I forgot to turn it off.'

'Maybe it's important,' Jennifer teased her. 'I don't know, a sexual emergency.'

'I doubt that.'

'Oh, come on, put it on speaker, it might be fun. Last time I had to guess what they were saying on the other end of the line and, as your ringtone says, it's business. Can you afford not to collect that fee?'

'Okay, but this is the last time. I'm not sure I want to continue with this line of business.' Ginger stood and fetched the phone from her bag. 'Pamela speaking,' she said in an attempt to do a raucous, sensual voice.

'Hello, babe, I'm John.'

'Hello to you, stranger,' and then she recited, at ultra-fast speed, 'SexyCall Inc. is the owner and operator of this line, charges are three dollars fifteen upon provision of a valid credit card. This conversation has a maximum scheduled duration of thirty minutes. By continuing this conversation, you acknowledge to have understood the terms of the General User Conditions. Furthermore, you acknowledge to understand that the services offered on this call are of explicit sexual nature and you agree that no liability on the part of SexyCall Inc. can ensue because of your use of the services offered on this call by SexyCall Inc. Calls can be monitored for quality and training purposes, terms and conditions apply. Do you accept?'

Jennifer burst out laughing. Ginger shushed her by putting a finger in front of her nose, then she mouthed 'Mia's idea.'

'Whatever, babe, yes, I do accept,' John said.

'The credit card number, please, expiration date and the security code. Read them slowly, sensually, we don't want this to end too soon, right?'

'Right,' the man obeyed and read the numbers.

Ginger had a small device plugged into her phone to collect the payment.

'I'm all yours, I'm glad you called me. Tonight, I'm super-excited.' Ginger walked towards the sofa and sat near Jennifer. She put the phone down on the small table in front of her and removed her shoes.

'What are you wearing tonight?' the man asked.

'I just took off a pair of stiletto sandals and placed them on the floor. Tonight, I'm wearing a skin-tight dress that shows my gorgeous curves. Red. Underneath, I have lace lingerie, very expensive, so be gentle.' Ginger opened up her dress slightly to show Jennifer she was telling the truth.

She received a thumbs-up. Then she lay on the sofa, resting her head on Jennifer's lap.

'But this is not my usual dress, you must know.'

'It isn't?' the man asked. The curiosity and the excitement were clear in his voice.

'Oh no. I'm a repressed librarian, nobody in the library gives me a second look, they're all busy with their studies, getting books, returning them. I wear big glasses and a large jumper to hide my femininity, but when the dark comes, I wear my best sexy dress and I go out to bars, hoping for wild nights of sex. Men or women, doesn't matter to me, as long as they're resolute in what they want. Are you resolute, John?'

Jennifer, who was caressing Ginger's hair, giggled.

'I... I am. Hey, are you alone? I heard something.'

'No, I'm not. Tonight, a very attractive Asian lady made me an offer that I could not possibly refuse. From the lust in her eyes it was evident she desired my body. She told me so. Gosh, it was embarrassing. I was in this high-class bar on Seventeenth Street in Manhattan, and a stunning woman came straight to me. "I desire you, I want your body" she said. "I'll give you a thousand dollars, but you will do everything I ask you to tonight." She has toned legs and small but perfect breasts. I could see her nipples hardening in front of me from under her evening dress. Can you imagine?'

'I can. Oh my gosh, what did you do?'

'She is clearly the wife of some rich Chinese tycoon and she is bored. I was planning to fuck her mind, then fuck her body until she screamed for mercy, but I'll let her go if you ask me to,' Ginger said in her most sensual voice.

Jennifer tilted her head and pinched her on an arm.

'Auch! Unless you might be interested in a threesome. You know, I can get rid of her, if you really want, or I could ask if she'd like to join the two of us. She is in the bathroom getting ready.'

The man on the other end of the line was breathing heavily. 'No, n… I mean, would you really ask?'

'Sure, I can do that for you, John,' and then Ginger shouted, 'May Lin, come here for a moment?'

May Lin? mouthed Jennifer.

Ginger shrugged. May Lin (Jennifer) pronounced her 'r's as if a kitten were purring.

'I'm coming, my dear,' Jennifer replied, moving her head away from the phone. 'I'm ready to explore your body, you will be mine tonight.'

'May Lin, I desire you! But I really go wild when someone hears me making love. Would it be okay if an old friend of mine listens over the phone? You will not regret it.'

'I don't mind, it will be my pleasure,' Jennifer answered.

'What is she wearing?' John asked.

'She came out of the bathroom wearing nothing,' Ginger said. 'She is tall and slim, a perfect body. She didn't shave down below, so I hope you don't mind. I like kissing a girl when she has a bit of a bush. It tickles my lips.'

'Oh-my-gosh.' John was breathing heavily.

'I can lay on her soft, beautiful body whilst you take me from behind,' Ginger suggested, 'and then you can have your pleasure with her. Ahhh, I can't take another inch of you, John, you almost hurt me…'

'Carry on, babe, I can feel you.'

'Use me, John, fuck me harder,' Ginger said, 'tell me what you're doing to me.'

The conversation went on for several minutes, and when John hung up, they both knew they had a *satisfied* customer.

'I cannot believe they are paying me for this shit.'

Jennifer caressed Ginger's neck and then slowly moved her hand towards her breast. 'To be honest, I'm excited. You're quite good at this stuff.'

'Am I?'

'A true professional.'

'I'm excited, too,' Ginger replied.

Jennifer lowered her head and kissed her passionately.

They made love on the sofa.

CHAPTER 31

On the fourteenth floor of the *Style Magazine* building, Keeley Rose Williams was sitting at her desk, sipping a cup of Oriental Beauty Taiwanese Oolong. Her secretary had to follow a specific ritual in preparing the tea, and it was known that predecessors lost their job for over-brewing it on a wrong day.

The intercom buzzed. 'The team is ready, Ms Williams,' said a soft, submissive voice at the other end.

'Very well, I'll be in the meeting room in five.'

Keely gave one last look at the list of articles that were ready for the next issue. Then she checked the one showing the work in progress. Still not enough.

The email count reached one hundred and fifty new messages, but she ignored it. The secretary filtered through them, giving her a summary of the important ones later in the day.

Outside, the sky was a dull grey. Snow was due later in the day, but the forecasters were uncertain on the matter. Either a blizzard or a couple of inches. Keeley loved the snow, and she toyed with the idea of moving to Toronto if she had the chance. A possibility that she never really pursued, like people who dream of winning the lottery and forget to play, because everything she needed was right there in

New York. A career going beyond any reasonable expectation, power, influence, a job that she loved.

Everything she achieved was due to her tenacious drive to arrive at the top. It hadn't been easy. After her degree in journalism and her first job in a national newspaper, she was relegated to the female section of the news. She hated that term. As if women were only interested in fashion, furniture, food, and gardening. Most infuriating, the newspaper didn't have a 'male' section. Of course it didn't, it was run by males. Each attempt she'd made to emerge and get assigned to a different sector, either crime or politics, had proved to be in vain. There was always a male colleague who was a more suitable candidate.

With rage running through her veins, she decided she had to change the way the female section of the newspaper was run. Three years later, she was chief editor of the department. The following year, when the online version of the newspaper changed to a subscription model, fifty-eight percent of the subscribers were women, and the female section was the most read after politics.

That was when she landed the position at *Style Magazine*. The owner had a strong view about not having another fashion magazine out there, and his ideas were a perfect fit for Keeley. Colleagues laughed at her—'You'll be back in six months begging to have your job back,' they'd said. The rest of her career was history.

Who was laughing now?

She took another sip of her tea then placed the cup on the desk. She hated Mondays, but the magazine didn't run by itself. She stood and walked to the meeting room were the editors were already waiting.

'Tony, what we got?' she asked before even sitting at her designated chair at the end of the long oval table.

'We're full steam ahead for the February fashion weeks, here, in London, and Milan. Still some legwork to do for Paris, but we're getting there.'

'I'm not expecting anything else. Paula, how are we progressing with that article on contemporary architecture? That should be ready by now.'

Paula Schellenberger was a brunette in her mid-fifties. Thick glasses and a determination gave her the nickname *the bulldog*. 'We are ready.' She checked her watch. 'It should be in your inbox by now for approval. The interview with Senator Gillis is also done. It will be controversial, though.'

'Madison?'

'I'll need another week. I'm opening a can of worms here. Those fashion consultants, or "personal shoppers", as they like to call themselves, are a bunch of crooks. Most of them anyway. We are going to make a killing.'

Keeley nodded and reviewed her notes. 'Seventy thousand dollar bill? It has to be a kill or I'll have trouble justifying these expenses.'

'No worries. We're taking pictures as we speak and then we'll return all of them, I got the receipts.

We came up with this idea of getting a model of ours to wear the clothes. We thought of calling it Horror Fashion Week. You know, it's not enough going around buying expensive clothes if there's no coordination or taste. Here, check these out.'

She slipped several photos over the table. Keeley looked at them very carefully and then passed them around.

'Gosh, this is a Halloween costume.' Tony threw away the pictures as if they were on fire.

Elizabeth, another senior editor, faked puking in a bin.

'Well done, Madison, it will go in next months' edition. Very nice haircut, by the way, it suits you.'

'Thank you.'

Keeley carried on with the tasks at hand, and when the meeting was almost over, she said, as an afterthought, 'I'd like an article on Allerton Groceries.'

'What else is there to say about them?' Tony interjected. 'It's like shooting a fish in a barrel. Everybody hates them, but they seem to be a necessary evil with their prices.'

'True, but this acquisition smells. I mean, they're obviously trying to get out of that hole they dug. This merger is giving them an area of legitimacy, they're aiming to become a *fair* supermarket. I don't buy it. Paula, start digging into them. If they have gaps in gender pay, I want to know. Working conditions, harassments swept under the carpet, the whole lot. We take a shot at Allerton's from a female perspective. And bring Madison with you. You're too famous, and they'll smell a rat if you show up too often at their door.'

'I prefer the term notorious,' Paula replied, 'but it will be done.'

People laughed. *The bulldog* was carrying her nickname as a badge of honour.

'Very well, folks, back to work!' Keeley said.

The journalists closed their laptops, picked up their block notes, and left the meeting room in a hurry. They were a good bunch, the backbone of the magazine. She felt lucky. A word that hardly had a place in her vocabulary. Only Paula remained behind.

'Are you sure you want to go after Allerton?' she asked.

'Hundred percent. What's your concern?'

'It might backfire. You're known to distribute favour for the people you care for. I know you and I don't care about rumours, but other people might.'

Keeley pondered an answer. Paula was an old and trustworthy colleague; she deserved the truth. 'I've never actually done any real favours for anybody. I'm a good judge of talents. Take Heather Graham, she's a top-notch political editor and she deserves her place on national television. Gracie Hensley is a fantastic model, and she's now in her first blockbuster movie. No, I didn't do them any favours, they had talent on their own and I just showed them the way. Worst thing they can say about me is that I'm a disaster in my love life, that's all. I wouldn't lose any sleep on that.'

'Okay then. I wanted to clear the air before I start digging. Allerton had better be cleaner than a pussy on prom night.' She collected her laptop, muttered a 'See ya', and off she went.

Carlton Allerton. Amanda had pledged to let it go, he wasn't worth the effort, she said, but Keeley thought different. Her mind went back to her first job, the way men had always conspired to keep the best jobs for themselves. The prevarication despite her success. No, Allerton was dirty, and if she had half a chance, she'd love to bring him down. There was no space anymore in the twenty-first century for people like him.

Eventually, she stood and went back to her corner office.

'Call Aaron from the legal department and ask him if he can pay me a visit this afternoon,' she said to her secretary.

The gloves were off.

CHAPTER 32

'Need some help! Pleeease!' Ginger shouted, bringing a suitcase so big it wouldn't have looked out of place in Ellis Island one century before.

'Bloody blimey, how did you manage to bring it here, not to mention even lift it?' Xander dragged the case into the office, complaining about a bad back, war injuries, herniated discs, and muscles pulled.

'Pussy,' Ginger muttered.

'What was that? I didn't catch it, come again?'

'I was just saying: thank you for your help, there are more. I borrowed the car from a cousin.'

Xander dropped the suitcase on the floor. 'A car? How many clothes you got?'

Ginger laughed. Her head went slightly back, showing a perfect line of teeth. 'A lot. Mostly bargains, but I have also some expensive pieces. And racks. I've got racks in the car that need assembling.'

'You what?'

'Your idea. Don't stare at me like that.'

'Okay, I'll deal with the clothes in a minute but first I have to make a phone call.' He checked his watch. Ten-thirty in the morning was a reasonable time. 'You okay in sorting the website?'

'Not a problem. As a matter of fact, I started yesterday afternoon. It's not my first website, it's going to look a million dollars.'

'Cool.' Xander sat and placed his feet on the desk, wishing he had a cigar. He flicked to his contacts on the mobile phone and when he found what he needed, he dialled.

'Hey, Richard, Xander here.'

'Hey, what time is it? But most important, do I owe you money?' a sleepy voice on the other side of the phone asked.

'Yep, three grand, and you've been ignoring my calls for the past two months. Bailiffs will be at your door shortly,' Xander said in the harshest voice he could manage, 'and because you asked, it's ten-thirty in the morning, when decent, ordinary people have already had breakfast and started working hours ago.'

'Xander, is that you? Damn, man, I'm still asleep and it's fucking Monday. Really, what's up, dude?'

Xander thought for a moment what would be the better way of facing the issue at hand. 'I have the most appealing business proposition of the century. Something really exciting, and guess what? You're the first lucky bastard to hear about it.'

Richard grunted. 'As long as it isn't one of your ideas where you ask me to work for free. Or *in exchange for visibility*, as you might say. I'm becoming royalty, I landed a job with *Style Magazine* and I start next week.'

It actually was one of Xander's come-to-work-for-free ideas.

'No, I would not dare. But my partner in crime and I will need some of your expertise in the field of photography, in particular, in the fashion area, just to get started. Instead of visibility, I can offer you a percentage on my next novel royalties. Something, if you ask me, you should consider without further ado.'

'I'm not asking you. Get straight to the point, man,' Richard said. 'Damn! I think I'm a vampire. I opened the curtains, and the light coming in is painful.'

'Consider it as a consultancy. A crash course on fashion photography. We're smart people and we can pick up quickly if you show us the ropes. You'll be rewarded with our gratitude, pots of hot coffee and, as I said, the ticket to richness in the form of a small, negotiable, percentage of my next bestseller. Are you free this afternoon?'

Ginger, who in the meanwhile had assembled a rack and was starting to hang her clothes, looked at Xander with amusement.

'Sorry, man, I don't do Mondays. To be honest, I don't do Tuesdays either or the rest of the week, come to that. I tell you, I'm becoming royalty and I'm enjoying some quiet before they squeeze every inch of my photographic superpowers in exchange for an outrageous fee.'

Xander sighed. Things were not going as he'd expected. *Could we do this alone?* he asked himself. Of course they couldn't. They'd have to learn by doing, spend umpteen hours outside in the cold with unpredictable results. Time they didn't have and time that would be taken away from semi-lucrative business. It was something he and Ginger could simply not afford. Not for an idea that Xander knew was half-baked at most, a shot in the dark. He still had one last option.

'I'm glad you're having some success now, Richard. If you ask me, it's well-deserved. If I just think about how you got your first job...' He didn't finish his sentence. Now the ball was in Richard's court.

The man went quiet.

Xander heard the noise in the street, cars honking, the sound of the city that never slept. He loved New York; he wouldn't want to be in any other place.

'Are you cashing in that favour? I thought we were friends,' he said eventually.

'We are,' Xander replied, 'and that's what friends are for. They help each other when there's a need. Come on, man, your help is essential. I promise we'll be on our own, just show us the direction and we'll take it from there.'

'Bastard! Okay, text me the address. I'll be there in a reasonable amount of time. Damn, Xander, it's fucking Monday, you make me break one of my most sacred vows.'

Xander sent him the address as soon as he hung up.

'Is he coming then?' Ginger asked.

'Yeah.'

'So, what was the favour?' she pressed.

Xander told her how they'd met at university and became friends. Richard had a passion for photography, and he could not shut up about Ansel Adams, Cartier-Bresson, and Helmut Newton but, apart from that, they got along just fine. 'The problem was that he never had the money to buy any decent equipment. We shared a flat for a period of time, and all our earnings were going on beers, junk food, and rent. All I needed was a half-working laptop, but as for photography, it's a never-ending game. Dozens of lenses, flashes, filters, Photoshop, and all sort of wizardries and gadgets. Bottom line, I took some of Richard's pictures and showed them to an uncle who shared the same passion. I said they were mine, and he lent me his old equipment. You would not believe it, stuff worth a few grand a piece. I told him, here you go. Richard almost cried, and he promised that if I ever needed something he'd repay me.'

'It was a nice gesture,' Ginger said.

'You know what he did afterwards? At some point he kept nagging me he needed a tripod: *Does that uncle of yours have one?* The old guy moved to Florida, so I couldn't really go there and ask. Well, that Christmas I got a big present from Richard as a way of thanking me. You know what it was?'

'Not a clue,' Ginger said. 'What was it?'

'A bloody tripod. The cheeky bastard.'

One hour later, a white, battered van parked in front of the shop. Richard walked through the door and looked around, then he spotted Xander behind a desk, furiously typing on his computer.

'I thought I got the wrong address. It says Legal Services outside.'

Xander stood and shook hands with him. 'Thank you for coming, I really appreciate it. This is Ginger, my partner in crime.'

'Hello, gorgeous.' He squared the woman from head to toe. 'Are you considering a career as a model? I could really help on that front…'

'Richard, hands off,' Xander said. 'Come on, let's have a coffee.'

They sat around the table, and he explained what he had in mind.

'A shootout across the city? We can do that, but it's not going to be easy, especially if you have to do it on your own. Too much to learn in a short period of time.'

'We're clever people, Richard. We don't aspire to be professional but we need some guidance. We need to stand out from the crowd. Just talk out loud when you're shooting, what you're looking for, your mental process. Something's gotta stick.'

'Very well. Load the van with as many clothes as you can. Think about combinations, you don't want to spend half a day getting changed in this bloody weather.'

'In the van?' Ginger asked.

'You either change in the van or you and Xander go to the nearest bar, he drinks a coffee, and you get changed in the toilets. Your choice.'

'We take the van,' both answered with one voice.

Ginger got busy sorting clothes, Xander loaded what his companion threw in the suitcases, and few minutes after they were hitting the road in the general direction of Brooklyn Bridge.

'Here we are.' Richard suddenly stopped on a secondary road. He went to the back of the van, followed by Xander and Ginger, and started explaining the basic concepts. Wide angles, telephoto, depth of field, the use of a flash.

Ginger checked her outfit and said she was ready.

Richard stepped away a few paces and directed her, making her walk towards him, explaining what he was doing and his mental process. They moved on to a different location.

'Here, stand by the crosswalk,' he instructed her. 'You see,' he showed Xander, 'see those horizontal lines and how they break her figure into different sections?' He took several shots, then walked away and took some other pictures of Ginger, asking her to position her hands in a certain way, then holding a Starbucks' cup, changing her hat, then asking her to walk by, pretending to read something on her phone.

After an hour of moving locations, changing clothes, and shooting, they stopped in a bar to get warm. Richard fired up his laptop and put some pictures on the screen.

'Wow,' Xander muttered.

'You see here?' Richard explained, 'the idea is to make them look casual, as if Ginger is passing by and someone took a shot, but pay attention at those buildings.' He took a piece of paper and drew lines. 'The background has to complement the image, like in this picture. Or in this other case, it's neutral, only a door and grey behind. Here you isolate the subject.'

Xander was taking notes, doing small sketches on paper and nodding. The photographer carried on explaining how to manage shadows by using a reflector in addition to a flash. 'It's really a three-person job, to be honest. Photographer judging the light, assistant with the reflector, and a makeup artist. You're lucky you don't need any,' he said to Ginger, 'but attention to detail is everything. It takes a lot of work to make it look casual but perfect at the same time. Hey, do you want to give it a try next?' he asked Xander.

'I… Sure, why not.'

They spent the rest of the afternoon driving around, shooting, changing clothes, and then shooting again. Eventually, they returned to the office.

After a well-deserved brew, Richard handed over two huge bags full of equipment. 'This is mostly still your uncle's stuff. I changed the camera, obviously, but, after all, it's something you lent me. It served me well. Don't worry, I have plenty of new stuff in my studio. Just promise you won't use your bloody phones to take pictures.'

'Richard, I'm really grateful...'

Ginger's words were suddenly cut off by a hand gesture from Richard. 'Don't mention it.' He downloaded the pictures on a portable drive and handed it over to Xander. 'You can sort out the ones you like, just mention my name somewhere if you're posting them.'

'We will.'

Richard left the office, and Xander and Ginger relaxed on their chairs.

'A three-person job,' she pondered. 'We need to grab Jennifer when she's not working at the hospital.'

'I was thinking exactly the same thing.'

Ginger turned on her computer. Outside it was dark, and the traffic was getting heavier. It was commuter time, and a flurry of snow fell. She uploaded the photos onto the website, and it was glorious.

'We need some blurb,' she said.

'I can do that.'

'You know what?'

'What?'

'I think you were right.'

Xander nodded. He was sure they were onto something, they just needed to tread carefully; too many times he thought he had the right idea, and too many times reality proved otherwise.

'Come on, let's go to Corrigan's. I'll buy you a well-deserved drink.'

They walked out into the night, arm in arm. The pavement started to fill with snow.

CHAPTER 33

A few months had passed since Mia had joined her new firm, and Christmas came and went as if it was an ordinary day. The city was covered in snow and ice for what the news declared to be one of the coldest winters since nineteen thirty-six. Central park was completely white, and the Hudson had almost frozen. Not that she had a chance to see any of it—she'd caught a glimpse on the news the evening before. Her day started at 6.00 AM when it was still dark and ended at nine in the evening. When there wasn't something urgent to deal with, which was often the case.

The rare spare time at her disposition and her lunch break were taken up by organising a wedding that, so far, was going nowhere. She spent her evening crashing on the sofa after a takeaway as she had no energy for a meal out and the occasional bad sex with Carlton.

He'd changed.

She justified that by telling herself they were both busy. Allerton's merger with King General proved more difficult than she thought, and that was for sure the reason for Carlton's permanent bad mood, and her job was extremely demanding. She had been assigned to Gareth Szymansky's team, defending in court the rights of a well-known oil company. They'd found gas deposits near Alamosa,

Colorado, and gotten all the necessary permits to start fracking.

Two years later, the first serious incident happened. Carl and Bertha Miller reported the smell of gas to the local authorities several times; no investigation took place. A few days later, when the old couple were shopping at the mall in Alamosa, they heard a loud explosion. When they returned home, they found that the explosion had levelled their house and three more in the neighbourhood. The count was five deaths, including two children, and an old man who lost his legs. Three months after, a family was taken to the hospital. All of them showed signs of heart palpitations, sinus infections, and growth of the thyroid, symptoms that became quite common in the area. Another major incident followed few months after, where the whole city had to be evacuated for almost a week.

Myerscough, Nibley, and Holton were fighting on behalf of the oil company on a double front, a class action from the people injured on one side, and against the town who wanted to put a halt to the whole fracking process in the area on the other side.

The strategy brought forward by Gareth Szymansky was simple. Dismiss as many cases as possible on the class action and find a weak case for a separate trial. On the other side, it was decided to prolong as much as possible, the trial brought forward by the town of Alamosa with the intent of bankrupting them. Create as much paperwork as possible, invent motions to dismiss with little merit, drag their feet for months, if not years. After all, the oil company had deep pockets, and Alamosa would not be able to keep spending at the same pace. No money, no trial. That was what Mia was working on.

It was a Sunday, and still she was in the office preparing for her trip to Colorado the following day. That was her second visit on-site. She had come to hate Mondays since she started working for Myerscough, Nibley, and Holton.

CHAPTER 34

Xander had done it.

It was at the third revision of his newly written thriller, and still he thought what he'd written was half decent. He knew it was not a hurried-up novel, despite the short time it had taken to write it. It was not the usual light story filled with bi-dimensional characters that was typical of his erotic novels. No, this was something else. For once, he knew he'd nailed it.

Funnily enough, he hadn't felt drained, as usually happened to him in the past after finishing a novel. Having to write articles day in and day out, ten hours a day, made his life easier. He felt like a well-trained runner; he knew he could go the distance now without any effort. It didn't matter what subject he was writing about. The white page in front of his screen was not a problem anymore, he just knew that he had to fill it, and after typing a few words he wouldn't stop.

He needed fresh air.

He put his boots on, grabbed a heavy coat, and carefully placed his laptop in his backpack. He then ran down the stairs and went onto the street. Brooklyn was blanketed with snow and ice. He stopped for a second, wondering if he'd done a backup of his files. He recalled he had.

There wasn't much traffic, and the few people walking by were looking at the ground in front of their feet. He thought he'd better do the same. To reach the local Starbucks it was a five-minute walk, and that was enough to almost lose all the heat he had accumulated in his apartment. February was the best month of the year, especially if it was a record cold winter. The only other place where he'd consider living would be Oslo in Norway. In winter. Other than that, it was because the wine down there was too bloody expensive. No, better stick to New York.

Starbucks was fairly warm that day, and he peeled off his layers of clothes, then ordered the biggest coffee they had. He knew it would not be his only one that day.

He opened the computer and went back to his novel. This time he'd listen to it. He had a free text-to-speech programme which read chapter by chapter and send the output to his earplugs. A monotonous but clear voice in the background. It was an exercise he'd picked up from his new girlfriend. 'Let the sound of the words be in the background. If you hear an error, your brain will pick it up immediately,' she'd said.

He sat there, staring at his coffee whilst the software narrated his latest work. He checked his bank account. He had enough money to pay for a copy edit but he'd talk to Ginger first. Things were slow, and the website and Instagram account were not going as he'd hoped. Some traffic, but nothing to be excited about. Another failure.

He typed Ginger's website address in his browser. A mere eight hundred visitors, despite the site looking like a million dollars. They spent every weekend taking pictures, filling it, writing all sort of articles, and still nothing. He couldn't see where they'd made a mistake.

Two hours and three coffees later, his mobile buzzed. He was almost dozing off, despite the large dose of caffeine, listening to a dull voice that recited word by word of his thriller. He almost fumbled it. It was a WhatsApp message from Ginger.

- Are you awake yet?

No, I'm bloody not, and I'm depressed.

- Sure, what's the matter? he texted back.

- Buy a copy of *Style Magazine*, NOW! Page 36, and call me back ASAP.

Xander shook his cup to ensure it was empty and then gave a glance outside the window. It was snowing again, and this time it was serious. *What the heck?* He closed his laptop and went out into the cold blizzard. The newsagent was a hundred meters away. He bought a copy of *Style Magazine* and went back to Starbucks for a refill.

He flicked through the pages until he reached the spot indicated by Ginger. The article was titled Horror Fashion Week, and in the top-left corner was a familiar face. He read the caption, which said the woman was Madison Turner. Madison... He then clicked — she was the lady Ginger had helped out. He started reading avidly.

'What can I get you? Sir?'

Xander awoke from his daydreaming. 'What?'

'Sir, may I take your order?' the barista asked again.

The small queue in front of him had suddenly disappeared. 'A double espresso and a cinnamon bagel, please.' He paid and went back to the same table where he'd sat before.

The article was ferocious. The journalist had spent weeks going around with personal shoppers and getting advice. It was a name-and-shame list as you could find in specialised consumer magazines. For each personal shopper, there was a picture of what Madison had bought, worn by herself and by a model. The first one resembled roadkill, a horrible combination of clothes. Madison's article went on abusing each and every one of the personal shoppers she had enlisted with, also quoting total expenditure for the day out and fee asked. They surely had worked with their legal department, carefully analysing each individual word. They were flowing but they never crossed the line of objectivity. He finally reached the name he was searching for, Magdalene O'Sullivan.

Two pictures as per all the others, Madison's and the model's, and they didn't look that bad. *But what do I know?* he asked himself.

He exhaled and started reading.

The last personal shopper we worked with is a Magdalene O'Sullivan. Don't bother searching, you will not find her on Yell or on the specialised pages that usually advertise this sort of service. Her website, at the time this article was written, was under construction. No, Miss O'Sullivan's name came to me via a friend of a friend. Word of mouth, so to speak. They swore about what Miss O'Sullivan did for her, but I could not verify it first-hand, so I decided to try her out. We still had three thousand dollars in the budget, so we thought of giving it a last go before going back to the editorial room and licking our wounds.

Miss O'Sullivan is an attractive redhead and gave me an appointment near a corner shop in Brooklyn. I loved the mystery, it reminded me of a rendezvous at Checkpoint Charlie where spies needed to be exchanged. Our personal shopper for the afternoon arrived by taxi accompanied by an attractive young man who seemed extremely bored and kept checking his mobile. He was apparently our safeguard in case we got lost. Still to this day I've not understood what his role was, as he barely spoke. On the other hand, Miss O'Sullivan, who promptly asked me to call her "Ginger" never shut up, asking question after question about my life and taste in clothes. She could have had quite a success as an interrogator for the FBI, if you ask me. She was well-dressed but not over the top, and I couldn't spot any of the most expensive brands on her. Nonetheless, she appeared extremely elegant.

After she checked about my budget, a mere three hundred and eighty dollars, I was expecting a visit to the mall, or that she would give up completely and find an excuse to leave me there. What can you really do nowadays with that budget? A pair of Jimmy Choo's, a couple of other items, and bang! Your budget is blown in ten minutes. I wasn't there to buy stuff, I made it clear, I wanted a "style".

Ginger stood in front of me and didn't flinch at the latest "Mission Impossible", Brooklyn version, and she took me to a local shop that I'd have overlooked even if I had to walk that road day in and day out for my commute.

Whilst our male chaperone was sitting on an armchair, bored stiff and probably typing email number one hundred and twenty-five, Ginger explained, with tact, what kind of clothes would better suit my curvy shape. Nothing that I didn't know already—after all, I'm surrounded by people who deal with fashion on a daily basis—but nonetheless, what I found refreshing was that she took time explaining to me her thought process. We came out of the shop with some inexpensive, but still very nice, clothes.

The same happened in the next shop. By then, if I was a novice, I'd have totally embraced what my personal Virgilio was saying and where she was taking me. I knew straight away she'd do her best to guide me out of Hell. And she did.

I felt confident, empowered, and the result was that I got what I was asking for. A personalised style.

But Ginger was not done with me, she had one last trick up her sleeve. A visit to a hairdresser. I panicked for a moment; I hadn't changed my hairstyle for over fifteen years. Not an option. I know what I like and I know what I *want in that department. But for the sake of this article I decided, reluctantly, to play along. It might have taken me a few months to go back to my old style, I might have regretted it, but at that point, Miss O'Sullivan had completely gained my trust.*

You can see the result yourself in the pictures. I never thought anything would surprise me in life, but Miss O'Sullivan did, once again. She whispered some words in the hairdresser's ears, and half an hour later I had everything I asked for. And more.

Ginger was doing a spectacular job with me, but my old cynical nature was not completely satisfied. I asked if we should buy some more and, contrary to my expectation, she declined. I mean, who is going to reject money nowadays? Instead, I got a lecture on how to stick to my budget and not overspend. Who could have guessed? Bottom line, I came home with a new style which (I already knew) was going to suit me, a brand-new haircut that awed colleagues, a person who I'd trust with my life if my bank account suddenly dried out, and I still wanted to look elegant. And all this for a mere seventy-dollar fee.

You can find Miss O'Sullivan's website address below, if it's not still under construction, otherwise your other option would be to know someone in that secret society of her clients who is willing to pass you her number.

Xander's jaw dropped. He read the whole piece once again to be sure. Ginger was the only one not to be slaughtered by Madison Turner. On the contrary.

He picked up his phone and dialled Ginger's number.

'Did you read it?' she asked without even saying hello. The excitement was palpable in her voice.

'Yeah, that was good. Strike that, it was GREAT! Did you know she worked for *Style Magazine*?'

'Not a clue. Hey, the website is lighting up as if it was a January fire sale.'

'Really? I checked it a couple of hours ago and it was as dead as a dodo,' Xander said.

'Not now. I've already got five requests via email, and visitors have bumped up to four thousand. Jennifer wants to put me on Valium as she said I'm overexcited.'

'I bet you are.' Xander fired up the computer and looked at the website. Indeed, the counter was up and kept climbing. 'Check your Instagram,' he suggested.

'Fifty thousand followers and rising.'

'Okay, but don't get too excited,' Xander continued, mostly to calm down his own elation, 'it might dry out.'

'Party pooper!'

'Just trying to be realistic. Okay, catch you later. Hey, Ginger, well done!'

Xander sagged in his chair. He saw a glimpse of success, for the first time in his life, in something he was part of. It had never happened before, and he felt ecstatic.

CHAPTER 35

'I didn't hear your squeaky voice calling an objection, Miss Crawford.'

Mia woke up from thoughts of motions, briefs that still needed preparing for another case, wedding plans going down the drain. But most of all, what took her attention away was a brief she saw just earlier that morning in the office. Contrary to office practice, the paper was left in the copy machine and was a litigation against Compassionate American Purse. She recalled being at one of their events months before with Carlton. She glimpsed the stack of paper and learnt some disturbing news. First, the charity was getting loads of money from several high-profile individuals and celebrities. What was also evident was that the organisation, of the several dozens of millions raised in the past year, had only used a mere seventy thousand dollars for actual charity donation. The rest of the money went back to the donors as fees, gifts, and commissions. She could spot a tax avoidance scheme (when it was not clearly tax evasion) just by glancing at the document. Most disconcerting was that Carlton was named on the board of directors' list. He surely knew what that "charity" really was. She deposited the paper back on the copy machine but couldn't stop thinking about the implication of what she'd just read.

Judge Lamarr was staring directly at her, and so was the defendant's attorney.

'Ehm, I don't think I have a squeaky voice,' she managed to say whilst her brain was catching up. She knew she had lost concentration and missed several minutes of the proceedings.

'That is debatable, although that is not the point, is it? Do you have an objection?'

Mia regained composure and answered, 'I certainly do. Objection on the grounds of hearsay.'

The judge seemed amused. 'A decent try, but not good enough. Try something else, Miss Crawford, and let's hope we stop at two out of three.'

'Compound question?' Her mouth twitched, a clear tell-tale of her wild guess.

'Very well, Miss Crawford. Sustained, and don't let me catch you sleeping in my court anymore,' and then addressing the defendant's attorney, he said, 'One question at the time, Mr Wilson.'

The defendant's attorney looked at the judge as if he had suddenly dropped in the court room from Mars.

'What's the matter, Mr Wilson?'

'I think she is supposed to object, Your Honour, not have you remind her when to do so.'

The judge nodded. 'Let's not object on the objection. You will have grounds for an appeal in case you lose. Hurry up, I want to hear the closing statement today. '

COLETTE KEBELL

'Yes, Your Honour.' Mr Wilson asked the two remaining questions and declared there were no more witnesses.

Both lawyers proceeded with the closing argument, and the judge ruled in favour of the defendant. Mia pondered for a second if a jury trial instead of a bench one would have brought a different result, but she dismissed the thought. She knew she'd dropped the ball.

'I'm sorry, Mr Layden.'

Her client nodded. 'I had my day in court, that was what I was hoping for, to be heard. If the justice system thinks I wasn't in the right, so be it. I thank you anyway.'

That was the last client Mia had from her old legal clinic. The vast majority of her clients decided to find a different lawyer. She stood, exchanged greetings with Mr Layden, and exited the court room. She had to hurry back to the office, but for a second, she sat on a bench in the corridor. She knew she'd let down her client but most of all she'd let herself down. Sitting there, whilst lawyers hurried up to go to their next case, she couldn't avoid thinking about how her life had changed.

Only months before she wouldn't have lost that case. The clinic wasn't what she wanted, but she never knowingly disappointed any client. They needed help, and nobody else was ready to take care of their problems. And now, she was on the other side of the barricade. She thought about her recent trips to Alamosa. How different it was from what

270

she'd been doing. First of all, there wasn't a client, not that she could think of. There were shareholders, that was for sure, but they couldn't care less about her, they just wanted results. The closest she came to her client was her weekly report to their in-house lawyer. On the other side, she met with the people in Alamosa too many times. It was a small community which reminded her of Camden, Maine, the place where her parents lived and where she'd grown up. The woman in the local bakery could have been her own mother, and she saw her crying during a filmed deposition. How she'd lost her husband, the terror when she had to abandon her trailer and drive away from the place she had lived her entire life, without knowing if she could ever return. The other depositions were of the same tone, people scared, people wanting to live in peace and carry on with their lives.

Mia had buried her head in the sand. She kept working hard, studying similar cases and occupying every single moment of her time with work, but deep inside her, she knew what she was really doing. She was avoiding her conscience. Though, this was what she'd desired when she was a student, dealing with the most complex cases she could come across, making history. But her dreams were always foggy; she imagined herself arguing cases in the Supreme Court, battling for civil rights. She never once thought or desired to represent an oil company trying to bankrupt a small town.

How she could have changed so much?

She felt tired. Talking to Carlton about her doubts was not an option. She'd tried once and got a *business is business* in reply. He never had to see the faces of those people in Alamosa. He never had to look at a sick child knowing she had to do her utmost to deny justice. Because that was what Mia was required to do. Deny justice. Delay, stall, play a chess game with the people in Alamosa in the clear attempt to ruin them, for them to go bankrupt before a case could be heard. And if they won, she'd appeal and drag them into court again.

She always criticised her father and her mother for being ordinary people. Mia was not ordinary anymore, she knew that, and she also knew she didn't like one bit of her life.

She stood from the bench and walked towards the exit. *Come on, Mia, you have to soldier on, you can't pick and choose what you like in this life.*

It was a sunny day, and April was fast approaching. It wasn't warm enough to be considered spring yet, but pleasant. She took a long breath, and in that very moment her head spun. She reached for a handhold, and one second later the darkness wrapped around her.

'Need some help here! Call nine-one-one,' was the last thing she heard before the nothingness.

Mia woke up and looked around. In the semi-darkness, she recognised she was in a hospital room; the distinctive smell of disinfectant filled her nostrils. The bed and the monitors on her left were also a clear giveaway. How she ended up there she couldn't recollect.

Mia closed her eyes, trying to revive in her memory what had happened. She was in court and she'd lost a case, then nothing, everything went dark. She lifted the sheet that was covering her—no evident injuries on the legs, no pain whatsoever. She still had all her fingers.

The curtain opened a few minutes later, and Jennifer appeared. 'You're awake, finally. How do you feel?'

'Jennifer…' Mia tried to sit on the bed, but her friend hurried her to lie down. 'What happened?' she eventually asked.

'You collapsed, simple as that. I ran all sort of checks, and you're fine, apart from a small bump on the back of your head when you fell to the ground.'

Mia instinctively brought her hand towards her head. The "bump" was more of a ping-pong-sized protuberance. It hurt.

Jennifer continued, 'Exhaustion. You pushed yourself too hard, and your body reacted. It just said it was time to take a break. You slept for two days.'

'I did what? No, no, that can't be true. Two days, you said? I'm supposed to be in Colorado, I have tons of paperwork to do…' She tried again to rise, but Jennifer stood in her path.

'Listen to me, Mia. You collapsed in the middle of the road. It will happen again if you don't take care of yourself.'

'Where is Carlton?' Mia didn't want to hear any reasoning; she had a job to do and she couldn't just collapse. Maybe she could negotiate a few days of sick leave and work from home until she fully recovered. She needed to talk to her boss as soon as her mind cleared a bit further. Jennifer's face was of stone. 'Where is Carlton?'

'He passed by this morning, but you were still sound asleep. He asked us to call him as soon as you wake up as he had some business to attend to. I've got his mobile number, don't worry. But if you're up to it, I've got some other visitors for you.'

Mia didn't know what to say, she still felt confused and foggy. She nodded.

Jennifer opened the door, letting in Xander and Ginger.

'Keep it quiet,' she said to the two newcomers, 'and remember she needs to rest,' before leaving the room.

'Xander, Ginger, oh my gosh. Thank you! How long have you been here?'

'About a day and a half, give or take,' Ginger said.

'We stayed around most of the time," Xander said. 'Jennifer bribed the charge nurse to let at least one of us in here after hours. The other slept in the waiting area. I told this bunch of sawboneses all you needed to wake up was a kiss from a prince charming like me, but they didn't want to hear any of it.'

Mia smiled. Her friend hadn't changed one bit during those months. The smile disappeared as soon as she realised for how long she hadn't seen them. 'I'm so sorry I have neglected you. I was so busy and kept repeating to myself I had to meet you, and then something else popped up. I have no excuses. How long has it been?'

'Four months,' Xander said, 'but who's counting?'

Mia nodded, a guilty feeling arising within her. 'I'm a terrible friend. I'm really sorry.'

'Don't mention it. You were busy.'

'So, what are you up to these days? Still working together?'

Xander and Ginger looked at each other as if to decide who had to go first. He took the lead and explained how Ginger was becoming a celebrity in the world of fashion, from that day when they'd met Madison Turner to the article in *Style Magazine*. From then, things only got better. A few million followers on Instagram, companies paying for Ginger to be a brand ambassador.

'Can you believe it, five thousand dollars for a single post.' Xander was unable to contain his excitement. 'Not to mention her website. She can pick and choose who to work with and what to charge. We're even considering hiring some people as we can't keep pace with the demand.'

'And it's all legit,' Ginger interjected, preventing further questions from Mia. 'And Xander here has some good news also.'

'You do?' Mia asked, 'are you getting married?'

'Nah, nothing of that sort, although I might propose soon. Got a novel out, and it's selling like hot cakes. I'm not in *The New York Times* bestseller list just because they count sales in physical bookstores, but the book is in the top charts on Amazon and has been there for a while. Publishing companies started stalking me for a contract. I'm far from being a millionaire but at least I can say I can make a living out of my writing.'

Mia sighed. She missed all of that, the moment where her dearest friends were starting to have success only because she was too busy making an oil company even richer. She wouldn't forgive herself. A tear trickled down her cheek.

'I'm so happy for you two,' Mia sobbed, 'and you, Xander, you deserve it.'

'Thank you. But I wouldn't have done anything if it wasn't for Ginger here. She pushed my book on her website, she contacted all the people we worked for, asking to spread the word. We're a team.'

Jennifer returned and smiled, seeing the three talking as if nothing had changed in the past four months. They were the same friends even if Mia had dropped the ball. 'It's time to go,' she sentenced, 'Mia needs a good rest.'

'Can you prescribe her a therapy of Barolo, three times a week, to be consumed at Corrigan's?' Xander asked.

'I'll see what I can do. Now you really have to go.'

Ginger kissed Jennifer on the lips and said, 'See you later at home.'

Mia's jaw dropped. 'I didn't see that coming.'

'You missed a lot. I'm going to be honest with you. As a doctor, I can give you a sick notice for a week and then you are back to your routine, you can go on killing yourself working twenty hours a day. As a friend, I'd really want to know what happened to you.'

Mia told her about the case she'd lost and, most importantly, why. Her head was somewhere else. 'I don't like what I'm doing, Jenny. I mean, the people in Alamosa. They could be my parents, my old neighbours in Camden. Their lives are ruined, and for what, so someone could profit, me included, out of it? I hate it from my gut. Life is miserable. I go home and all I want is to sleep and cry; Carlton is hardly there, and even when we have a chance to talk, he's not listening. I'm not saying he doesn't hear my words, it's just… He is one of them. Profit's his god.'

'So, what are you going to do about that?'

'I don't know, I feel lost. I'm questioning everything, even my relationship with Carlton. I knew about his past and the differences between us, but somehow I swept them under the carpet. I thought love would prevail and we'd find a way of dealing with our differences. But it doesn't, does it? I lived in a bubble, ignoring signs of our incompatibility, hoping that time would bring us closer. I don't really know what to do.'

Jennifer nodded; her face was sad. 'Maybe you should go back to the legal clinic.'

'I can't do that. I mean, have you seen them, they're happy, they made all that happen by themselves. It wouldn't be right for me to go back.'

'Take a break then,' Jennifer suggested, 'a couple of months of sick leave. Call your parents, even go there for a while, clear your mind, but most of all, get some rest. Get out of this city and that toxic environment you got yourself into. And as Xander said, Barolo three times a week—killing some of those brain cells of yours might do you good.'

'I have too much to do, I have the wedding...'

Jennifer's face hardened. 'So, where is he?' she said, looking around. 'I swore I wouldn't get involved, but you have to pull yourself together. Mia, you never did it for the money, not the job, nor the wedding. It's your twisted way of thinking about what success is; if you ask me, I think you were pretty successful at the clinic. You were complaining, but you were happy, and your work made a difference. Maybe it's time you put aside salary and status and think about what is really good for you. You know the alternative, collapsing on the road. Have a rest, see you tomorrow.'

Mia fixed her gaze on the ceiling for a time that seemed eternal. She felt empty, without energy to even counter what her friend was saying. She didn't want to, and she knew it. She closed her eyes, incapable of even thinking about what she'd do next.

She fell asleep and dreamed of her parents' house collapsing, the smell of gas filling her nostrils, her mother crying. She dreamed of her boss, Gareth Szymansky, counting piles of dollars in front of Carlton, the two laughing, sharing a cigar and congratulating each other.

She woke up in a pool of sweat. The clock on the side table marked half past three in the morning on its red dials. Mia knew something had to change.

CHAPTER 36

Mia looked around the impressive lounge one last time.

It was a fine apartment with a spectacular view, but it was also a bachelor pad. How she could not have realised that before?

She'd discussed the matter at length with Carlton the previous day, and things went much easier than she'd first anticipated.

Everything that had happened in the past few months made her understand she'd never been in love with him, and she was sure Carlton never loved her either. They were fond of each other, but love was another thing, something they never experienced together. No, she was not being romantic, she knew.

And what they discussed the previous day hadn't changed her mind. Yes, Carlton had been apologetic about not showing up at the hospital, about being too busy. But that was the point. Career came first, something she could relate to until not long ago, but today that wasn't enough. Career was a means to achieve what Mia desired in life, stability, prestige, security, which would form the basis for a solid family. It was evident that Carlton didn't think that way.

Her mind went back to all the details that were screaming at her not to marry him. The difference in taste, his change in temper, how he always seemed very casual in how he dealt with relationship matters. Even the proposal was halfhearted, something that came out of his mouth to fill a gap in their dialogue rather than the will to live with someone else for the rest of his life. The evening before he'd proved her point. His attempt to put forward his reasons were weak, tepid, and he accepted what she was saying without putting up a fight. Who didn't fight for the love of his life?

The three suitcases were ready by the door. Her only possessions. When she'd moved in with Carlton, she'd sold in bulk the little furniture she had in her apartment.

The flight to Bangor was booked, and a taxi would be waiting outside in twenty minutes.

Her phone rang.

She looked at the display, which showed Gareth Szymansky.

She swiped to the right and answered a polite, 'Good morning, Mr Szymansky.' The clock showed 7.00 AM. She pressed the record button on an app on her phone.

'What is this story that you're sick?'

'There is no story there,' Mia replied, 'the HR department got a sick note from my doctor, that's the end of it.'

'Yeah, exhaustion. Two bloody months? What have you done, run marathons in your spare time?'

'Mr Szymansky, I don't have spare time; you make sure every single hour of my life is sucked up in your firm. The lack of care for your employees brought me to this. Now I need a good rest.'

'Like hell you do; you have a job to do in Alamosa and an important client depending on you. You knew it was a demanding job, and we're paying you a hefty salary for your services.'

Mia was fuming. How dare he call her at seven in the morning on a Monday, when she was supposed to be off work. 'May I remind you, Mr Szymansky, that if you continue on this line you open your company to be sued?' She stopped right there, she didn't want to pick a fight with a senior partner, but in that moment, she wouldn't have it. She knew she couldn't let it slip. She'd stand up for herself no matter what. No more compromises. She'd done that too many times already in her life and she wasn't prepared to anymore.

'Be my guest, it's not lawyers to defend ourselves that we're lacking. At best, you have a *he said, she said* scenario here. Get your arse down to Alamosa and do your damn job or we can make sure we can prove your performance was less than stellar in the past months. Even if I have to make up the paperwork myself!'

'My performance was just fine, and nobody mentioned anything about it until now, when I got sick. Only, try to fire me whilst I'm off sick, and no jury will believe a word of what you are saying. I'll make sure of that, and you know you can't win this. You're going to pay me, Mr Szymansky. Your only choice is to either pay me my salary whilst I'm off sick or to pay a much larger compensation fee later on, when I take you to court. I'm recording this conversation and I remind you, New York State is a one-party consent when it comes to recording. And I give my consent, by the way.'

'Bitch!'

'Still recording…'

'Okay, turn that damn recorder off, and I'll tell you what I'm going to do.'

Mia pondered what the senior partner was saying and turned off the recorder. 'Go ahead, Mr Szymansky.'

'Six months' salary starting from today, and then you are out of my sight. I can put it in writing.'

'Make it one year, and I can live with that. Send me the proposal in the post, and I'll review it. I'll text you the address,' Mia replied. For a moment she pondered if she could ask for more. No, she was in no condition to take them to court, and they'd make sure to drag the case for years; she couldn't afford it.

'One year it is then, but I want a non-compete agreement here in New York. Best and final offer, otherwise you'll have to take your chances. Not that anybody will hire you in this city if you take us to court. I'll make it my personal pet project, ensuring no firm will touch you with a stick otherwise.'

'I'm glad we came to an agreement as civilised people would do. I'm looking forward to receiving the letter.'

Gareth Szymansky grunted. 'My secretary will type it this morning, and it will be in the post by the end of the day. And now go to hell, Miss Crawford,' and so said, he hung up.

What a start for a Monday morning, staring at the black screen of her phone. In that very moment, she swore to herself she would not do Mondays for the rest of her life, no matter what.

She texted her parents' address to Gareth Szymansky and got to the door. It was time to leave the city for good.

In the hall, she handed the keys of Carlton's apartment to the concierge and moved the three large suitcases onto the street. Her taxi was waiting, and the driver hurried up to help her load the lot in the trunk.

'Where to, madam?' the driver asked in a thick Middle Eastern accent.

'Newark airport, please.'

She looked, for what she knew was the last time, at the tall buildings in Manhattan. She'd never return, not as a lawyer. What was left of her experience in the city? Not much. She'd joined the rat race at the top, she was made redundant, she worked for pennies, she later found a job that people would kill for, only to almost kill herself in the process. Now, everything came to an end.

The positive things she was left with was her friendships with Jennifer, Xander, and Ginger. And the feeling that, on final balance, those friendships and what she did as a lawyer helping people in need was the only thing she'd gained in what, otherwise, she had to consider as a failure. Her relationship with Carton included.

She didn't feel sad or sorry. On the contrary, she felt elated, finally free. She didn't know what to do next and, for the first time in her life, that didn't make her worry.

Who would have thought?

Newark Liberty International airport was in sight, and so was a new chapter in her life.

CHAPTER 37

'The article is ready, and the legal team gave us the thumbs-up to publish it,' Paula Schellenberger said.

Keeley flicked through the printed pages she had in front of her, nodding with satisfaction. 'How did you manage to get Bill Ross on the record?'

Paula smirked. 'He's suing Allerton for wrongful termination and he ranted for hours about Carlton Allerton. The biggest part of the job was actually cutting down what he had to say to a reasonable amount of words. He'd worked for the firm for years and was contrary to the acquisition. In his expert opinion, Allerton Groceries skipped due diligence and gave a pass to some accountancy practices carried out by King General that can be considered creative at best. Dodgy and unlawful in the worst-case scenario. I tell you, Keeley, if we are going out with this, it's gonna be an earthquake.'

The meeting room on the fourteenth floor of *Style Magazine* was as quiet as a church on a Tuesday, everybody holding their breath for what escaped from Paula's lips.

'Well, folks, I guess if you have shares in Allerton Groceries, now it's time to cut your losses,' Keeley said. 'Any questions?'

One of the senior editors raised his hand. 'None of the financial newspapers are even close to the approach we're taking; they've talked about the merger very favourably.'

'Which will make this article an even a bigger bombshell,' Keeley said. 'At first they'll dismiss it, they'll throw all sorts of crap at us. *Stick to fashion*, they'll say. But someone will dig eventually and prove us right. Paula, this financial situation, how soon will it affect Allerton?'

Paula flicked through pages in her black notebook and eventually found what she needed. 'They'll have to disclose it before the end of the financial year. With the cat out of the bag, their only option is to issue a statement. They cannot deny the trouble now and suddenly discover it in the future. They'll look stupid. And If they don't deny, their stock will plummet to the floor. No way out.'

Keeley nodded and then added, 'And our legal department said we have grounds to publish.' She'd said this more as a reminder to herself than a question. 'Let's go ahead, we print it in this edition. With the other material you got, we'll follow up in the next issue of the magazine. It might be old news by then because some shark in the newspapers had smelled blood and they started investigating, but it doesn't matter. We got there first.'

A secretary entered the room, tiptoeing as if she was disturbing a speech from the president of the United States and murmured some words in Keeley's ear.

'I do apologise, I have an urgent matter to attend to. Tony, please take over the meeting and send me a summary later. Paula, a job well done, I will remember this when we come to discuss bonuses.' Keeley left the room and hurried to her office.

'Honey, what's going on?' she said, answering the phone.

'He's back.' Amanda's voice trembled with fear. 'I don't know how he did it, but he tracked my new phone number. He wants to meet me and he's been quite insistent. He told me a lot of bullshit about breaking up with his fiancée and wanting me back. I'm scared, Keeley. How did Carlton manage to get my number? What if he finds out where we live and shows up whilst you're at work?'

Rage mounted in Keeley. Allerton again. This time he had to pay. 'Listen, Amanda, you take a taxi to my office. No questions. As soon as you're here and safe, I'll take care of him, I promise.'

She hung up and called her secretary. 'Get me someone from Legal, and I mean NOW!'

A young attorney in a white shirt, grey tie, and a dark suit arrived few minutes later. 'How can I be of assistance, Miss Williams?'

Keeley explained what she had in mind.

'A restraining order for Allerton? This is not what we usually do, Miss Williams, it's not our area of expertise.'

'Then get me someone who knows what to do. We do have external counsellors; we use them all the time. Get on the phone and sort out an appointment. One of our models has been threatened, and I'm not going to sit here and do nothing.'

'But... But Mr Allerton?' the young lawyer was clearly panicking.

'Young man, to whom do you report to?'

The lawyer mumbled, 'Gregory Hartman.'

Keeley looked at the internal directory on her laptop and found the details of the senior legal counsel. She dialled the mobile number and explained what she wanted to do.

'Give me half an hour.' Gregory Hartman's amusement was evident in his voice.

'You can go now,' she said to the young lawyer, who was red in his face by being embarrassed in front of his boss.

Amanda arrived ten minutes later, and after twenty minutes, as promised, Gregory Hartman arrived, accompanied by an elegantly dressed woman.

The senior solicitor nodded to Amanda and shook hands with Keeley. 'This is attorney Pamela Eusebio, who specialises in domestic abuse. I thought you'd appreciate the help of someone who deals in these matters day in and day out.'

'Thank you, Gregory. Nice to meet you, Mrs Eusebio, please sit down.'

They took two chairs on the same side of the table as Amanda. Keeley repeated to them what she'd witnessed at Amanda's apartment and the events of that morning.

'We'll need an affidavit from you, Miss Williams and Miss... '

'Parker,' Amanda completed the sentence.

'And Miss Parker. Very well. We can obtain a temporary civil restraining order almost immediately. You're aware that there will be a hearing to attend to make it stick. If need be, a clerk who owes me a favour might even slip a copy of the order to the press. It would be unfortunate for Mr Allerton, but hey, leaks happen all the time.'

Amanda looked at Keeley, seeking reassurance. Going against Carlton Allerton was something she wouldn't have ever considered in a million years.

'No problem, we'll be there,' Keeley stated.

The two lawyers left the room after exchanging information, phone numbers, and pleasantries.

'Keeley, I didn't want to cause trouble…'

'Not another word, Amanda. I told you, no, I promised you, that he would pay if he only tried to contact you again. That's on him. Come on, cheer up. Come with me, I want to show you some new arrivals we got from Paris. They'll look wonderful on you.'

Keeley took Amanda's arm in hers, and they walked together down the corridor. She felt Amanda was good for her; when her girlfriend was around, Keeley smiled as she never thought she was capable of. She never dared mention the word happiness, no such thing in her world, but on more than one occasion she thought she was getting close to it. She shivered thinking about it, and she liked it.

CHAPTER 38

The three suitcases were on the conveyor belt, but Mia had no chance of getting all of them quickly onto the floor. She dragged the first one and then waited until the other two came back, after a full merry-go-round. The bags seemed much heavier than when she was in New York, and the only explanation she could come up with was that the adrenaline from her conversation with Gareth Szymansky had just worn off. She still had the company laptop and phone and made a mental note to ship them back as soon as she arrived in Camden.

She sat for a second on one of the suitcases, and her hand went to her pocket, where her phone was. She looked at the dark screen, realising there was no point in checking her emails or messages. She didn't want to hear from Carlton or anything work-related. All her time spent working and with her ex fiancé was a total waste. Having a phone was pretty much useless, and the only friends she had left were in Brooklyn. Her life had completely changed, again. She needed to think carefully about what she'd do next, but in that moment she felt exhausted, empty. Better to follow Jennifer's advice and do nothing for a while. *I will find an answer but I don't need to find it right now.*

Mia stood and pulled her suitcases towards the exit. The familiar face of her father was waiting among the sparse crowd; he approached her and took the three suitcases from her as if they were empty. He kissed her on her cheek.

'Welcome home, darling.'

'Thanks, Dad.' Mia followed him to a battered pickup truck.

'Your mother was a bit cryptic about your return,' Gregg said.

'I'll explain later, but the bottom line is, you were right.'

'About what?'

The driver's door opened, and Ethan circled around the pickup truck to help load the luggage. 'Hey, Mia!'

'Hi,' she answered and automatically passed a hand through her hair to comb it. Considering her jeans, winter boots, and heavy coat, she wished she'd had a shopping session with Ginger. 'I didn't know you were coming.'

Ethan smiled broadly and lifted the first suitcase. He answered from over his shoulder, 'Your dad and I had an errand to do here in Bangor, so I decided to tag along.'

Mia shrugged. She thought about how many times Ginger had said to her she had to do an errand and Mia knew she was up to no good. She'd turned out well. Once in a while, she checked her Instagram and her website. Who knew? She was on the road to becoming the most influential fashion blogger in the state.

Her father had run errands her entire life. Fixing windows, doing occasional plumbing work for the neighbours, obviously in his spare time. Now that he was retired, he had even more free time to do "errands". Apparently, Ethan was walking the same path.

'Do you mind if I sit in the back,' Mia said, 'I'm totally exhausted.'

She climbed into the old pickup truck and laid her head against the window. The snow was still everywhere, giving a sense of peace and quiet to the surrounding area. She dozed off almost immediately. The occasional laughter and banter between the two men sitting in the front snapped her away from a dream. With her eyes closed, she thought about the relationship between Ethan and Gregg. It wasn't a father and son one, they were more like buddies, best friends, despite the gap in age. The wheels crushing on the snow were like a lullaby, and Mia lost the notion of time. She thought about her youth in that part of the country, running in the snow chased by Ethan when they were both just teens, their first kiss in her father's barn.

She woke up to Gregg's voice.

'Mia, we are home!'

She opened her eyes and looked around. Ethan was nowhere to be seen, and she wondered if she'd dreamt he'd come to the airport. No, he was real. As soon as she exited the car, she shivered. Her father had already brought the luggage into the house. She walked slowly and, once at the entrance, carefully

293

removed her boots, not to bring any snow or mud inside. The scent of hot chocolate and vanilla was in the air, although she knew her mother was still at the shop. She excused herself from her father and went upstairs for a warm shower.

That evening, during dinner, Mia narrated the most recent events to her parents, from when she'd collapsed to the struggle she'd had, working on behalf of the notorious oil company.

'I was the evil one in that game,' she said. 'We were going to bankrupt Alamosa knowingly. It could have been Camden. I looked at them sitting in front of me. Their anger was visible on their faces; I was there to perpetrate a tort towards them, and they hated me for that. I lost a case because I wasn't focused enough, and you know what my client did? He thanked me.'

Her parents didn't say a word, clearly trying to imagine what their child was going through. They both nodded as a way of encouraging Mia to keep talking.

'At that point, I collapsed.'

'What about that fiancé of yours?' her father asked.

'My friends had taken turns to sit beside me, and he was too busy running his company to show up. He's no different from my employers or whomever own that oil company. I'm not even sure if I loved him or if I loved the idea of being with him. He was the promise of what I thought would be a perfect life, and it turned out to be just a bad dream.

The career, an important husband. Carlton was a wrong choice.' Mia explained her conversation with Jennifer and the phone call she'd that morning with her former boss.

'I'll take a few days to mull it over,' she said eventually. 'I'm quite sure I don't want to go back to New York. What's with that smug face of yours, Crow?'

'Me? Nothing, nothing.' Her father held his hands high, as if to surrender. 'I'm glad you're home. You did the right thing, kiddo. Everything a decent parent wants is for their children to follow their dreams. You did that, and I'm proud of you. It was only the wrong dream. You'll have other chances; we never know what the future holds for us.'

That was something Mia tried to figure out during the trip to Maine without coming to any conclusion. She knew what she didn't want to do, but nailing down what she *wanted* to do, that was a different matter.

CHAPTER 39

Boredom took over after a week. Mia had received the letter from Myerscough, Nibley, and Holton. She read it twice and, not finding any loopholes, signed on the dotted line. A couple of problems less to deal with and a bank account that had never been healthier in her entire life.

Reading the news online, she spotted an article in *The New York Times*. Carlton Allerton was being slammed with a restraining order from a model, an Amanda Parker, whom she'd never heard of. She looked pretty. Everybody was innocent until proven guilty, but the fact this Amanda had hired a top gun like Mrs Eusebio spoke volumes about Carton's behaviour. She'd never met Mrs Eusebio, but her reputation was top class, and she must have had some compelling evidence to go full steam ahead against the Allerton family.

Mia sagged in her armchair. She did a mental calculation and realised Carlton must have been messing around the whole time they were together. Good riddance, and thank God she'd left him before she'd found out after the wedding. Mia was surprised she didn't feel angry at him; at most, she was disappointed. He had a past of turbulent relationships, and her thinking she'd be the one to make him change proved to be an illusion. Another misplaced dream of hers. She thought about all the times Carton was late, every time he had a sudden meeting, and the evidence he was cheating had been in front of her all the time. She'd just chosen to look the other way.

She turned on her mobile and texted Jennifer.

- Did you see about Carlton?

- Yes. WOW. I think you saved yourself by the skin of your teeth. I'm sorry, babe.

- I agree. No need to be sorry. I should have listened to all of you. I'm the one who needs to apologise.

- Don't mention it. How's Maine?

- Cold. But nice. How things are going there?

- Great guns. Xander stopped complaining and is getting some success with his novels. A big contract is in the air, apparently. Maggie's as lovely as ever. We're happier than I could ever imagine we could be. I still saw bones and bring sanity to the group. We're missing you at Corrigan's.

- Miss you, too. Got to be ready for work now.

- No work, doctor's orders. I thought you left the old one.

- A new one, in my mom's bakery.

- That's allowed. Wrong career move, though, you should open a wine bar.

- I'll ponder that. Thanks for the advice.

- Free consultation. Catch you later?

- Count on it.

She put down her phone and went for a shower. *How do you dress for a first day in a bakery?* Mia reminded herself of the last time she was there and opted for some comfortable sneakers, jeans, and a jumper. Her mother would insist on her wearing an apron and a hat. She could do that.

Her mother was waiting for her down in the lobby. Thank God she didn't have to go to the bakery at five AM and now she'd get some help with the hard work.

Mia spent half of the morning serving customers and learning about all sorts of bread and pastries, and the other half answering questions. Her mother introduced her to what seemed to Mia the whole village. The most amazing thing was that everybody remembered her and had all sorts of anecdotes to tell, even the ones she couldn't recollect. At some point, she thought of pre-recording the answers to the most common questions. *Oh dear, you really grew up. How long will you stay?* And the most annoying two variants of *Are you married now?* and *Do you have a boyfriend?*

That was exactly how she remembered the place. There were no secrets in town; everybody knew everything about everybody. It was not for gossip, people cared about each other, and especially for the older ones, it was a way of keeping in touch. A bakery-café like that would go bankrupt in New York, too much chatting. However, this was Maine, things were going at a different pace, people took time to exchange greetings, having a few words before moving on to the next task. It sounded strange to her, but she needed to adapt again.

'Good morning, Mrs Clark,' Mia's mother said, 'how are you today?'

'Oh, good morning. A bit of the usual. I'm doing some nursing; little Harold is sick, and I thought a chocolate cake might cheer him up. But don't tell his mother, please.' Mia's old teacher hadn't changed one bit. Same old white hair, same hairstyle and, from what she could remember, same old coat.

'I think I have something special in the back,' Mia's mother said. She returned with a stunning cake in her hands. 'Do you want all of it or only a portion?'

'Let's say half,' Mrs Clark said, 'although I will have to hide the rest, or those little pests will eat it in no time. Oh, hello, Mia, I didn't know you came back.'

'Yeah, I'll stay around for a while, that is, if my mother doesn't get annoyed with my clumsiness.'

'Don't be daft. Now that I remember, Mrs Clark always said she wanted her will sorted, why don't you have a look into that?'

Mrs Clark was enthusiastic. 'Will you do it for me, Mia?'

'I... I suppose I could. When would you like to discuss it?'

Mrs Clark shrugged. 'Even now. I'm of an age where it's better not to delay things much further, if you know what I mean. We could get a coffee at one of the tables to start with.'

Mia looked at her mother.

'Go on then,' the mother replied, seeing the doubt in Mia's expression. 'I ran this business for years without you, I'll cope if you are not around for a few hours.'

Mia dried her hands on her apron and followed Mrs Clark to a window table. The old woman had a smile on her face. Mia remembered that smile, it was the same she'd seen many times over when she was a student. She wondered what it would be like being a teacher, seeing young people growing and moving on with their lives and then do the same year after year. There must be some sense of achievement in there. She was determined to make her old teacher proud.

Mia explained to her she needed to know about her financial status and assets in order to make some proposal and pay taxes in an efficient way. 'And I'll need to know who will be the beneficiaries. Do you know what the house is worth? Have you asked for an evaluation?'

'I haven't thought about that. I was thinking of leaving something to my grandchildren. Jonathan now has a great job, and he doesn't really need the money anymore.' The old woman seemed to have an idea. 'I have all the paperwork still at home. Why don't you go there one of next few days? Here are the keys,' the old teacher said, 'I keep all the documents in the large sideboard in the lounge. Feel free to go through it if you need.'

Mia took the keys in her hand and weighed them. 'Sounds good to me. Do you want me to have an estate agent around for an evaluation?'

'Please.'

The old lady left, and Mia sat at the table for a bit longer, looking outside the window. It was nice to do some legal work again, even if it was a favour for her old schoolteacher. 'Mom, do you mind if I take a short break?'

'Not at all, dear. Enjoy.'

She put her coat on and walked around without a destination. The hill behind the town still had snow on it, and the fresh air was reinvigorating. There was no rush, people took their time going around, no honking or screaming at the traffic. What a lovely town. People came here on vacation, but Mia started thinking about living there full time.

'Hey!'

She turned to see who was calling and came face to face with Ethan. He was wearing a lumberjack red-and-black-squared jacked and a beanie. He had three days' worth of stubble that made him look better than usual and a contagious smile stamped on his face.

'Hello, Ethan.'

'Visiting town? I can give you a tour if you like.'

'Just taking some fresh air. Hey, are you busy?' she asked.

'Is that a trick question? I mean, if I say yes then I have to explain why I'm wandering around. If I say no, sure like hell you give me something to do.'

Mia laughed. 'I take it you're not busy then. I was wondering if you could drive me to Rockport? I'd like to visit Mrs Clark's house.'

Ethan nodded. 'She moved, you know? She lives here in town now.'

'I know, I met her few minutes ago, she wants me to take care of her will. I was thinking of having another look at the property. It's been ages.'

'I can drive you there, although I doubt she'll need a will. That old wren will still be around when you and I are in retirement age.' Ethan turned in the opposite direction and, without waiting, he said, 'Follow me, I'm parked down there.'

Mrs Clark's house was a few miles from the centre of Camden, and if it were summer, Mia could have easily walked there, but the forecast was for heavy rain later in the afternoon and the lift by car came in handy. Ethan's pickup was somewhat newer than Mia's father's but still could almost be considered 'vintage'.

He parked in front of the old Post and Beam two-storey house. The front was deceivingly small, but Mia knew that the building was on a slope, and on the other side there was also a full walk-in cellar. It had a red shingled roof and was a typical Cape Cod style property, two windows on each side of the door and two dorm windows.

'It could do with a lick of paint.' The seaside weather had removed most of the colour from the front, and in places the bare wood was visible.

'And some gardening, too,' Ethan added. Overgrown bushes surrounded the orchard. 'Pretty much the whole five acres. The roof is in good condition at least.' He pointed at the red shingles with a smug grin on his face.

'It has five acres? I remember picking apples, peaches, and cherries. I always thought the garden was huge, but you know how it is. Growing up you find disappointment in what you thought was something exceptional when you were a kid.'

'Are you disappointed?' Ethan asked.

'No, not at all. Actually, I find it even more beautiful than I remembered, even if it needs attention. Shall we?' She opened the front door. Inside, most of the furniture Mia remembered was gone and only few pieces remained. There was a beautiful oak floor, posts, and beams were clearly visible and in good order.

Their steps resonated in the empty space.

'What are we looking for here?' Ethan asked.

'I need to get a feeling for the place, and Mrs Clark said I could get her files for a will.' Mia approached the old sideboard and opened it. Neatly arranged were several folders. She flicked through some of them and, satisfied, she put them on the floor. 'I didn't manage yet to go to the art gallery and check out your paintings, but I plan to do it as soon as possible, maybe this weekend.'

Ethan sat on the floor, without prying into the files, and added, 'We can do better than that. If you want, I can show you some of the things I have at home.'

'I'd love that. When do you think we could do it? I couldn't see much through the gallery window, but they looked lovely.'

'When you've finished here, if you like.'

Mia made a pile of the various folders and picked it up. 'Let's do it now. I can examine the documents later when I'm home.'

She placed the folders in the car and closed the door behind her. She didn't know it yet but she'd set foot many times in that property in the future.

CHAPTER 40

'Mom and Dad moved to Florida,' Ethan said, parking on the driveway just off the High Street.

Mia detected a tone of embarrassment in his voice, and she wondered why it was there. The house was immaculately white with green shutters, a New Englander farmhouse built in the nineteenth century, and it was huge. Sure, on the same road there were possibly some of the most beautiful buildings in Camden, but even then, the property could have been on the cover of any country-style magazine. It had been in the family forever, from what she knew, passing from generation to generation. Now it was Ethan's turn.

'I cannot believe they moved. They so much belonged here,' Mia said.

'I know, but Mom had knee problems, and the humidity didn't help, especially in winter.'

Her thoughts went to their childhood. The game of hide and seek in a house that had four bedrooms, nine rooms in total, and more hiding places anyone could find in any reasonable amount of time. She remembered that house was in constant maintenance, all the wood to repaint, the timber and flooring needing regular attention. Not a path too dissimilar to the one chosen by Mia's parents. Most likely a money-pit in maintenance.

They didn't enter via the main entrance and instead went in through the orangery on the side, overlooking the garage.

'Wow, this is a change,' she said.

The sofas, the armchair, and an old chest that had being there forever had gone, and instead the space was full of paintings and equipment, brushes on a table, tubes of colours, palettes. Ethan had expanded his painting activity into the adjacent room, from what she could see.

'This is the room with the best light, you know, with all the windows, it's ideal.'

Mia wandered around as if she was in an art gallery. There were different styles, some more old-fashioned countryside paintings, some still life, and others completely abstract. She tried to understand if there was a path she could follow, from an older style to the next, but she failed. Most of the painting seemed recent.

'When did your parents move to Florida?' she asked.

'It's been three years now. I rented a flat by the marina, which was also a workshop for a while, but then as soon as they went, I moved here. I love this place, lots of memories.'

'I have lots of memories, too.' Mia stared at the emptiness in front of her.

'Hey, do you want a glass of wine?'

'I'd love one.'

'I'll be back in a minute.'

She looked at him walking in the direction of where, she remembered, the kitchen was. She flicked through a set of canvasses that rested against the wall and then moved on into the next room. Here there was a large table with many paintings on paper. She recalled how Ethan used to buy, years before, cheap white wrapping paper from the local store, cut it in sizes of one meter by one and paint on it. 'Cheaper than buying a canvas,' he used to say. There were hundreds of foils, one over the other. She came across a portrait of herself, made with a sanguine pencil. It was only a sketch, but then she noticed other portraits of her, more detailed. Some were stunningly good. In another section of the room there were sponges, canvasses on easels covered by old dustsheets, and rolled sheets of plastic foils.

'Those are experiments, not sure I'm ready to show them yet,' Ethan said from behind.

Mia winced, as if caught doing something naughty. 'Sorry, I hadn't meant to pry.'

He passed the glass of wine to her and slowly walked towards the lounge. He sat on a small armchair near the fireplace, and she sat on the large sofa in front of him. The room had less furniture than when his parents had been around, the two white bookcases were also not so crammed. Only a few books, elegantly placed and some ceramic vases. She recognised a couple of those as hers.

'Gewürztraminer?' she said as soon as she tasted the wine.

'My guilty pleasure. With wines, I like to wander freely, although eventually I'm drawn back to the Traminers. You can visit the world from your dining table in this way.'

'Exactly what I think!' she replied, with the same enthusiastic emphasis that was only visible among people who shared the same passion, 'and this is a decent wine. May I see the label?'

'Never judge a book by the cover, a man from his shoes and a wine from the label,' Ethan pronounced.

'What?'

'Never mind, I just made that up.' He passed the bottle to his guest.

'Domaine Weinbach. Never came across this one, I'd have to make a note.' She then decided to test the waters. 'Have you ever tried the Sciacchetrà from the Cinque Terre in Italy?'

'I have indeed and I love it. Although it's quite rare to get here. But as we're talking about Italy, I got a bottle of Ortrugo.'

Mia thought hard and searched in her memory.

'Do you have any problem in mixing wines?'

'Nah. The only problem I have is when people mix wines with water.'

She watched her host leave again and walk towards the kitchen. Her thoughts went immediately to the friends she'd left in New York, their common love for wines. She'd never really stopped and thought about the most recent events in her life. That evening Ethan was making her feel less lonely.

He came back a few minutes later. On the tray there were crackers, some cheese and ham.

'Wow, I'm being pampered,' she said.

'I'm going to have my share, don't worry. Here is the Ortrugo.' He poured the wine in Mia's now-empty glass. 'Very inexpensive compared to other wines. It's made in the hills around Piacenza. I think I became a geography expert. Old Mrs Clark would be proud of my results.'

They both laughed, but Mia knew exactly what he was talking about. She spent hours looking at regions where good wines were produced, what grapes they used, what made them unique.

'So, what's the verdict?'

'I could have it any day of the week.'

They sat in silence for a minute or two, tasting the wine and nibbling from the tray.

'You've changed,' Mia said.

'Maybe. Perhaps some things are different for me, but I don't think I changed my values or who I am. I'm still the same Ethan I was back then. I only have a bit more experience.'

She nodded. Her thoughts went to the paintings she just seen. 'I like your painting, but what I haven't understood is where you're going with them. They're so different one from the other.'

'Depends on the mood I'm in. I never really focused on a style although I think my painting is evolving somehow.'

'Much better than the rubbish my father used to do.' She waved the empty glass at Ethan.

He grabbed the Traminer's bottle and filled it. 'I'd not be so hard on him, after all, he's the one who taught me, remember?'

'Yeah, an *apprentice that surpasses the master* situation. It must have taken you a whole week…'

Ethan laughed. 'You should cut Gregg some slack.'

'You're probably right. I've been too busy being a rebellious teenager to really pay attention to what he was saying, but you did,' Mia reflected. 'You're very fond of him.'

'Best buddies, despite the age gap.' Ethan stood from his armchair and took the tray. 'I need more crackers.'

'I need more cheese,' Mia retorted.

'Shall we stick to Italy with a Sassicaia, or may I tempt you with a trip to France in the Bandol region?'

'You're taking advantage of me, that is a low blow. Bandol, please.'

'Back in a minute.'

When he returned, he opened the bottle and put the cork on the small table, right in front of Mia. She laughed and threw it in the fireplace. 'You're not getting me that easily.'

'I see.' Nathan poured the wine from the new bottle and passed over the glass.

'A friend of mine suggested to me that I open a wine bar here in Camden, now that I've got a big payoff and I can't practice in New York anymore. Fancy doing a fifty-fifty venture?'

'We would go bankrupt within a month and end up in a rehab centre.'

Mia nodded and spread some cheese on a cracker. With her mouth still half full, she said, 'I'm tipsy. Let's stick to art. I might want to buy one of your paintings but I need to have a good look at them. How much do they go for?'

'Depends. A thousand in a gallery, when they sell. Which they don't. Definitely not in Kowalski's range.'

'Do you like Kowalski? He's my personal hero.'

'Love the guy, yes. Although I tend to prefer the previous works. He's been around for what, over twenty years now? The first ones were masterpieces, but lately his work is a bit different.'

Mia sat forward. 'I disagree. Of all, I found it more specific, better focused.'

They kept talking and sipping wine. Outside, the sea wind was blowing, and a light shower of rain wet the roads. Two hours later, when Ethan took the empty bottles to the kitchen, Mia was dozing off on the sofa.

'Shall I take you into one of the spare rooms?"

'Hmmm…' she managed to mumble, but she couldn't speak a word.

He placed a pillow under her head and covered her with a warm duvet.

He kissed her on the cheek and softly said, 'Welcome back, Mia.'

'I love Mondays, especially if they start like this,' she muttered to herself.

CHAPTER 41

The corner table by the window at the Crawford's bakery and café had become Mia's semi-permanent office. That morning, she had a meeting scheduled with Mrs Clark.

Her mother was the supreme architect of Mia's start-up business. Whilst working in the bakery, she had spread the word to every single customer who entered the shop, and Mia had to quickly come up with what could be considered reasonable fees for Camden. A nod from her mother meant regular price, a wink implied a discount for those who couldn't afford the full price. Something far, far below what she could have charged in New York.

'May I get you anything else, my dear?' Mia's mother asked, approaching the table.

'A coffee would be nice, thank you, Mom. So, Mrs Clark, here is your will. I put all the documents back in the house.'

The old woman flicked through the pages, nodding her approval once in a while.

'There is a thing I'd like to mention before you sign, though. I understood you'd like to leave the house for your great-grandchildren to cover their university fees, but that property needs some attention. The weather here is inclement in the winter, and the more the time passes, the more the property status will deteriorate.'

'I'm not selling! And then even if I put the money aside, bankers are crooks. I don't trust them as far as I can throw them, and at my age, I couldn't even lift one.'

'I know, I didn't mean that, but have you considered other options? For example, renting the house. A tenant would look after the garden, you could agree on maintenance of the property. You said your family doesn't need the money now, but they will have to spend something to keep the estate up to order. The agent said you could get a rent of almost two thousand dollars.'

The old teacher pondered Mia's words.

'My son is close to retirement and will pass the fishing business to his sons. So far, I've managed to keep the house, but if the expenses will increase I'd need to ask for money from them. I can't do that. What if I need to sell the place in a hurry?'

Mia nodded.

'Why don't you live there?' Mrs Clark asked.

'Sorry, I don't understand.'

'You live there. You're a grown woman now; you can't stay with your parents forever. You might want to have a family of your own. Yes, you could live there and take care of the property, for as long as you want, or until these old bones decide it's time for me to go and pay a visit with my deceased husband.'

Mia passed a hand through her hair and sank back in her chair. 'I cannot possibly do that, Mrs Clark!'

'Of course you can. I'm telling you something. Several years back, my son lost his boat. I was still living in the property, and half of the roof collapsed. I had to make a decision: either help my son in getting a new boat or have the roof repaired. My grandsons were still teenagers, his income was the only one in the family. You can guess what I did. I used my savings to help him out, but that left me bone dry. I didn't have a penny for repairs. Your father and young Ethan did all the job for free; they didn't even ask me to pay for the materials. "That is what good neighbours do," he said. Trust me when I say you could live there as long as you want. I wouldn't have that property anymore if it wasn't for your father.'

Mia fell silent for a spell. She did a mental calculation on what repairing a roof cost. Typical of Gregg. She was also reminded of Ethan's comment about the roof; he knew and he hadn't said anything. She enjoyed being at her parents' but she was aware she was lingering there exactly because it was a temporary solution. She could find a job in Chicago, or in whatever state had reciprocity with the New York Bar. Renting wasn't as strong as settling but still involved buying furniture, having bills. *Do I really want to go to Chicago or Los Angeles?*

'I couldn't do that, but I could pay you rent, at market value, if that's okay for you.' It was a snap decision. Recently, she had made a few.

'Nonsense, I owe your family a lot.'

'Mrs Clark, that is something between you and Gregg, and what concerns me... I'll tell you why I can't accept. You're my first customer here. I prepared a will for you, and what do I get in return? Free rental of your property? How would it make me look?'

The old teacher nodded, pondering what to say next. 'You are a Crawford, no doubt there. Very well, if you're interested in renting the property, I'll leave it to you. You can pay what you think is fair.'

And there she was, renting a house in Camden after she'd spent a lifetime trying to get away from the place. 'I'll prepare the paperwork this afternoon for your review.'

Mrs Clark stood from her seat. 'Don't forget to send me the bill or I'll have to have a word with your mother. Oh, Rodney Brown is in need of a probate, and I took the liberty of passing him your number. He'll call you today or tomorrow at the latest.'

'Thank you, Mrs Clark.'

On a stool in front of the coffee machine, Mia's next client was waiting.

A week later, she'd paid the deposit, got Mrs Clark house keys, and sorted out the paperwork for what she had in mind. She picked up her phone and dialled a number. Ethan answered at the third ring.

'Hey, are you busy?' she asked.

'Is that a trick question?'

'Not at all, and you'll be handsomely rewarded for your time with rivers of quality wines.'

315

'I see, an offer I can't refuse. Give me one hour. Where are you now?' Ethan asked.

'At the shop.'

'See you there.'

She placed the phone in her jeans pocket. The weather was turning good, and the sun was shining through the bakery's window. Maine in spring was worth a visit. The clear sky, the blossom, people buzzing around. The ideal weather for a Saturday shopping spree.

Ethan arrived one hour later, as promised, parked in front of the bakery, and honked twice. Mia picked up the case of bottles she'd ordered a few days before and loaded them on the back of the truck.

She kissed him on the cheek when she entered the truck. His stubble lightly scratched her lips. He smelled nice.

'So, where are we going?'

'I need a guide. I've rented Mrs Clark's house and I'm in need of some basic furniture. And a fridge. And a sofa. And a new mattress and bedding.'

'And a lawn mower, from what I saw last time.'

'That one as well, but I can borrow it. By the way, are you free next Saturday?'

'Is that a trick question?'

They both laughed.

'Indeed it is,' Mia said.

'Hang on, if you rented the house it means you'll stick around for a while, right?'

Mia nodded and looked out of the windscreen. The main road was getting busy. A couple of white clouds were lingering in what was otherwise a bright-blue sky. 'I think so. I might not make millions but also I doubt I'll collapse due to too much work. A fair trade if you ask me.'

'Right. Just browsing or are you planning to buy? I was thinking that maybe we should get Gregg's van.'

'No plans and no hurry, that's my new philosophy. If we fill your pickup we call it a day and have the rest delivered. That makes me think I'll need a car, too. Secondhand.'

'I know of a place.' Ethan turned on the engine.

A few hours later, they had a mattress and a sofa. The fridge was going to be delivered the same day, after a lengthy negotiation. They stopped for a seafood lunch in Rockland, Ethan's recommendation, and despite the rustic appearance from the outside, the food proved to be delicious. Mia settled for a lobster claw roll and Ethan for a plate of calamari. He gave a rough update on what was going on in Camden, and Mia carefully avoided talking about her old job in New York. She did mention, though, a few of the schemes Ginger had set up throughout her career.

'A post-atomic food blog?' Ethan asked with disbelief painted on his face.

'Indeed, and then she sold the website. That was one of the legal ones. She came up with all sorts of recipes for preppers, all done using canned food. I

317

never dared to try one, nor did she from what I know, but they sounded reasonable. I can't tell you about the illegal ones I had to put a stop to because I'd breach client-attorney privilege, but some of those were strokes of genius. She could have made serious money before ending up in a penitentiary.'

'And now she's a celebrity fashion blogger?'

'Indeed. What do you reckon, shall we ask for the bill? I have a car to buy. Any suggestions, by the way?'

'Nothing too flashy, no Audis or things like that. You'll need a four-by-four, maybe a Rav4 or a Subaru. They won't guzzle gas and will be in line with your new friendly, economic law firm.'

'Ahaha! Okay, I'll follow your lead. I have a question for you. Do you think that kiln my father built could be moved? I'm sort of in the mood to start doing ceramics again.'

Ethan pondered the question. He scratched his stubble. 'It's huge. Of course, we could dismantle it and rebuild it using the same bricks, but maybe Gregg can call in a couple of favours and we could move it as a whole. Leave it with me.'

'Cool. Hey, we will need to stop and get some seafood, cheese, and crackers on the way back. We need solid food for the wine-tasting session I have in mind for this evening. I mean proper food, not that bunch of scraps you put together last time.'

'Oh, I see. Yeah, seafood will work well with those vinegar bottles you placed in the back, which you insist on calling wine.'

'Food. Drive. Silence. In reverse order,' Mia said.
'I know my place.'
Of course you do.

CHAPTER 42

'You got it?'

'Yep! Keep it sliding,' Ethan said.

The sofa wasn't extremely heavy, but nonetheless, heat mounted under Mia's clothes. They'd done the same with the mattress a few minutes beforehand. Holding, sliding, bouncing against a wall, and then pushing it up the stairs. Thank God Mrs Clark left a bed frame behind.

'New York made you weak,' Ethan stated, seeing her struggle.

'Wait until I take you to court for bullying in the workplace and you'll see who's the weak one.'

'I have the judge in my pocket. They don't like newcomers here.'

She huffed and puffed. 'Mind the doorframe, or I add property damages to my claim.'

'I sort of preferred you when you were in New York. Are you always this bossy? You used to be a lovely girl back in the day.'

'Always been ruthless. You just didn't notice in the past because you were wearing rose-coloured glasses.'

They managed to squeeze the sofa through the doorframe and placed it in the centre of the room. Mia looked around to get her bearings and then dragged the sofa farther towards the fireplace. Ethan unloaded the wine and the bedding, and on the next trip out she followed him. There was a wardrobe to assemble. How they'd managed to get all that stuff on the back of the pickup still baffled her. But there she was—she had some basic furniture, and utility bills had been redirected so she was ready to move in. It'd be spartan at the beginning, no frills. Her mind was already set. She'd stay in Camden, but there was no point in splashing too much cash from her payout until the lawyer work picked up. That would take time, she knew that.

In a moment of panic, she went into the kitchen and rummaged through the drawers. Good Mrs Clark was old-fashioned—she'd left cutlery, pans, and the basics, corkscrew included. Mia also found some matches, which she put in her pocket. The chimney and the stairs to the upper floor were in the centre of the building, and actually divided the ground floor into four main spaces. Was it better lighting up the fireplace or the stove in the kitchen? The stove was less romantic but would carry the heat for longer, so she retraced her steps back to the kitchen. It was easy enough, a couple of fire starters and some kindling; once again, her thoughts went to Mrs Clark who had left some coal around. She went to the lounge and turned on the electric heating as well. She thought she was back in the fifties for a moment, and she smiled.

A knock on the door announced the arrival of her brand-new fridge. Ethan opened the door. There was a stocky guy who could have been a linebacker. Maybe he was. The second delivery man was thinner than a corn harvest in January; he seemed tired. The linebacker examined the entrance, evaluating spaces, making mental calculations and nodding. Then he looked at the half-empty house.

'Newlywed?' he asked.

Ethan froze. Mia noticed it and decided it was a good moment to tease him.

'Can you believe it, guys? We got the house today, and what does he do? Instead of carrying me over the threshold like any decent man in this country would do, he asked me to help him move furniture in.'

The linebacker glanced at Ethan, but it was evident what he was thinking was: *Good luck, my friend.*

'Okey dokey, we unload and then we need a signature. Leave the fridge unplugged for twenty-four hours.'

'Twenty-four hours?' Mia asked. 'Ethan, are we going to drink *warm* champagne on our first night in?'

The two delivery men got their paperwork signed and run like hell from the place. They had a story to tell their friends that evening.

'Thanks for that,' he said.

'My pleasure.'

'I'm sure it was. Come on, there's a wardrobe to assemble.'

Two hours later, they were both downstairs crashing on the sofa.

'Thanks, Ethan, I really appreciate you slaving away to give me a hand.'

'I thought I was getting paid with wine and a dinner worth a Michelin star.'

'You will.'

He turned towards her. 'I'm glad you're back.'

'Still trying to find my bearings, but I'm pleased to be here,' and then, after a moment of silence, she added, 'and I'm glad you're also around.'

Throughout her life, Mia had planned everything. She liked things that way, trying to overcome difficulties by breaking a big problem into small, manageable pieces. It was her way to protect herself, to analyse things, approach a task from many different angles until she was sure she could achieve her goals. Now she didn't have a plan. She didn't have one when she accepted a lump sum to leave New York and never come back as a lawyer. She didn't have a plan when she'd rented that very house.

She didn't have a plan when she got closer to Ethan and kissed him on the lips.

He kissed her back. His hand caressed her cheek, and his fingers got lost in her soft, dark hair.

Mia brushed off a rush of memories that came to her mind; she didn't regret going to Harvard, she only regretted letting her ambition get in the way, between her and Ethan. She knew that moment that he'd never let her go and, in the depths of her heart, she knew she hadn't let him go either. Sure, she'd had other boyfriends, she'd almost got married, but what she felt for them was only the pale shadow of what, now she was more aware of it, she had felt for Ethan.

They sat on the sofa, kissing, playing with each other's hands in silence. Each one of them didn't dare to speak, fearing to break the spell, until the darkness came. What a journey—she was lost but she'd found her way home, eventually. Nothing else mattered, not her career, not her ambition. She'd be okay now that Ethan was by her side again.

'Someone promised me a wine-tasting session,' he whispered.

'Right, I better getting cracking.' Then she looked around and laughed.

'What's up?'

'No table, nor chairs.'

'Are you free tomorrow?' Ethan asked.

'Is that a trick question?'

They both burst out laughing.

'No, it's not. I have some spares in the barn, we could fetch them tomorrow. They are a bit rustic, though.'

'Rustic is the new glass and steel. I'm sure they'll be perfect.'

'Then it's a deal,' he said and stood. 'Come on, let me help you with that food. You city girls don't have a clue on how to cook *properly* on a stove.'

'Camden, Maine. When the police arrived at the scene for what appeared as a family dispute, they found instead the body of Ethan Miller lying on the floor. After a preliminary examination, the coroner declared him deceased. The murder weapon was a bottle of Amarone della Valpolicella, 2015.'

'A bit drastic, don't you think?'

'Maybe, yes. A bottle of Frascati would take you to the floor in the same way.'

'You won't need to hit me in that case, just let me drink it; it would have the same results,' Ethan said. 'Okay, back to work now.'

They kept bantering for the rest of the evening, sipping wine and nibbling. That night, they made love as if it was the first time.

CHAPTER 43

Carlton Allerton threw the newspaper against the
wall.

The storm began when a fashion magazine
wrote an article about the acquisition of King
General. *A bloody fashion magazine!*

Carlton had to ask his secretary to buy a copy.
The article was divided into sections. The first one
was a reportage of the acquisition—it showed leaked
documents belonging to King General and some of
their accounting practices. Transactions had been
artificially inflated, and Allerton Groceries skipped
due diligence during an acquisition that should
never have taken place.

In the second section there was an interview
with Bill Ross, former legal counsel for Allerton
Groceries and recently fired by Carlton Allerton,
CEO.

Ross went into lengthy detail on why he was
contrary to the acquisition, and he had shown,
according to the interviewer, "plenty of documents"
proving so. "Carlton Allerton is a controlling and
demanding individual", Ross stated, "and he clearly
knew what he was doing. He repeatedly ignored our
counsel and, when push came to shove, he illegally
fired me for speaking my mind on what, in my
opinion, was by far the dumbest acquisition in the
history of Allerton Groceries."

Ross went on talking about his legal proceeding against Allerton Groceries for gross misconduct when they pushed him out of the door after decades of service.

The nail in the coffin was the third section of the twelve-page article: a crude profile of Carlton Allerton, his celebrity status, and the countless relationships with models and starlets, culminating with a restraining order preventing him to contact, directly or indirectly, the rising model Amanda Parker. The magazine even put pictures of him, tagging each item of clothing with a price sticker, the expensive watches collection, the cost of his Rolls-Royce and his apartment in Manhattan. "When people struggle to make ends meet and sometimes they have no option other than to turn to Allerton Groceries, you can bet Mr Carlton Allerton paid full price for his expensive lifestyle. No fifty percent discount for him, that's for sure."

After that, the stock price lost twelve percent of its value in a single day. The following days, the stock didn't recover, and the major newspapers in the city smelled blood. TV channels interviewed Paula Schellenberger, who was now one of the most sought-after persons in the evening news. Everybody was baffled about the change of direction taken by *Style Magazine*, under the firm hand of Keeley Williams.

The real damage came when the financial newspapers started digging and sinking their teeth into Allerton's. Then came the news that the

Securities and Exchange Commission decided to open an investigation. That sank the stock price another ten percent, and the board of directors pressed for a statement to deny any potential write-off of the merger.

The intercom buzzed, and Carlton's secretary announced, 'Mr Allerton is here…' She couldn't complete the sentence when Jason Allerton, his grandfather, stormed in the room, with a murderous expression. His cheeks were a burgundy red.

'YOU BLOODY IDIOT,' he shouted, slamming the newspaper on Carlton's desk.

It was nothing new to him, the old man had only two expression in his repertoire, angry and angrier.

'What are you doing here?' Carlton asked. 'I think I made it clear that you…'

'I regained the majority. Even you might have noticed that our shares are worth nothing. People won't touch them with a barge pole, which means buying back my own company became easier than I thought possible.'

'You don't have the capital to do that, even if you sell all your assets; may I remind you…'

'Oh, but here is where you're mistaken, boy. Jason Allerton's name still counts for something. I got some backing from people who owe me favours. Of course, I had to promise a radical change of direction, starting with a new CEO. The board of directors agrees. You can either resign now or be fired later this afternoon. The company will not defend your actions in court, and I'll personally make sure we will claim any losses towards any asset you possess.'

Carlton was in an indefensible position. 'Grandpa, I…'

'Don't Grandpa me, you had your shot and you messed up. Most of all, you never listen, so listen to me now. Get out of that door straight away before you do more damage to this company, and I promise I will not hand over to the newspapers what I know about you. Thank God I have another granddaughter and my legacy will not end up with you.'

Carlton glanced at the laptop opened on his desk. *Company asset.* He looked at his office for the last time and then mumbled a 'very well.' He stood and walked out. Two security officers were waiting to escort him out of the building. *Bloody Mondays.* He'd come to hate them.

CHAPTER 44

Not too far away, in the editorial room of *Style Magazine*, a celebration was underway. Instead of notepads and laptops, the large table was covered with glasses and bottles of champagne.

'I wanted to congratulate...' Keeley tried to say, but the buzz was too loud.

People were standing and chatting, patting each other on the shoulders. *Ding, ding, ding.* Keeley resorted to bashing her pen against an empty bottle of champagne until order was reestablished. 'I wanted to congratulate the whole team for a job well done, you are superstars. The owner has also asked me to pass his personal congratulations to Paula for writing an article that will leave its mark for years to come in the history of *Style Magazine*.'

The room burst into a spontaneous round of applause. Paula nodded slightly as a gesture of appreciation.

When the clapping faded, Keeley resumed her speech. 'Today this magazine is a force to be reckoned with in the editorial space. There is no limit to what we can achieve if we keep working at this standard. Every newspaper in the city—scrap that, in the whole country—are talking about us. We have beaten financial analysts, investigative newspapers, financial papers that were supposed to come up with this kind of news in the first place. All this is because of you.'

More applause.

'For today we celebrate, tomorrow, business as usual.' She raised her glass and shouted, '*STYLE MAGAZINE!*'

The crowd cheered in return.

Paula Schellenberger and Madison Turner approached Keeley.

The senior journalist was the first to speak. 'We've got an idea.'

'Fire away.' Keeley understood long ago that when Paula wanted to run something, the best course of action was to give her head and let her do her magic. Recognising talent and giving them free rein, that was Keeley's strength.

'Magdalene O'Sullivan.'

'What about her?'

'She is becoming the hottest thing in town, raised from being a nobody to stardom in a few months. She has some cool, fresh ideas, and both Madison and I followed her blog for a while. There is raw talent there, and we thought we could give her a regular column on the Magazine.'

'After all, we discovered her,' Madison pressed.

Keeley looked the two editors in the eyes, first one, then the other. 'Make it happen!' She wasn't *exactly* sure what they had in mind, but there was no doubt that if someone could pull a trick like that, it would be Paula.

The two editors nodded and went back to celebrating the day.

Madison's idea, but she didn't dare bring it forward by herself so she sought Paula's opinion. I have to let those two work together more often.

Keeley returned to her office to find Amanda waiting for her.

'Hey, you look stunning today,' Keeley said, kissing her on the lips. 'I love the floral-patterned Valentino, by the way.'

Keeley's heart skipped a beat every time she saw her. She gently caressed Amanda's arm.

'I wore it for you, I thought you might appreciate.'

'By the way, what are you doing here? You don't do Mondays.'

'I've come to love Mondays,' Amanda replied.

'Since when?'

'Since when it marks the beginning of a brand-new week with you.' Amanda slowly walked to the sofa and sat.

Keeley followed.

Amanda took a small box out of her bag and opened it. Inside, there was a stunning diamond ring. 'I'd like to propose to you, Keeley. You're everything I always desired in life, and I want to grow old with you. I have no doubts. Will you marry me?'

Keeley put a hand on her mouth and started crying. She didn't remember the last time she'd cried in front of someone. 'Yes! Yes, I do want to marry you!'

Amanda took the ring from the box and gently placed it on her companion's finger.

They kissed.

CHAPTER 45

Mia had a house.

And a boyfriend.

And a job that was paying the bills and fulfilled her.

What scared her most when she was in her teens was to end up living like she was doing now, an ordinary life, as an ordinary person in an ordinary town, and guess what? She was happy. How much money did she *really* need? That was one of the recurring questions coming out of Kowalski's work, and she came up eventually with an answer. Not much.

People came to appreciate her work as a lawyer, although someone still insisted on calling her *Gregg's daughter*, or the *little Crawford*. She was good at what she did and charged reasonable prices. Would she travel the world? Most likely not, or at least, not in a single trip. She wouldn't have had time to travel the world in her previous job anyway, too busy slaving away, paying outrageous rents in New York and having zero time for herself. New York was the place of postponement. Eventually, she would have been rich. Eventually, she would have travelled the world. Eventually, she would have found love. But everything was in the future in New York. No time for the present.

In Camden she had time. Time to work, time to connect with people, time to live her life with her wonderful boyfriend. She had also coined a brand-new word to describe her life with Ethan: *wonderfun*.

She had reconnected with old friends and she made new ones. Working was no longer the only goal in her life, she didn't have anything to prove anymore. Being in Camden was her choice—a choice, she knew, she wasn't going to regret. She had felt some guilt towards how she'd behaved with her dad when she was a teen, but Gregg brushed away her attempt to say she was sorry. 'Nonsense,' he'd said, 'you just needed to find your own path.'

And a path she'd found indeed: being part of a community. She didn't regret anything. The only thing she missed were her friends back in New York. Xander, Jennifer, and Ginger.

She followed Ginger's blog and Instagram account. Who knew? Also, who could have known that Xander would eventually have a break? She called them regularly and invited them for a visit during peak season; she wanted to introduce them to Ethan. It didn't really matter if they were living in New York, there were other ways to still get in touch.

She could say that pretty much everything was perfect. Except that it wasn't.

It was Ethan who spotted the clouds on Mia's face that evening, when she returned from work. Her house now had furniture, and he had a key. They alternated days and weekends between her place and the larger house Ethan owned.

'What's the issue?' he asked her, pouring a glass of red. A good one, given her thunderous expression.

'Nothing. Work stuff.'

'Come on, I've never seen you like this. Something is definitely bothering you,' he pressed.

Mia sipped her red wine and sat on the armchair in the lounge. She removed her shoes. 'It's about the Libbys. They're going to lose their house. The bank repossessed it, and it's going to be auctioned.'

'Damn!'

They both knew the Libbys. A family that had been around for ages. They ran a tour in the countryside near town and they also operated excursions off the coast in their boat. It was a seasonal business, but it generated enough to make a living out of it.

Mia explained about Meghan Libby, how she had a terminal illness. The insurance initially paid for the medical bills but eventually stopped when the Libbys reached the insurance cap. From then on, they used their savings, they skipped mortgage payments to cover for medical expenses, and ignored the warning letters from the bank.

'They lost it,' Mia said, 'as if everything else in their lives didn't matter anymore. They were so absorbed in working towards finding a cure, spending on specialists and hospital bills, that when

they realised they were in deep trouble it was far too
late.'

'Isn't there something you could do?'

'That's the annoying part. I could have helped if
they only came to me much earlier. But you know
how these things work, you ask a lawyer only when
you're deep in it, up to your neck. I'm not sure if I
could do anything.'

'What are they going to do now?'

'They moved onto the boat. Damn, you should
have seen them. They were crammed in that small
boat; thank God it's good weather. But the auction is
next week. Not good.'

'What's going to happen?' Ethan asked.

'It's an auction. The bank will sell the house to
the highest bidder. They'll collect what's owed to
them, and the rest of the money, if something is left,
will go to the Libbys. Who in the meanwhile are
living on credit cards and borrowing, so when they
clear their debts they'll be left with nothing.'

'Damn!' Ethan said again. He scratched his
stubble and went quiet for a moment. 'I've got an
idea. Sorry, but I have to leave for a few hours. I'll
meet you here at one AM. Don't fall asleep.'

'At one AM? Why?'

'Because we're going to do something illegal,
and illegal stuff is better carried out in the dark.' He
had a grin on his face.

'Hang on...'

Mia couldn't finish her sentence. He kissed her
on the lips and stormed out of the house. Her head

was spinning. Something illegal? Would he burn the Libby's house? No, that was plain stupid, the insurance would never pay, and Ethan was *definitely* not an arsonist. If they were in the Appalachians, maybe he'd run a batch of moonshine, but how much moonshine would you need to pay off the bank? A rough estimate placed it in the *boatload* ballpark. She couldn't imagine what Ethan had in mind. She was a lawyer; she wouldn't allow him to do anything stupid.

At one o'clock, she was fully asleep and didn't hear him coming in. He gently tapped her on the shoulder.

'It's you! I thought I was going to be kidnapped by a ninja,' she said, looking at his black overalls.

'Very funny. Come on, we got to go.'

Mia stood and scratched her eyes. 'Ethan, we cannot possibly...'

'Shh. Follow me. The faster the better. And no questions. Not yet. I'll explain later.'

They drove in silence until they reached the Libby's property. It was outside the town limits on the outskirts and fairly isolated from the neighbourhood. Ethan climbed down from the pickup and retrieved several white tubes and a large bag from the back of the truck. Mia recognised them; she'd seen them in his house previously. The door was slightly open. There was an echo when they entered the room, and their steps resonated in the empty space.

'Breaking and entering,' Mia said in a muffled voice. 'Minor misdemeanour, carries a one-year sentence which could be lifted as we both don't have previous convictions, and a fine. I can kiss goodbye to my career as a lawyer.'

'We are not breaking anything,' a voice said behind her.

Mia jumped in surprise. 'Dad? What are you doing here? And *breaking* is just a saying. The sole act of pushing the door constitutes breaking.'

'I told you she was a fine lawyer.' The smirk on Gregg's face was barely visible in the dark.

Ethan chuckled.

'Okay, maybe we could work on having the charges changed to criminal trespassing. Still trouble, if you ask me.'

Ethan removed some huge stencils from the long tubes he'd brought in from the car. He then started lining up spray cans of colours.

'What are you doing?' she asked.

No answer.

Ethan and Gregg worked as one, pushing the stencils on the wall and adding Sellotape to keep them in place.

'You'll need one of these,' Gregg said, passing a mask and goggles. 'It's going to stink.'

They sprayed on the stencils and, by the aid of the moonlight that was filtering through the window, Mia finally realised what was going on. A Kowalski was being painted on the wall in front of her eyes. Ethan removed the stencil and carefully placed it back in one of the tubes. Then they worked on the next wall, and the next.

It took thirty minutes, but when the two men had finished, Mia found herself in what looked like a Kowalski exhibition.

'You… you are Kowalski?' she asked Ethan. Her voice and her legs were trembling by the revelation.

'He is,' Ethan said, pointing at Gregg. 'I'm only taking over the business.'

'You're too modest, kiddo, it has been what, four years now?'

'Something like that.'

'Come on, take some pictures and let's get the hell out of here before the sheriff turns up.'

Mia couldn't believe what was happening. The street artist she'd admired her entire life was… her dad. And her boyfriend, too. She recalled all the artwork she remembered, the feeling she had in numerous occasions that Kowalski was speaking— strike that, painting for her—to pass a message to her personally. She'd always dismissed that idea. Of course, Kowalski was not sending her messages via his artwork, but now she realised that was exactly the case. Her dad and Ethan *were* sending her messages. Their paintings had a larger audience, they were the moral compass for many people, not only for her. But some of the minor work, those people struggled to understand, resonated immensely with her.

'Do you think they're going to chop them and sell them piece by piece?' Ethan asked.

'I doubt that. But here we have the best lawyer in town. What do you think, did we increase the property value? Can you ensure some greedy banker doesn't get their dirty hands on those?' Gregg asked, pointing at their work on the wall, 'and the money goes to the Libbys?'

'Leave that with me,' Mia said. Her voice was firm and assertive. When it was the time to make good for one of her clients, nothing would stand in her way.

'Time to get lost,' Ethan said.

They picked up bags and stencils and ran towards the cars.

I'm Kowalski's daughter, and the other Kowalski is my boyfriend, she thought whilst Ethan was driving. She giggled.

'I take you're not upset with me about not telling?'

'Oh, I am, buster, you'll have to fill my cellar with wine before I'll speak to you again.'

'I can do that, as long as you allow me to taste some.'

'Only if you're a good boy,' she teased him. 'Damn! Kowalski is my dad... and you! Did you have a laugh, you and Gregg, that evening when I came back and I kept talking about Kowalski's work? I can't believe I even showed *you* pictures on my mobile.'

Ethan grimaced. 'A bit,' he said. He shrank his shoulders, waiting for a hit on the head, which didn't come.

'Bastards! How much does a Kowalski sells for nowadays?'

'We don't sell many, but anything between a hundred thousand and half a million. I mean, that's not the goal. We make a few paintings, maybe in an area that's depressed, on a wall of a gym that's doing good for the community, it doesn't matter in what city, things like that. They get the spirit and they don't make a profit out of it.'

'I remember that boxing gym in Chicago. They sold the door at auction and renovated the gym.'

'Exactly,' Ethan continued, 'they keep serving their community. Once in a while, we sell one, anonymously. Mrs Clark's roof was paid off with a Kowalski. We do a donation here, a little help there. All over the country.'

'Does my mother know?'

'Of course she does, since the beginning.'

'Stop the car,' Mia said.

'What? We've almost arrived.'

'I said, stop the car!'

Ethan parked on the side of the road. He turned around to look at Mia.

'You know it will be your duty to report to the authorities such act of vandalism,' he teased her.

'Oh, shut up!'

She kissed him. The most passionate kiss she could give.

The pictures posted on Kowalski's website got nationwide resonance, and all the national newspapers reported the news. Several television crews asked to visit the Libby's property, and a deputy sheriff was permanently stationed in front of the house to protect the artwork.

The following Monday, the property sold for one-point-five million, the auction was even televised. The Libby's story was all over the place, and journalists queued for an interview.

'Do you know Kowalski?' they asked. 'How did Kowalski come to know about your situation?' Doctors and hospitals volunteered to take the Libby's case at no expense.

The Libbys were more baffled than the journalists, but when they'd been asked what they'd do with the money, the answer came out spontaneously. 'We'll clear our debts, get another home, and carry on with our lives. What's left will go into the community.'

Mia pushed away the tears in her eyes.

CHAPTER 46

It turned out that moving the kiln was not an option. The monster was a half tube about four meters long, built with two layers of refractory bricks and rendering. Taking it apart meant losing maybe half of the bricks, having to transport everything to Mrs Clark's house and spend ten days rebuilding it.

It was an Anagama kiln, Gregg explained, built on a slope and with a refractory arch. He went to the house and brought back to the barn all the plans and the research he and Ethan had done to build one to specification. Mia couldn't believe the length of effort her father had gone to in order to build it. She'd walked around it, looking at the ventilation holes, had walked into it from the arched opening on the front. She knew what needed to be done—the pottery would go at the back, and depending on the distance from the fire, they'd cook in different ways, the ones at the front affected by the smoke and the ash produced by the fire, the ones at the back receiving a different treatment. She also looked on the internet on how to deal with such a monster. Not an easy task. It could require days and days to cook a set of pots properly, and because it needed a huge quantity of firewood (Ethan had come up with a new imperial measure, *the shitload*), it needed constant attention, day and night.

Realising she couldn't spend ten days of cooking just for one piece of ceramic, Mia prepared a batch of thirty. The first result was disappointing. She kept openings during the day, between a client appointment and the next to ensure she could drive to her parents' and add more wood to the kiln. Her dad took the first night shift, and she would wake up early in the morning.

The second batch was not dissimilar. Lots of work and results that Mia considered mediocre. The major concern was the amount of wood she was burning, despite using reclaimed wood and old dead trees they foraged from the surrounding area.

'It's not worth the effort,' she said a few times to Ethan.

Then, one day whilst driving to the office, she understood.

She was doing pottery, not art. There was no point in replicating what other millions of people were doing, on a small or on a large scale. She knew she had to do something unique. If she had to fire up that monster of a kiln and make it worth the effort, she had to produce *art*.

The wheel was an essential part of her work, but now it wasn't the only one. She started experimenting with sprigging techniques and moulds. The first piece came out after a month, and it was a beautiful, enormous orchid. Mia had to be creative to ensure it didn't collapse, but after a couple of attempts, she achieved what she wanted. The second piece was a big vase. She used a trimming tool to carve beautiful herons and flying cranes on it, geometrical patterns and stylised rivers. She then filled the gaps with other clay in different colours. When everything was dry enough, she removed the excess clay with a spatula, making the vase smooth.

'That's a piece of beauty,' Ethan said.

'Two weeks and two full weekends to do it. This thing is sucking the life out of me, and it's huge,' Mia said without turning her head from the vase.

'Look at it from another perspective. You're giving life to it, you're infusing your time and care into it. Your love and passion are in that piece.'

'It still very time-consuming. It will take me months to have enough pieces to fire the kiln again.'

Ethan shrugged. 'It takes what it takes. Are you in a hurry?'

'Not really, it's just…'

'You have done the quick and fast work. You didn't like it. If you were to write a book, it'd take you months anyway. Don't put anything in the kiln that you're not one hundred percent satisfied with. If it takes one year, so be it.'

Mia dropped the spatula and caressed the large vase. It was perfectly smooth; the tips of her fingers couldn't find any imperfection. She liked what she'd done, it was a good piece.

'Take me out for dinner, will you,' she said. 'I need to be pampered tonight.'

Months had passed, and finally Mia was ready to fire the kiln. Her friends from New York were due to visit her soon, and she wanted to finish her ceramic work before they arrived. No point in having friends flying over four hundred miles and then not being able to see them.

Everything was ready; she and Ethan carefully loaded the kiln and bricked the door. Yes, that was a step they had to do every time. Brick the whole front entrance and then smash through once the batch was cooked. Ten days after.

Everything was in place, there was just a small opening to feed the fire. Both were covered in dust, and they had concrete on their hands.

Ethan passed a bucket of water to Mia. 'Here, wash your hands. I've got a surprise for you.'

'A surprise?'

'A new Kowalski I'd like to show you.'

'Here?' Mia asked, surprised. She looked around to ensure nobody was watching.

They were completely alone.

He took her hand and walked her outside, to the rear of the barn. A dustsheet was hanging on the wooden wall. 'Come on, unveil it.'

'Ethan, this is my parents' barn…'

'Shhh! Go ahead.'

She removed the sheet with a yank, and there it was. A painting of Mia standing in a white candid dress and, on his knees, Ethan, handing her a ring in what was clearly a wedding proposal. She gasped and put her hands on her mouth, unable to speak. She turned, and Ethan was there, on his knees as well.

'Will you marry me, Mia Crawford?'

'I… Yes, Ethan. Yes!'

He took her hand and carefully placed the ring on her finger, then he rose. They gazed into each other's eyes and kissed. And then they kissed again.

'We can't leave that one there, Ethan!' she said, pointing at the painting on the wall.

'Not to worry. It's chalk and charcoal, and tonight the forecast is rain. But I will take a picture of it for our private album. Come on, let's light up the dragon.'

CHAPTER 47

A few days later, Xander, Jennifer, and Ginger arrived. The taxi parked in front of Ethan's house. It was the one with the most rooms, and Mia barely spent time at Mrs Clark's house anymore.

'Wow,' Xander said, looking around. 'Good move.'

'Jennifer...' Mia noticed her friends' growing tummy. 'You're pregnant!'

'Never ask a woman if she is pregnant,' Xander said. 'Last time I did it I got a ticking off from a *slightly overweight* woman. I don't even make the gesture to leave my seat on the subway anymore. I just pretend I have to exit at the next station and, nonchalantly, I vacate the seat. Then the woman can do what she pleases...'

'Shut up, Xander,' Mia said. 'For how long?' she asked Jennifer.

'Three and a half months.' She was holding Ginger's hands and turned and kissed her on the cheek. 'We're as happy as we ever will be, and so far the pregnancy is going very well, fingers crossed.'

'I'm happy for you—no, I'm ecstatic! What have you been up to all this time?'

'Same old, same old,' Ginger said. She explained the latest development of her career, the column she had now in *Style Magazine*, and the never-ending number of followers on her website and Instagram account. She was doing great.

'I couldn't have done it if it wasn't for you and them,' Ginger said, pointing at Jennifer and Xander.

They were sitting in the lounge and sipping wine, one of their favourite activities. Ethan was listening and barely speaking.

'No, I think you had it in you from the beginning,' Mia said.

'I was lost, Mia, and you know it. I'd have ended up in jail eventually. But what about you?'

'Got my own firm, and I practice law here in town. A reasonable number of hours.' She winked at Jennifer who, in exchange, raised her glass. 'Ethan and I got engaged, so you're all invited as soon as we set a date.'

'Congratulations!'

'And you started working with ceramic also,' Ethan interjected. 'Come on, show them some of the things you took out of the kiln yesterday.'

'Follow me,' Mia said.

They went in the orangery, where some of Ethan's work was also on display, and Mia placed her latest creations on a large table.

'They're beautiful,' Jennifer said.

'Wow, that is art!' Xander added.

'Do you have a website?' Ginger asked.

'A what? No, I haven't gotten around to doing one yet.'

'That's something I can help with,' Ginger said. She took pictures of Mia's artwork and then went back to the lounge and fired up her laptop. Half an hour later, Mia was online.

'Wow, it is beautiful. You really are talented.'

'Crafty is the word.' She took her mobile and posted a few of Mia's work on her Instagram, with the caption, "Check this out. Mia Crawford, Camden, Maine" followed by the newly born website.

'Hey, did you have a chance of looking at Kowalski's work here in town?' Xander asked.

For a moment, Mia and Ethan fell silent.

'I mean, your favourite artist, Mia, and what is he doing? A set of paintings right in the town where you live, what are the odds?'

'We've been lucky,' Ethan said. 'One of the policemen guarding the house was an old friend, we had a sneak peek. Amazing guy, don't you think?'

'Indeed,' Xander said.

Mia burst out laughing. 'Sorry. Yes, that was the most amazing coincidence.'

'You seem so happy,' Jennifer said. 'I'm glad it all turned out well for you.'

'I've been lucky,' Mia replied, 'but yes, I'm happy.'

'I could live here,' Xander said. 'You can write from whatever place.'

'You leaving New York? Not in a million years.'

'Do they need a doctor round here?' Jennifer asked.

Mia knew they'd never move from New York, but nonetheless, she appreciated what they were saying. Camden was a beautiful place to live, and she'd found love and a renewed life.

It was time to pour some decent wine for her beloved friends.

CHAPTER 48

The article was titled "The rise and fall of Carlton Allerton". Mia read it for a second time.

It described his earlier years when he'd taken over Allerton Groceries, the numerous acquisitions and expansion that led people to believe he was going to become the Steve Jobs of supermarkets. His maverick attitude brought the attention of the media, his lifestyle was the envy and the hate of many. The path followed by Allerton Groceries with rock-bottom prices, rudeness of the employees, and dubious quality had always been controversial, but it was also a life-saver for many who simply couldn't afford the alternative. One thing was clear at that time, he was destined for greatness. And then things started going south. The acquisition of King General proved to be one of the worst financial disasters in this decade; he lost his job, and the subsequent legal action from a starlet dried up what was left of his fortune.

"Nobody gave a second thought to what happen to Carlton Allerton after that," wrote the journalist, "until he resurfaced a couple of weeks ago in a small town in California. On the 17th of July this year, a video emerged on the internet and went viral immediately. A scruffy, bearded individual was filmed in a bar in San Jose, CA."

353

Mia went on reading, unsure if she felt amused or relieved there was no mention of her in Carlton's past. The journalist went on to say how Allerton started racially abusing a couple nearby, in a long tirade about how that couple didn't belong and should go back to their country of origin. A waiter and a waitress intervened, and Carlton Allerton was escorted off the premises.

"Soon afterward, the hunt on Twitter to recognise the individual started. It soon became apparent that the abusive man was Carlton Allerton, despite the long beard and the rough attire. A brief research on LinkedIn showed he was now CEO of a minuscule IT company, with just a couple of employees. The company didn't seem to be anything cutting-edge and most likely barely in business, but nonetheless, the Twitter community called out all the major companies to ensure nobody was doing business with Allerton's company."

The video was now plastered on all the major online newspapers and had reached national television. Carlton Allerton went from being one of the most powerful millionaires to one of the most hated and despised individuals in the country. He'd lost his fortune, his dignity, if he ever had any, and now an enquiry from the San Jose police was ongoing. They would soon press charges, according to the police spokesperson.

Mia deposited the newspaper on her workbench and shrugged. She felt as if her previous life was light years away from where she was now and she didn't regret her decision to move to Camden one bit.

She had important business to do.

The lady turning up at her doorstep that Monday morning was a representative from the MOMA, the Museum of Modern Art in Manhattan, and she had travelled all the way to see Mia's work. The gentleman was an art dealer and was proposing to organise a tour of the States, exhibitions in every state, from New York to Los Angeles, meeting with collectors, the promise to exhibit her work all around the world. By coincidence, they arrived the same day, almost at the same time.

Mia knew the man's name.

He could make it happen.

She declined the offer. 'My life is here in Maine,' she said to him. 'I'm not really interested in doing great exhibitions, nor travelling.'

She could see he was disappointed. It was a once-in-a-lifetime opportunity, but she wasn't prepared to leave everything behind to chase that dream. She had clients in her, now, part-time law firm that she didn't want to disappoint. She had a partner and she enjoyed what she was doing. No change allowed.

She thanked the man for the opportunity and accompanied him to the door.

The lady, a Reese Marsden, was a different story. She genuinely was interested in her artwork, and they spent hours talking about techniques and what she was creating. Mia even showed her the monster kiln.

When she left, Mrs Marsden took a beautifully crafted vase with her to be displayed in the museum. In exchange, she left a cheque with a decent sum written on it, and the promise that Mia would feature in a documentary the museum was preparing.

She sat on the sofa, staring at the ceiling for a moment.

She laughed

She had fought with her father just to discover, later on, he was her personal hero.

She'd abandoned her career as a top lawyer and found happiness in the very place she thought she had to leave in order to be successful.

She didn't hate Mondays anymore. Mondays had changed her life, although not in a direction she had foreseen.

Ethan was waiting, and she had some good news to share with him.

THE END

I DON'T DO MONDAYS!

Printed in Poland
by Amazon Fulfillment
Poland Sp. z o.o., Wrocław

62366903R00201